D1240019

The
Starve Hollow
Affair

P.A. Schoenfeld

deVia Publication LLC
Contact: P.A. Schoenfeld pschoenfeld410@gmail.com

Written by P.A. Schoenfeld
Susan Pohlman, Developmental Editor
Ann Howard Creel, Editor
Beth Deveny, Copyeditor
Cynthia Kiefer Ph.D., Writing Coach
Design by Deborah Perdue, Illumination Graphics
Illustrated by Tara Thelen

Hardcover: ISBN-13: 978-0-9997636-0-5
Paperback: ISBN-13: 978-0-9997636-1-2
Ebook: ISBN-13: 978-0-9997636-2-9

Dedication

For Donald, the love of my life,
whom I miss every day

For my children
Chip Page and Amy Doi

For my grandchildren
Dylan Page and Jesse Page
Max Mangini and Devia Doi

Vallonia Home, 1913

Acknowledgments

Thank you to my loving children, Chip Page and Amy Doi. To you Chip, thank you for always cheering me on. The 1930's music you sent, put me in the spirit of the times as I wrote the novel about your grandmother. And to you Amy, for so patiently putting up with me every single day while I obsessed over writing this story. You have been my rock.

A special "thank you" to my best friend Connie McGuckin for giving me the push I needed to write this story in the first place. Your words still play across my mind and I often hear you emphatically say, "You can do it!" You were so insistent that I could. You planted the ideas in my head while we sat on your patio in N.J. that summer. I'll never forget it.

I will be eternally grateful to Cynthia Kiefer, my dear friend and absolutely awesome coach. Thank you for taking me under your wing. You were so patient and encouraged me every step of the way. I cannot express how special you are and how happy I am that you are in my life. You have taught me much more than I ever expected to know about writing a story. You are the best coach ever!

Thank you, Margie Grady, my darling niece who kept the letters safe for me and returned them sixteen years after mother's death. I'm sure, if it hadn't been for you Marg, I might not have had the opportunity to write this romance novel at all.

Thank you to my second cousin Joe Peters of Brownstown, Indiana who has given me so much of our family history on a personal level. You have been a wealth of information.

And, to my adored Aunt Kay, whom at age 98 is the only living family member in this story. Thank you for giving me so much history and insight into your life growing up in a family of ten in the small town in Southern Indiana. You are so loved by your children, your nieces, nephews, grandchildren, your friends, and especially by me.

Chapter One

Relaxing in my favorite recliner late one night, I was startled to hear the screen door squeak open. I watched the front doorknob slowly turn and thought, *How on earth could I forget to set the deadbolt?*

Fear overtook my senses. My heart pounded, my stomach churned, and my legs felt cold and numb. I struggled to get to my feet, but before I could fully escape my recliner, two men dressed in dark clothing stormed through the door and shoved me back into the chair with one swift motion.

The larger man leaned in, and with his face inches from mine, demanded in a slow gravelly voice, "Give us your money, bitch."

"What money? I have no money," I lied.

Both men moved threateningly closer, and the smaller man said, "If you don't give us your money, we'll tear your house apart and look for it ourselves. Is that what you want?"

I begged them to leave. I even tried appealing to their sense of decency, asking, "Can't you see I have nothing?" However,

I sensed their anger rising, and it occurred to me, I might not survive this robbery.

Losing his patience, the larger man yanked me up from my chair and dragged me from room to room by my hair. I began screaming, but it only made him jerk me around harder, slamming me into walls and doorways. I was terrified and in pain, but I couldn't stop screaming.

The men looked in the refrigerator and anywhere they thought I might have hidden some cash. The smaller man pulled out the drawers and opened every cabinet in the kitchen, tossing the contents aside when he found nothing of value.

In my bedroom, the intruders clawed through my dresser drawers and argued about what to take. Finally, they discovered the rolls of bills I'd stashed in a small space in the back of the desk. I should've given up the money right from the beginning.

The larger man, enraged, began punching my face. I struggled to protect myself, but he didn't let up until I almost couldn't see. The searing pain in my face and arms was intense, and my scalp felt as if it were on fire by the time he tossed me back into the recliner. I was exhausted and nearly unconscious.

The smaller man rolled my walker into the next room and stuffed my telephone cord in his pocket. They pulled the door closed behind them and left. The room around me began to fade as I thought, *Is this how it's going to end?*

⊛

I woke to the sound of beeping and nurses' chatter. I couldn't see through my swollen eyelids, and I had a terrible headache. I managed to stay awake just long enough for Miss Allen, my nurse, to explain that a friend had stopped by my house the morning after the attack and found me barely conscious, still slumped in my recliner. The police found an emergency medical form taped to the front of my refrigerator and notified my children.

My daughter, Patty, and son, John, arrived at the hospital by early morning and stopped at the nurses' station to speak with my doctor. When they came to my bedside and saw me, I could tell they were shocked by my bruises and wounds. The brutal injuries I'd sustained were much worse than they'd imagined. I began to cry—as much for them as for myself.

"Don't cry, Mom, we're here now. It's going to be all right," Patty said. She leaned over to kiss my forehead while John gently clasped my hand. I finally relaxed, feeling more secure in their presence.

"I wish I had listened to you two when you told me I needed to move to a better neighborhood. I wasn't trying to be stubborn. There were just too many years of wonderful memories in that house. Those memories will never live anywhere but in the house Dad and I built together. The thought of leaving sixty years of memory behind was just too much, but I'll never feel safe living there again."

John and Patty stayed with me until I became drowsy. Before they left, Patty bent over to kiss me good-bye. I pulled her close and whispered, "When you get to the house, I have a few special belongings I want you to save for me. I want my old picture album, my letter box, and the green lock-box sitting on top of it. Look in my bedroom closet, way back in on the left side. Promise me you won't let anything happen to them. I never want to go back into the house again, so just get rid of everything else."

"Don't worry, we'll find those things and put them aside for you," she assured me.

❦

The next evening when they came to visit me, I could see they were both upset.

John's jaw tightened as he slowly shook his head, "We were sickened when we went in the house and saw the mess the robbers left behind. What low-life creeps. It was disgusting."

I could see Patty's eyes fill with tears as she listened to her brother describe what they found when they'd entered their childhood home. It was obvious it was time to make plans for my departure from Phoenix to a facility in Utah near John.

Each evening they came to the hospital and kept me updated on their progress in the house. It was a huge undertaking, but there was nothing I could do to help. After all of my resistance, I was finally ready to move on. One thing was certain—I was lucky to be alive.

⚬⚭⚬

"Mother, we found the items you wanted from the house. We'll keep them safe for you, like I promised, but . . . that letter box has me intrigued," she said. "Why did you hang onto those letters for all of these years?"

"I don't know. I just did. That's all." I brushed her off, explaining I was too tired and in too much pain to talk right then. I had never told my children the story about my love letters and didn't want to now. How could I explain that there had been *two* great loves in my life? I doubted that they would be able to understand my struggle to choose between the two men or my desire to hang onto both relationships through those letters. I couldn't bring myself to part with them, so I secretly kept them safely stowed away in the back of my closet.

Then, when I mentioned I was in pain, I could see John become visibly concerned. A little crease appeared between his eyebrows, as it always did when he worried.

As he and Patty were leaving that evening, he alerted the nurse about my increasing pain. I had already started to doze when my nurse quietly entered the room to administer my shot.

"Anna, your son said you're having a lot of pain. Dr. West has ordered something to relieve your pain and help you to sleep," Miss Allen said.

"Oh, thank you. I'm so weary. It's been almost too much for me today. I feel exhausted."

I calmly lay there in silence with my eyes closed. I wanted to stop thinking about the terror of the attack and reflect back on happier times. I wanted to dream about the love of my life who wrote me beautiful letters and called me "Glorianna." We'd had a good life together, and I still missed him every day. As the shot began to take effect, I started to feel fuzzy, as though I were floating. My mind drifted back to my senior year of high school in Vallonia, Indiana, and the love story I had kept to myself for nearly seventy years.

Chapter Two

A month after my seventeenth birthday on August 6, 1927, I began my senior year at Vallonia High. Out of habit and just being nosy, I stopped at the mailbox on my way to school and was pleasantly surprised when I found a letter addressed to me. It was from an older Vallonia boy, who had moved out of town a few years before. The letter piqued my curiosity, but I wanted to make sure I got to school on time that first day, so I tucked it in my pocket and hurried on my way. At recess, when I went to the girls' lavatory, I opened the letter.

September 7, 1927
Hamilton, Ohio

Hello Kiddo,

I trust you've had a nice summer and are back in school by the time you get this letter. I was wondering if you have any news you can share with me about how things are in Vallonia. How are our old neighbors and

other folks who live there? Anything new
going on at the school or with the teachers and
classmates? Who's your teacher this year? Is
there any gossip going around the town? I
was wondering how your brothers and sisters
are doing. I'm trying to get used to Hamilton,
but folks are very different here.
Write when you have time.
Dale

It was an exciting first day at school, and my friends were glad we were back together to catch up on the latest news and begin our senior year. After school let out, I saw my cousin Delores just ahead and hurried to catch up with her. The thought of the letter had played across my mind so many times during class, and I was bursting to share it. When we stopped for a chat, I couldn't wait to tell her I'd heard from an old friend.

"Delores, do you remember Dale Stevens?"

"I do. I remember the family was poor and lived in an old abandoned cabin in Starve Hollow."

"That's right. They did."

"Didn't he move away a few years ago?"

"Yes, and you won't believe this. On my way to school this morning I stopped at our mailbox and found this from him. The return address is Hamilton, Ohio."

I read the letter to Delores, and noticed her surprised look and thought she was probably wondering why he had chosen to write to me. We'd both gone to school with Dale since we were eight, and he was almost eleven.

"Anna, did he just write you out of the blue?"

I tried to make light of her question, but we both had wondered the same thing. Why *had* he written to me? Even I was puzzled about it.

"I *am* curious, but I think it was a short, just-to-be-in-touch, kind of letter. I plan to write to him and answer his questions. I'm interested to see if he writes back."

"Do you remember Liz, that skinny, pin-straight blond-haired girl who lives about a mile east of here?"

"No, I don't think I do. Why?'"

"She was in Dale's class and apparently crazy about him for years. Carolyn told me, not too long ago, Liz had bragged about him coming to see her after he moved away, and that she was in love with him."

"Goodness, Delores. I hadn't heard any of that and never heard anyone mention seeing him since he moved away."

"I only vaguely remember Liz and never thought much of her. The boys said Liz was 'good and easy,' and behind her back, they called her 'Lizard.'"

"Ha-ha, that's funny. Now my curiosity is definitely peaked. I don't understand. If he's interested in Liz, why is he writing to me?" *I'm going to ask him about her.*

❧

I decided there was no harm in exchanging letters with Dale, especially since he lived so far away. I could at least give him some news about the school and townspeople. I admit I felt special he'd singled me out and a little grown-up that an older boy might be interested in me. At least, I hoped he was interested. I shared the news about the letter with other girl-friends. They were envious that an older boy had written to me and were sure he had romantic intentions—which I denied, of course—but I hoped he didn't have any interest in Liz, and that the rumors about him visiting her weren't true.

The day after I received the letter, Delores continued to press me about Dale's purpose in writing.

"Anna, you never told us why he started writing to you."

"I don't know. It was a surprise to me too."

"Were you two good friends?"

"No, not exactly. We were friendly, but I wouldn't say we were especially close."

"Carolyn thinks there's something more going on here."

"I don't. I think he was just curious about what was happening at school and wanted some news about Vallonia—our neighbors and town gossip."

"I always thought he was sweet on you."

"Come on now, I think he wrote the letter because he was just bored and homesick."

"When I told Carolyn you received a letter from Dale, she said she remembered him always watching you at school."

"Well, if he was, I sure didn't know it."

"Do you remember the time in sixth grade when the boys wanted to play tag with us, and if we were tagged by a boy, we had to kiss him?"

"Yes, I remember that. I just thought it was a game the boys invented."

"It seemed Dale always tried to tag you, but not any of the other girls. Don't you remember him kissing you on the cheek when he caught you?"

I shook my head in response. "No, I don't remember ever kissing or being kissed by any boy. Ever. But I do remember how different he looked his senior year. I noticed he was becoming more handsome with his deep blue eyes, red hair, and clear skin." I was blushing at this point, and tried to hide my embarrassment from Delores.

Since Dale was a few years older, it made me feel attractive and mature to think someone of the opposite sex would pay attention to me. I didn't want to show it, but I was thrilled when another letter arrived three days after the first. I was hoping his quick response meant he definitely *was* interested in me.

Vallonia, Indiana
September 10, 1927

Dear Anna,

I'm here in Starve Hollow and will be here for another ten days. I received your letter yesterday morning in Hamilton before I left.

I saw your folks at the carnival up at Seymour yesterday, and talked to your sister Laura Mae. I sure wish you had come with them. I asked in my last letter when you would be available to see me because I'll be starting to do some tree-trimming around the 24th, but you didn't answer. I'd very much like to see you. Gosh Peachy, it sure is a pretty night. A great big moon, and it seems ages since I last saw you.

Well, goodnight, Kiddo,
Dale

As time went on, Dale wrote more frequently. Soon it became several times a week, and I'd answer back just as often. He addressed me as "Peaches," in one of his letters and I started to feel maybe I *was* special. Secretly, when I passed the mirror in the living room, I'd make romantic gestures, teetering on my tiptoes like a ballerina, slowly drifting along as though the wind were whisking me away. I'd lift my eyebrows and smile ever-so-subtly. Then I'd give a little twirl and look back over my shoulder at my long golden-brown hair flowing around me. I'd sometimes flutter my eyes and even talk to myself in a soft whisper as I imagined a romantic heroine might do. Receiving mail from a boy was a splendid feeling, and it tickled me so much, I often found myself lost in romantic daydreams about the two of us.

I'd known Dale for many years, but he hadn't seen me for a long time. I wondered whether he'd recognize me. Maybe he'd been waiting until I'd reached the proper age? I wondered if he'd think I was pretty now. Or like my blue-green eyes? I was no longer the young girl he remembered. I was outgoing enough, and had lots of friends, but I'd never dated anyone. In fact, I'd never even been asked.

I felt genuinely perplexed about Dale's sudden interest. Maybe he merely wanted a friendly contact in Vallonia for the times he would come back to visit, but when he again called me "Peachy" and said he wanted to see me, I wondered if he had something else in mind. His intentions puzzled me since I'd just heard he'd been seeing Liz.

Vallonia, Indiana
September 20, 1927

Dear Dale,

I enjoy getting mail from you and hope you feel the same about my letters. Do you think the letters I write are silly?

You wanted to know if I had a boyfriend at school. I assure you, there are no interesting boys here. Prospects are limited in our small town of Vallonia. I'm still looking for the man of my dreams, the tall, strong fellow with black wavy hair, and brown eyes. Ha!

I'll be here if you want to come on the 13th.

Anna

Chapter Three

It was the end of a sweltering September afternoon, and I was anxious to get home from school, change clothes, and cool off. Lying on my bed, I became totally lost in my daydreams. I wondered what the year ahead might bring until I graduated, and what my future might be like—especially if I could afford to attend college. Our parents wanted all of us to get a formal education. Just the thought of college life was exciting, but also somewhat frightening. I'd certainly need to live away from home since the nearest university was fifty miles away. More than anything, for years, it had been my dream to graduate from Indiana University. I wanted to earn a degree and secure a career for my future.

I remember one evening when I was about eight years old, Dad commanded our attention. He called us all together for a family meeting. We gathered around the dining room table, looking inquisitively at each other, and we knew whatever it was, it was serious.

"Children, you know Mother and I have always insisted that all of you go to college. I've come up with a plan making it possible for all eight of you to get through school and earn your degrees. We'll help Roy through his first year, since he's the oldest."

"So, how is that going to work?" Truly asked.

"Now that Roy is eighteen, we'll chip in to cover most of it, but he'll have to work also to help pay his expenses. When he's about finished with his third year of school and has saved money along the way, he'll have to help you, Truly, since you're next in line. Each one of you will have to do the same so that you will all have help getting through. I've spoken to Roy and he's in agreement with the plan."

I counted on going to college, even though it was an unimaginable dream, especially for any girl, since money was so tight. Roy did help Truly and Dad's plan seemed to be working. Our parents encouraged each of us to take on odd jobs however we could to earn money. Since the population in Vallonia was less than four hundred, the opportunities were limited and most of the jobs were on neighboring farms. Near town we had a hardware store, my uncle's general store, a cannery, and a farm equipment repair shop. My brothers were occasionally hired at the going rate of ten cents an hour to help out in the shop. The flour mill was further out of town and seldom hired young boys.

Most of us learned to be frugal, primarily through the teachings of our mother. She could make anything and do just about everything. I heard it said more than once that "Mother could make a purse out of a sow's ear," and we all believed she could. Most of her day was spent in the kitchen and she was an excellent cook. Her usual attire was a cotton print dress covered with a bib-apron. Her dark hair, swept up into a bun on top of her head, gave her stocky build a matronly appearance. She was generally good-natured, but took no nonsense or backtalk from any of us. She spoke English but it was even harder to understand her when she was excited, due to her thick German accent. Her parents and grandparents only spoke German. It was her first language.

Mother had gone to the German school in a largely German community in Vallonia. She finished her education in the eighth grade. Even though she could read German, her ability to read English was minimal, and she couldn't write in English. Her limited schooling, however, didn't dissuade her dreams of having her children complete a formal education. All eight of us.

One morning, I was lying on my bed daydreaming about college when Dude came into my room. He was the youngest boy in the family and loved to pester and tease his sisters.

"Hey, Sis, I have something of yours," he said hiding it behind his back.

"What is it, a book?"

"No, guess again."

"Gimme it," I said impatiently as I lunged toward him. "What is it—for heaven sake?"

"It's a letter from your boyfriend. Hee-hee-hee. You'll have to catch me if you want it."

Dude ran down the hall, slammed the door, and held it closed. I struggled to get the envelope away from him in one piece.

Dale wrote that he was coming to visit on Saturday. I definitely wanted to see him, but it was my weekend to do most of the house cleaning in the main rooms. I ran home after volleyball practice on Friday and began my chores.

Cleaning was no easy task since our living room and dining areas were large. At the end of the long dark-blue sofa was a round table with a crocheted doily, a large hurricane oil lamp, and Dad's Bible. Near the front entrance, an upright piano and three comfortable chairs sat waiting for those who wanted to listen to music. For me, dusting was always the best part of cleaning. A black wooden clock, which was a wedding gift to my parents, sat on the mantle. Next to it was a family picture taken in front of our Victorian home during the summer of 1913. Dad held me while Mother cradled Laura Mae, who was just one-year-old at the time. Roy, Truly, and Ken stood between my parents, close to the picket fence. We loved that picture, even though the next three children, Doc, Dude, and Kay hadn't been born yet.

We ate most of our family meals on a large table in the kitchen. The spacious dining room accommodated a table for ten, but we only used it when we had company. A sofa for overnight guests crowded the far corner of the dining area. I finished cleaning everything, including the living room rugs while most of the family enjoyed the porch swing or threw horseshoes in the yard. I was anxious to see Dale the next day and wanted our home to impress him.

"The house looks beautiful," Mother said as she began preparing supper.

"Thank you. I can help with supper, if you like."

"I'll take that help. You're happy Dale is coming here, aren't you? Your father asked me what you see in him."

"He's just someone I like to talk to. He's so smart and he reads all the time. We like writing to each other and he gives me suggestions on books he thinks I might like."

"There must be something else. You know how he was raised, don't you?"

"I'm learning. We've known each other at school for a long time."

"Well, a little warning. Keep your eyes open and be careful," she said heading into the pantry.

Even though curious about her advice, I wasn't going to ask what she meant by that comment.

⁂

I woke up early Saturday and donned my pale pink dress, the one Truly had made for me to wear the first day of my senior year. It had been a long time since I'd seen Dale, and I hoped our visit would go well. I must have looked out the window at least twenty times before he finally arrived. I was casually sitting on the swing pretending not to be overly excited.

"Good morning, Dale. It's good to see you. Would you like to go inside?" I said holding the door open.

"Gosh, you've changed since I last saw you."

"You have, too," I said pushing my hair back behind my ears.

"I think you're taller and your hair is much longer. I don't think I ever saw you with curls."

"Curls? Oh, yeah, I thought I'd try a little something different for a change."

"Well, it looks good on you."

When I glanced up at him, I noticed his face was a little red and wondered if he were blushing after the compliment he'd paid, so I thanked him and kept walking.

"Come on in the kitchen. Want something to eat?"

"No, I ate not too long ago, but I'll sit with you and chat if you don't mind."

"Hello, Mrs. Fosbrink. It's been a long time."

"Yes, it *has* been a long time. Anna said your family moved to Hamilton."

"We did. We moved after I graduated."

"Do you like it there?"

"It's all right, I guess. People aren't as friendly, and I've had a hard time finding any work to speak of. Just odd jobs—nothing steady."

"That's the way it is these days. I have work to do in the garden. We'll talk again." She put on her straw hat and left out the back door with her basket.

"Anna, after you finish your lunch, let's walk over to the school. I'd like to see it again, and maybe we'll bump into some old friends."

We walked around town, and Dale clearly enjoyed being back in familiar surroundings where almost everyone was friendly and knew each other. We visited with Delores and Carolyn and met up with a few of the boys who had been in Dale's class. I was amused by the expressions on Delores's and Carolyn's faces when they saw me with Dale. Delores's knowing face and winks told me she felt my excitement, but Carolyn's questioning face looked as if she may have doubts about us being together.

On our way home, Dale said he enjoyed reminiscing about his years living in Starve Hollow and graduating from Vallonia High. I liked being seen with him while we walked around town, and I admit I felt an overwhelming attraction to him. Actually, much more than I'd expected to.

❦

When we returned, I asked Dale if he'd like to join me on the porch swing a short while before he had to head back to the cabin. We sat in silence for a moment, then I said, "I noticed you often write about your dad, but you haven't mentioned your mother."

"Sorry, I guess I never told you about her."

"No, I don't recall that you ever did."

"I have no memory of my mother because she died when I was three."

"I'm so sorry. All these years I've known you at school, I had no idea."

Dale leaned forward with his arms crossed, resting on his knees, and just staring at the porch floor.

"My dad talked about her all the time, and I grew up loving her through the stories he told me."

"It's good he had such nice memories of her. Sometimes the scars of a losing a loved one makes it hard to talk about."

"I suppose some of the kids at school may have thought she was alive because of the way I spoke of her."

"It must have been hard for your dad, losing his wife, with her being so young and leaving you and your two sisters behind."

"It *was* hard. I think that's why he wrapped himself around us so much when we were little. He tried to make up for it by spending time holding the three of us near as he sat telling stories and reading to us. I grew up loving to read."

"I love to read, too. Mother thinks I hide with a book to get out of doing chores, but that's not so. I just like to get lost in a good book."

"Same here. Dad and I read every day and I loved sharing what I read with him. He often told me how much he loved being with me, even from the time I was an infant. Then, when I was older, he taught me to ride horses, shoot guns, and hunt rabbits, possum, and squirrel. I liked to hunt— still do."

"My dad taught me to hunt, too. We should go hunting sometime."

"I'll take you up on that—maybe the next time I'm here."

"Sure, that'll be something to look forward to. Hunting squirrel is great sport."

"Dad also taught me how to raise pigs and chickens to sell at market. I think the closeness I have with him is especially strong because we all lived together for many years in the cabin. It was always a struggle—living out there away from everything."

"I'm sure it was hard for all of you."

"Now, looking back, I see how poor we were. When I was younger, I didn't think about how differently we lived from everyone else. We had so little to eat and sometimes nothing at all. We went to bed hungry almost every night. Now we live with my sister and her family, but I still like the cabin life better. That's my home."

Quietly listening to Dale describe how they struggled to survive, I was aware we had come from different worlds. Extremely different worlds. It was hard to imagine living his kind of life. Then, I don't know why, but suddenly the disquieting mental image of Liz flashed in my mind. I lunged forward on the swing and abruptly blurted out without even thinking, "You remember Liz?"

Dale instantly turned toward me with a pained expression. "Whatever made you ask that? What about her?"

"Just curious," I said, realizing how awkward the inquiry sounded.

"What made you bring her up?"

"I heard she was your girlfriend."

He appeared annoyed, shook his head, and momentarily gazed into space, then said, "Where did you get that notion?"

"I just heard it somewhere."

"But, where? Who told you that?"

"She wasn't your girlfriend?"

"Nope."

"I heard she was in love with you."

"Maybe, but I never was in love with her, if that's what you want to know." He nervously ran his fingers through his hair and turned to look back over his shoulder at me.

"Is she just a friend?"

"Yes, and I only saw her a couple of times. That's all. Don't worry, she's not my girlfriend or anything of the sort."

"You're sure there's nothing between you?"

"Anna. Why the interrogation? Of course, I'm sure!"

Then I realized I'd gone too far and gave a little chuckle. "I'm just picking on you. Don't get so upset."

"How do you like school this year?"

Dale changed the subject so abruptly, I wondered if there was more to their relationship than he was willing to admit. Clearly, he didn't want to discuss it further.

"It's fine. I love being on the volleyball team, and I'm thinking of playing drums in the orchestra. That and studying should keep me busy."

"You're not going to be too busy to write me, I hope."

"I probably can squeeze in a little time to write once in a while."

"Just once in a while?"

"Maybe."

I enjoyed being with Dale, and after he left I thought about our conversation. I felt sorry that his mother died when he was so young. I couldn't imagine growing up without my mother. Obviously, Dale had experienced an extremely different upbringing than I had, and I wondered if that difference might eventually become a problem for us. I also wondered if he'd told me the truth about his relationship with Liz. I could tell he didn't like being questioned. I wondered what the two of them actually had between them. I definitely didn't want another female entering into the picture, now that I was developing feelings for him.

Chapter Four

$\mathcal{I}$was more than a little spoiled and I knew it. When I developed malaria at age five, I was confined to bed for many weeks. It was a devastating illness which had a long recovery period. I was such a small child and so seriously ill at that age, my dad built a little bed so they could push me into whatever room the family occupied to keep me near them. Initially the disease left me weak and unable to walk, but with the constant attention of my father, mother, and older brothers and sister, I learned to walk again. I eventually enjoyed a good healthy childhood, but in the opinion of my brothers and sister, all of the attention left me spoiled. Truth be told, I was spoiled.

I think because I'd once been so ill, my father took a special interest in me. We had a bond I didn't share with my mother until my later teenage years. My dad's name was Henry Ulysses Fosbrink, but I renamed him "Hezekiah Perkins." I loved it when he'd refer to himself by that name. I imagined Dad might look just like a person named Hezekiah Perkins. He always wore bib overalls and an old felt, snap-brim hat which was a hand-me-down from Grandpa. He spent most of his time in the sand fields growing melons. Everyone in town knew Dad because he grew the sweetest melons in Jackson County and he enjoyed his reputation as "the watermelon man."

Dad and I were both passionate about riding horses. When he'd come home early from the sand fields, he'd tell me to come out back. I'd drop whatever I was doing and join him. I couldn't saddle the horses to get the cinch tight enough, so he'd saddle both Nellie and Spiffy, and we'd race to the hills. We'd dismount and just stroll along and talk. There was always so much to talk about. I loved my father and treasured our special bond.

On the other hand, my relationship with Mother was testy, especially during my teen years. It seemed there was often tension between us, and it didn't matter what we were doing. We often couldn't agree on how a particular task should be accomplished. It was a struggle for us both. Sometimes we'd have terrible arguments. I'd go out to the corn crib when it was empty and stick mean notes in between the slats. I remember it made her cry when she found them, but we always made up. One time, she took my note to Dad to read to her and I hid around the corner to listen in.

"Henry, I found this note in the corn crib. Did Anna write it?"

"Yes, it's Anna's handwriting, all right."

"So, what does it say?"

"Did you two have a quarrel today?"

"Yes, and she got mad and started crying. I told her she needed to help out with laundry and housecleaning more on the weekends. She stomped her foot and yelled, 'If you don't like the way I do it, then do it yourself!'"

"I wonder what made her so angry?"

"I'm not sure. I told her she just wants to get done in a hurry, then stay in her room and write letters to that fella, or go over to see Delores. She yelled back that I was mean and expected her to do more than any of the other kids. She became angry and flew out the door yelling, 'I hate you.'"

"Dora, don't get upset. The note just says she thinks you're unfair and mean. It's not good for you to get so upset."

"It hurts me when she storms out the door and says she hates me."

"You know how kids are. After supper, I'll ask her to go for a ride and talk to her. She shouldn't be acting that way. Maybe she had a bad day at school or something. Who knows? But, I'll tell her she needs to apologize . . . whether she wants to or not."

I usually *did* apologize because living with those feelings of conflict with Mother, always gave me a stomachache. Sometimes I felt the problems I had with her were just the growing up kind of troubles a girl has with her mother and not out of the ordinary. My girlfriends often shared the same kinds of stories about their mothers, and they didn't seem too different from mine. However, that somehow didn't prevent the next argument, which often invited solace during which I could lose myself in deep thoughts and daydreams in the quiet of my own room.

At times, I wished I could saddle Spiffy by myself so I could ride out to the hills to a peaceful spot I called "Arcada" to be alone in my own world. I liked the idea of having a boyfriend, but I needed to do some serious thinking about my feelings of insecurity in my relationship with Dale. I had many conflicted thoughts about him and I was still trying to figure out if he was right for me. My heart said he was, but in my mind, there were some doubts. And that Liz person? I was suspicious of her intentions and she ignited the worst thoughts I'd ever had of any female.

Chapter Five

It was early October when I was chosen to be a contestant at the State Latin Contest in Indianapolis. For me, it was a magnificent honor, and in three days I'd be competing against high school students from the entire state. I was lying on my bed thinking about what to wear when I heard my sister coming down the hall. Truly, who was six years older than me, had graduated from IU and lived in her own apartment just outside Vallonia. She was a take-charge kind of person—maybe because she was the oldest girl in the family and had looked after all of us growing up. Nothing was too much trouble for her when it came to family. I loved her sweet spirit and always looked up to her.

"Mother said you made the list for the Latin Contest."

"Yes, and I'm so excited. I still can't believe I get to go to Indianapolis."

"That's great. I'm so proud of you. Do you have a special dress for the occasion?"

"No, I was going to wear the pink one you made me for school."

"You need something better than that. Let's design a dress just for the competition. I think I can make it in the next few days."

"Could you make something in blue?"

"I suppose I can. I'll take a look around. What style are you picturing?"

"Something eye-catching and fashionable; something to make me look grown-up."

Truly was a creative and talented seamstress who always made her own patterns. It amazed us all how her finished garments fit perfectly, and it didn't surprise me that she'd offer to make me something special to wear to the event.

We sat on the bed while Truly sketched a picture of the dress and, after we made a few changes to the drawing, it looked even more beautiful and grown-up than I'd imagined.

The morning I was to leave for Indianapolis, Truly arrived at dawn with my new garment as promised. I couldn't wait to slip on the lovely cornflower blue dress. As I buttoned the several small blue buttons centered up the front of the bodice, I noted it fit softly over the bosom. The traditional white collar surrounded my neck, and the long sleeves slightly tapered to my wrists. The fabric gracefully draped into a mid-calf length skirt. In other words, it was perfect.

My sister Laura sat on the bed in awe while I modeled my new dress. Truly plaited my hair with a single long French braid down the back, adorned with a small matching blue moiré taffeta bow, tied a few inches from the bottom.

"So beautiful," I said as I gave a twirl and a curtsy in front of her. Her smiling expression told me how satisfied she was with her creation.

"I love the dress and I'm so excited to wear it."

"I can tell. Say, by the way, Mother said you've been writing to Dale and he's been visiting you. It surprised me that you've become interested in him," Truly said casually.

"Yes, we've been writing and I find him quite interesting."

"You know, I knew the family pretty well. I took violin lessons from his dad. I guess I never thought about Dale being your type."

I didn't want to defend that statement since my younger sister Laura was still in the room, so I grabbed my jacket off the bed and headed for the front door motioning for Laura to come along. I'd fill Truly in about Dale at another time.

"Thank you, Truly, I absolutely love how this all turned out."

"You look so pretty, and I know you're going to do good today. Come on, we'd better get to the train," Laura said.

"Just give us a call when the contest is over and let us know how you made out." Truly hugged and kissed us both goodbye.

❦

During the contest, the excitement of surviving each elimination, one after the other was both nerve-wracking, and exhilarating. I was anxious the entire time, but I won the contest and received a beautiful gold medal. What a perfect day!

Laura and I hurried along to find a pay phone to place a collect call:

"Hello, Mother?"

"Yes? Well, what happened?"

"I won first place and got the gold medal. Laura and I are heading to the train in a few minutes, so I'll see you at home. Tell Daddy I won."

When we returned home, my parents were so proud of me that Mother created a festive dinner celebration for us. My brothers and sisters were there to enjoy the supper and examine my gold medal. I remember that day so fondly, not only because I'd won, but also because I was the center of attention for the day. That didn't happen often when you share the limelight with so many brothers and sisters. I loved the special attention.

I couldn't wait to send Dale a letter telling him about my good news. A few days later, I received a congratulatory note from him.

October 12, 1927
Hamilton, Ohio

Dear Anna

*I think it's wonderful that you won the
contest. What a happy moment for you when
you received that prize. I wish I had brains
enough to win a gold medal like that.*

Dale

In his next letter, Dale said after moving to Hamilton, he entered
Columbia College in Chicago, but only stayed a few months. He ran
out of money and didn't think he was cut out for college life, so
he returned home. That surprised me. I wondered what made him
think he wasn't cut out for it.

For many months after he left college, he applied for jobs
around Hamilton and Cincinnati. It was even harder to find
work than he'd expected. Eventually, a conservation service
hired him and he began working as a tree-trimmer. The
company sent men to various locations wherever they could
find jobs for them. Dale claimed he was happy to have work,
since thousands of men were now facing even harder times
finding means of employment. Most jobs were day-labor pay-
ing twenty-five cents an hour. Shortly after he began with a
tree-trimming crew in October, 1927, he was sent to Chicago
to work. He was pleased when he learned he'd be on a team
where my brother, Ken, was foreman.

It was good that Dale had finally found a job. He said many
times how much he loved to travel and learn about new places,
and this provided that opportunity. But, I admit, the distance
between Chicago and Vallonia was a huge disappointment and
I wondered when, *or if,* I'd ever get to see him. I was aware
of my growing feelings for him, but still, he was so unlike me.

His preference was to travel and do day-labor, while I wanted an education and a future with security. I wondered how our relationship could survive if we were always so far apart?

Chapter Six

*L*ate in the afternoon, Delores stopped by the house. Motioning her to come in, I said, "I just had another letter from Dale."

"Does he like the new job?"

"You knew the job was in Chicago, didn't you?"

"I remember you said that. He's there already?"

"Yes, and he said it was a hot, miserable, dirty trip. The three men he traveled with saw a card in a boardinghouse window advertising, "Room for Rent" so they stopped in to see it. He said it was a two-story building with twelve rooms, two men to a room, and each room had a double bed and a chair."

"That doesn't sound so bad." Delores said.

"Not yet, but wait, listen to this. The worst part was, he'd have to share a bed with another man."

"What? Share his bed with a stranger?"

"The part I didn't like was that they can only get a bath once a week. All those men work on trees in hot weather and need to bathe often."

"So, Anna, is he leaving? Is he going back home?"

"I don't know. Actually, no. He said, after thinking about it, he realized he had no choice but to stay because he couldn't afford a place of his own, and he didn't have any money to return home. Looks like he's stuck, at least for a while."

"Too bad he didn't know about it before he went there. Especially that part about sleeping with a strange bed partner. That gives me the heebie-jeebies."

I could tell Delores found Dale's new lifestyle disgusting—I did, too.

"And another thing—he said he felt it wasn't safe to be out on the streets of Chicago after ten-thirty at night. I guess Chicago must be pretty dangerous. There was one street the fellows called "the street of forgotten men." He said money was getting tighter, prices were rising, and jobs were getting harder to find. There were all kinds of men, women, and children out on the streets begging for anything they could get."

"That's awful. I'd hate to live there, wouldn't you?"

"What's worse—no, I wouldn't want to live there—hundreds of families were evicted from their homes because they couldn't pay the rent, and the little children were dirty and wailing because they were so hungry. He said the changes due to the Depression had become more obvious to everyone there. It made me feel terrible when I read his letter."

"Seems so different from here, don't you think? Our little town of four hundred, we don't even realize what others experience out there."

October 28, 1927
Vallonia, Indiana

Dear Dale,
I must have read your letter over a half a dozen times. You gave such interesting

*descriptions of the boardinghouse you live in
and the men with whom you work. I can't
imagine living like that and having to share
my bed with a strange person.*

*I've only been to Chicago once, but the
area where you are must be pretty bad if you
can't even go out at night. I think the most
upsetting part was reading about the people
who are out on the streets and don't have
anything, and those poor little children. It
makes me sad to think of them begging for
food on the street. Our tiny little town doesn't
realize how the rest of the country may be
suffering until we hear from others who see
that kind of poverty. Those signs of hardship
are so much worse where you are.*

*Take care of yourself and stay safe. I'm
happy you take the time to write so often. I
love getting mail from you. I hope you are
missing me as much as I miss you.*

*Affectionately,
Anna*

While I enjoyed my correspondence with Dale, it didn't keep me
from making the most of my senior year. I worked hard to earn good
grades and even took on some extra credit projects, along with joining
the orchestra. I couldn't wait to get home to tell Mother the good news.

"I just volunteered to be the drummer in orchestra and Mr.
Edwards is going to teach me after school."

"Goodness. Child, why on earth would you do that?"

"I thought it would be fun to learn how to play the drums."

"Isn't there enough noise in this house with the boys making
so much racket all the daylight hours?" She threw her hands up

in the air, then turned and headed back to the kitchen without another word.

I raised my voice to make sure she heard me, "I'll practice at school, and only at school. I promise. I'm excited to be the drummer."

When my brothers Doc and Dude found out I was the school drummer, they came back from the woods with small branches and made drumsticks. They began beating on everything they could find that would sound like drums. Dad had to quickly put a stop to it before he had to repaint the porch railings. Never a dull moment being the father of eight children. He had *the* patience of a saint.

I was so busy I didn't have time to write Dale as often as he'd like. He didn't hold back on the complaints that my letters didn't come often enough. Eventually he wrote, confiding that he'd become more and more discouraged about the men with whom he worked. They often had arguments about men of color and Catholics, whom they felt were odd anyway, and it bothered him. More than anything, having a bed partner was difficult to adjust to. He said the bed was soft and squeaked with each turn, often interrupting his sleep.

By December, Dale left the team and returned home. He told everyone he had to leave to care for his elderly aunt. I realized he wasn't happy with the living conditions and understood why he wanted to leave, but I felt it was unfortunate he'd given up his job. He told me his ninety-two-year-old aunt needed a lot of help after she'd fallen at home. She apparently had no broken bones from the fall, but she seemed as if she didn't want to get well. She was unsteady and had difficulty walking. Because of her weakened condition, she couldn't stand to cook, so she didn't feel like eating, which was evidenced by her thin, frail appearance. Her husband had been a Civil War soldier who was killed when a team of horses ran away with him. Since his death, she grieved for him, which made living alone an even greater challenge. She welcomed the attention from Dale, who, because of his strength, was able to help her in a way that some of the other family members couldn't.

I gave a lot of thought to Dale's reason for leaving the trimming service. Was it because his aunt needed him and he felt a strong family obligation, or was it something else? Was it because he was upset and disgusted by the men at the boardinghouse because of their criticism about the "men of color and Catholics?" Or, did he just not feel like sticking with it and took the opportunity to get out and gave the excuse that his aunt needed him?

While walking home from school late one afternoon, I had the misfortune of an encounter with Liz. She appeared out of nowhere and quietly followed me like a coati lizard. Moving closer, in little more than a whisper, she began harassing me about stealing her boyfriend. Her accusations caught me off guard because I barely even knew who she was.

"Listen here, girl. Everyone in town knows Dale is off-limits."

"I don't know what you're talking about."

"You need to stop bothering him," she threatened.

When I noticed she'd moved even closer, I picked up my pace. Pounding the ground with each step, she also picked up her pace and demanded, "You need to leave him alone. *He's mine.* I've been his girlfriend for years. Ha! Ha! Ha!"

"Sure, Liz, I'm sure you think so."

"He'll be here this afternoon. Just wait and see for yourself."

I hadn't seen Dale since he left the trimming service, but we'd exchanged letters and cards over the holidays. The weather had been uncooperative so he remained in Hamilton until mid-January. Now, I wondered how Liz knew he planned a visit to Vallonia today. That news troubled me so much, I stopped to see Delores who was picking flowers along the fence in her front yard. I told her how Liz had followed me, and how her accusations made me feel even more uncertain about my relationship with Dale.

"That girl is not only a sneak, she's a liar."

"It made me nervous that she was taunting me."

"That's the way she is and she threatens anyone who gets in her way. She elbows into everyone's business and tells so many lies—she actually believes them herself."

"When I asked Dale about her, he said there wasn't anything between them. I hope there's nothing to worry about, but she certainly makes me feel uneasy."

"That girl is creepy and if he's interested in her, you need to look elsewhere. Look, over there, here he comes now," she quickly lifted her head and pointed her nose in his direction. "I'll see you later."

"Hey, Dale. I didn't know you were coming to town until I saw Liz awhile ago. How did she know you were coming here?"

"I'm sorry Peaches, I wanted to surprise you. That's why I didn't write about my plans. Liz has been pestering me to visit her, and she even became friendly with my sister so she could keep track of me. I told her what Liz was up to and I had no desire to see her. I asked Sis not to tell her anything of my whereabouts."

"Then, I wish you'd tell Liz to leave us alone."

⋐⳾⳾⳾

Dale reassured me there was no room in his life for Liz. He said when he got to know her better, he realized she was a dishonest, deceitful girl who had made way too many bad choices. In the beginning, he felt sorry for her, but then realized she wanted more from him than he wanted to give. He said she didn't take it well when he told her he had no desire to be intimate with her. I hope the next time he sees her, he'll tell her to disappear.

After we returned to the house, he told me of the experiences he'd had working with the team, and how disgusted he became with some of the men. He planned to look for another job soon, but first he wanted to spend a little quiet time in the cabin and catch up on some reading. I felt reassured after having been in his company once again, that I *was* the special girl in his life that I wanted to be.

Chapter Seven

*I*t was early March 1928 when Dale wrote that he and his father were planning a trip to Starve Hollow. He'd drive his brother-in-law's car and bring his dad, who planned to stay a few weeks in the cabin. He mentioned that while he was home, he'd like to ride the horses, if at all possible. He said he was looking forward to seeing me again, and in fact, he was excited about the possibility. Admittedly, I had developed feelings for him and it tickled me to know he was excited also. I expected his visit to be another high point of my senior year, and I couldn't wait for him to come to my house.

Dale took his dad to drop off supplies at the cabin, then they joined my family for the afternoon and supper. My parents knew his father because he'd given Truly violin lessons, but they hadn't seen him in years. He was a self-taught violinist, but unfortunately, because they lived so far out of town there wasn't much interest in our community for music lessons. I remember growing up, towns-folk and also my parents spoke well of him. They often expressed compassion for their family so I was pleased Mother had invited them for supper.

Dale readily accepted my parents' invitation since it seemed to me, all he wanted was to know my family and me better. I was hopeful my parents would find them to be good company and they'd enjoy Mother's cooking. It had been raining for the past four days, so it was nice to stay inside where it was warm and our house smelled like roasting chicken and a cooling chocolate cake.

Everyone appeared to enjoy the visit, and I was excited to see Dale again. He looked nice, spoke so well, and his conversation engaged my entire family. I hoped it wasn't too obvious when I dropped my gaze each time he looked my way. I didn't want to appear blissful sitting across the table at supper, but I could scarcely take my eyes off of him. My parents entertained often and always made our guests feel comfortable. I was glad they were able to get to know him a bit better and I loved having him in my home for a leisurely meal.

"Dad and I thank you, Mr. and Mrs. Fosbrink, for asking us to have supper with you."

"We're glad you could come. It was our pleasure."

"I don't know when I've enjoyed a meal as much as this. And, Anna, the cake you baked was the best I've ever eaten."

"I'm glad you liked it. Just another thing I learned from Mother."

"Looks like we all enjoyed it. It's almost gone," Dad said wiping the icing from his lips.

"By the way, Dale, when do you think you might go back to school?" I asked.

"You know, Aunt Rita had a stroke and her arm was useless, but it's getting better, and she can use it some now. I spoke to her about my returning to school in the fall, but she said she doesn't believe in it. Besides, she has plenty for me to do at her place. I suppose if I don't stay out too long, I can make it up, but I don't know how I feel about it right now, anyway."

Dad and I were sitting across the table from each other and both briefly raised our eyebrows when Dale said he didn't know how he felt about going back to college. *What? He didn't know how he felt about going back?* His lack of interest in getting an education was so different than anyone in my entire family. I hoped he would eventually reconsider and see the opportunities he could have for his future.

Our visit was short, and it was nice to see Dale, but I was disappointed that we'd been writing for nearly eight months and had only twice been alone to talk. We'd exchanged so many letters and both of us were aware we had genuine feelings for each other. I was much more upset about the rain than I let on. I was so looking forward to riding the horses and our chance to be alone. At least I'd impressed him with my cooking, and, as my aunt used to say, "Good food is a sure way to attract a man." Now that I'd apparently attracted him, I definitely wanted the chance to be alone.

We continued to correspond several times a week. Some of his letters were as much as six handwritten pages. It pleased me that Dale took the time to write such lengthy letters. Since mail was transported by trains that ran seven or eight times a day, mail in Vallonia was delivered morning and afternoon. Regular mail required only a two-cent stamp. During holidays, mail was sometimes delivered three times a day, but with all my school and social activities, I struggled to keep pace and write as often.

Dale was unable to find work so it allowed him to visit me in early April. He usually stayed at his cabin and only visited during the weekend since I was busy with school. We were becoming fonder of each other all the time, but he still hadn't kissed me. I hoped that would soon change because I was constantly teased by my cousin and girlfriends wanting to know if he was a good kisser. They didn't believe me when I insisted there was no report card to share.

I was looking forward to seeing Dale and when he arrived early Saturday afternoon, I stepped outside to greet him as he reached the walkway.

"Hey, there. What did you do, walk from your cabin?"

"No, just got back from Hamilton and walked from the train station."

"Come on in. Want something to eat?"

"That sounds great."

"We all ate a couple of hours ago. Mother made a big pot of vegetable soup and hot bread."

"Where is everyone, anyway?"

"Mother went to check on Grandpa, Dad's at the sand fields, Laura's with Clint, and Dude is across the street with his pal Roger. And, I'm right here with you."

"Well, so you are. That gives me an idea— you just might need a peck on your cheek," he said leaning toward me.

"Oh, you think so, do you? With a grin, and slowly shaking my head, I leaned back and said, "With my luck, Mother will show up right in the middle of it."

"Alright then, I'll behave. At least for now."

"Since the weather's nice today, let's go riding. I probably have nearly two hours before I need to be back to help with supper."

"Great idea. I've been thinking about it since I was here the last time."

When we were on our way to the barn to saddle the horses, Dale hesitated and slowly shaking his head, he looked me straight in the eyes, "This brings back memories of the last time I was here. I can't tell you how much I loved our time together, even though it was terribly short. It pleases me that you've been writing such sweet letters."

I said, taking a deep breath. "I'm glad it pleases you. I enjoy writing to you and I love hearing all about your travels."

"You know, we've been writing each other for a long time. I feel I know you so much better and now I refer to you as my girlfriend when I speak of you to my friends. I tell everyone how beautiful you are."

Still having that jittery feeling, I thanked him for his compliment, but suddenly felt my cheeks burn and lowered my eyes. It was too hard to look at him when he said things like that. I wasn't used to it. Taking another deep breath to recover my composure, I said, "I think it's nice you refer to me as your girlfriend."

"You don't mind that I tell my friends you're my girlfriend?"

"No, it's fine. I like it. So, now I guess it's okay that I call you my boyfriend."

"Whoa, did I just catch you winking at me?"

"Who, me? What makes you think I'd wink at you?"

"Just that look on your face, and because you're blushing," he said with a chuckle.

"Stop laughing at me and just get on Nellie. Let's ride to the hills," I said, knowing full well my cheeks and neck were flame red.

We started out with a canter, then Dale wanted to flat race until we reached the hills. The lush green trees, and cool crisp air silently welcomed our arrival offering us a romantic backdrop.

When we dismounted, he gently took me in his arms, holding and kissing me passionately. Many times, I'd imagined what our first kiss would be like, and his kisses didn't disappoint. We held each other in a loving embrace while he slowly slid his strong hands down my back. What a wonderful sensation it was to quietly stand facing him while he wrapped me snuggly in his strong arms. It was a first for me and I loved every moment of it.

"Anna, I've dreamt so often about us having this time alone and have wanted to whisper in your ear so softly how I truly feel about you. Now I can hold you in my arms, and kiss you, and look at you. I love having this private time together."

My heart was pounding while hearing his soft whispers so sweetly in my ear. His warm breath and soft lips on my neck gave me the chills. I loved being the center of his attention. It was finally a perfect day to ride to the hills and escape into our own world. When we both said, we wished it wouldn't end, I realized I'd fallen hard for him. And, this time, I had high marks to put on my "kissing report card" so the girls would stop teasing me.

⎯⎯⎯

Dale appeared to love being at our home, so much that Mother had to chase him out this time. Her expression and tone told me she was annoyed he'd stayed so long. I was sure he realized it as well. The entire day had been so pleasant we didn't want to say good-bye, but I do remember wondering if it was his infatuation with me, or the pleasant nature of our home that made him reluctant to leave.

The next letter from Dale was full of apologies about Mother having to run him off. He said he hoped she wouldn't have to do it ever again. He'd try to be more courteous and asked that I give him a sign should he ever forget himself in the future. I told Mother, and she seemed pleased he'd apologized. I wanted to keep him on her good side. I wanted my parents to like him.

I went to my room and with a smile on my face, I fell back on the bed. I cherished the memories of our afternoon spent together horseback riding, the beautiful things he said to me and how I felt being kissed. I loved it, all of it, but still something was missing. Something that made me feel anxious, but I couldn't quite put my finger on it.

Chapter Eight

*M*y next letter from Dale said he'd been having a difficult time finding work. He'd applied at several places
around Hamilton and Cincinnati, then returned to Kent, Ohio,
to again join the team with the tree service. He said it wasn't
"labor work," but insisted it was "professional work." It was clear
he wanted me to understand the importance in his choice of
employment and was hopeful it would turn out to be permanent.
But, it was obvious to me, since his pay was twenty-five cents an
hour, it would be hard for him to save much out of his weekly
wage. In my mind, Dale was more inclined to do manual labor,
and I found this choice worrisome. How could he expect to ever
get ahead? I wondered how his future employment without an
education could be different than what he had at present. His
pay merely met his living expenses with nothing leftover at the
end of the week. Had he even thought that through?

It set me to wondering and I found it hard to understand
why a young, healthy man would just accept that kind of

lifestyle. Was it because of the way he was brought up? Was it too hard for him to abandon the past because his entire life he had lived in poverty? Didn't he ever dream of a future when he'd not be penniless the day after he received his pay? I imagined he probably never was given any encouragement or guidance from his father since, he himself, had lived such a troubled past. Was there no one in Dale's entire family that he looked up to who could influence him and help him to see there was more to life? I knew I definitely wanted more out of life. I had laid the plans for my future and dreamt that dream often. I wanted to graduate from college, have a good job, marry the man of my dreams, and have three children. That was it. That was my dream.

In his letter, Dale described Kent as a small town built on the side of a hill with a population of about five thousand people. The morning after he arrived there, he went to the woods and began to prune trees. The largest trees were about 125 feet tall by about 3 1/2 feet in diameter and the men mainly pruned only the largest ones. He described how they climbed by means of ropes, which were passed through to the highest part of the tree allowing them to swing eighty or ninety feet in the air if necessary. He said they'd climb to the top and go out on the farthest branches using the rope, but sometimes the limbs would break resulting in a fall. Many men left the job because they couldn't deal with the stress and fear of a tragic or fatal fall. That frightened me. I simply couldn't see how he envisioned a dangerous and transitory life as a "professional" tree-trimmer as a suitable future for himself.

Dale spent much of his time in the evenings reading or writing to ward off the loneliness. He was an avid reader and often shared his interest in books with me and I enjoyed reading the "book reports" in his letters. He frequently watched shows at the local cinemas which he loved to critique. He saw *Three Musketeers* and *Covered Wagon*, but based on his view, they weren't worth a nickel. Then he saw *Hunchback of Notre Dame*, which he thought would be worthwhile for me to see if I could. I didn't have a lot of opportunity to see shows since there was no movie house in our town. Occasionally I'd take my sisters to Bloomington so they could see a show, and I relied on Dale's critiques to make my choices.

The next morning, Laura and I set out for Bloomington to see *Hunchback* and talked about it all the way home. We thought Lon Chaney gave an excellent performance, but it was so frightening we thought we'd have problems sleeping for a few nights.

I wrote Dale telling him know how much we liked the show and thanked him for his suggestion to see it. In the letter, I included a special handwritten invitation for him to come to my high school commencement and banquet in May. I wanted Dale to share my big day with me and take me to the dance, so I'd have a date, for a change.

>*To Mr. Dale Stevens,*
>>*Please be my guest at the Graduation*
>*and Banquet at Vallonia High School.*
>>*Seven o'clock p.m. May 17, 1928.*
>>>*RSVP,*
>>>*Anna*

In return, Dale sent his congratulations for my accomplishments, but unfortunately, he wouldn't be able to attend the events. He'd just received notice that his company was sending him to Orange, New Jersey, a thousand miles away. He said he wasn't sure when he'd get back to see me. I was terribly disappointed because I'd envisioned ending my high school days with my beau on my arm for all to see. I began to feel even more unhappy about my relationship with a traveling boyfriend who was away all the time. It seemed hopeless for us if we weren't able to see each other, and now he was being sent even further away.

❦

Dale wrote upon arriving at the boardinghouse in New Jersey, he found the residence old, dirty, and unpleasant. It was a long, red brick building with only a few windows. The men shared a bathroom, which was at the end of the hall on each floor. Each room had two double beds, no closet, and only several large nails in the wall on each side of the room to hang their clothes. He said it was a dreary, cold, rainy day, and it was discouraging to look for a place to stay. His only good news was that he found a friend whom he had roomed with at Kent.

Orange, New Jersey
May 5, 1928

Dear Anna,

The service forwarded your letter to me. I've read it over twice and liked the part about you having me in your dreams. It would be nice if you would dream of me every night.

I was off from work today and early this morning, I went to the Atlantic. Just quietly standing on the sand, it occurred to me that I was sort of small and insignificant. I loved the sound of the ocean. As I looked out to the foggy vastness in front of me, I saw an ocean liner creeping slowly into sight, ever so quietly emerging out of the fog like a huge gray ghost. As I watched the waves rolling in and out, I felt as though a vast amount of energy was expended upon the breakers every time a wave crashed upon them. At first a queer feeling of helplessness and fear took hold, and the tremendous emptiness of being out there all alone seemed overwhelming. The water was blue-green and salty and the smell of fish prevailed all along the coast. There were a great number of fisheries located along the entire front, so one could easily tell the fishing grounds by the stakes, which stood above the water.

Through the day, the steady drone of airplane motors fills the air accompanied by the mingled shrieks of railroad engines and the lower moan of boat whistles. The entire day was a wonderful experience. I loved it all.

I do hope all goes well with your graduation. I wish I could attend and take you to the dance. But listen, Kiddo, don't let anyone steal my girl. I would love to see you again, and I often think of our last time riding the horses to the hills. I have such wonderful memories of you and that day.

Bye My Love,
Dale

As I lay on my bed and read his letter describing the Atlantic, I clearly pictured it in my mind. I readily imagined the rolling waves upon the beaches, the smell of the ocean, and the sounds he described. I realized he loved traveling and seeing new country, but his adventures consumed his entire life to the degree he actually might be avoiding developing a future goal for himself. I wondered if roaming the country, trimming trees, and living in horrid boarding homes with men of questionable values could possibly lead Dale to a bright future. I struggled with mixed feelings and the uncertainty about the survival of our relationship. I found it hard to admit to myself that I was falling in love with a man who was too unlike me. A traveling man who was never around. More than anything, I wanted him to want me.

Chapter Nine

Receiving letters from Dale was always a thrill, and he continued to write several times a week. While I was looking forward to graduation in May, activities and responsibilities made me wonder if I could possibly meet all of my graduation deadlines. Also, I was looking for a summer job to help with college expenses in the fall and spent time following up on those prospects. Because I spoke of it so often, my friends and teachers knew of my dream to go to Indiana University—if I could come up with the money. For myself, I didn't want to just make a living. I wanted to be well off and was determined to go to college to make that happen.

My high school graduation and banquet dance were drawing near, but Dale would not be there to help me celebrate. I was becoming discouraged about his continual absence and wondering how much longer he'd be away. He was constantly on my mind and I missed him every day. I had fallen hard for Dale, but I needed more than letters to keep me content. It wasn't that there were any better opportunities in Vallonia, but come September, when I'd arrive in Bloomington for college, that definitely would change.

Vallonia, Indiana
May 15, 1928

Dear Dale,

I feel I'm getting to know you so much better through our letters, but you're away all the time, which has been hard for me. I'm starting to get concerned about your absence, especially during the time I'll be in school in Bloomington. I'd like to know specifically how you feel about me dating. If you're going to always be away, I think I should expect some freedom to date others.

My commencement and banquet will be the seventeenth and I wish you were here to take me to the dance. But since you're not, I'll just have to look for that tall, good looking man of my dreams with the black, wavy hair and brown eyes. I'll be wearing the blue dress Truly made me for the Latin contest. It would be nice if you'd visit here sometime before I wear it out completely. Till then, I hope you are well.

Anna

Orange, New Jersey
May 19, 1928

Dearest Anna,

I hope to be back some time before you go off to college. You asked about having dates. I don't think it is good for one to have side dates. If one doesn't suit, start all over again with someone else. But, to be serious, Dear, it's acceptable to have dates if you care to because it will be a good bit before I will have a chance to be with you.

Please don't forget me altogether. I want to keep in touch with you, just for the sake of old times, but I definitely don't want anyone stealing my girl. Course, I would be ready to put up a big fight to keep someone from running off with you, so don't try it.

Say, if you get your picture taken in your blue dress, I would sure like one.

Yours forever,
Dale

I was surprised when Truly arrived home the afternoon of my graduation, and I looked forward to talking over my concerns about Dale.

"I'm so glad you're here. I admit I was feeling sorry for myself since I wouldn't have a date for the banquet."

"I agree. It would've been nice to have an escort," she said.

"My friends have been asking about Dale's absence, since tonight happens to be the biggest event in my life."

"We can still make it fun. The whole family will be with you. By the way, I love your new hairstyle and you look pretty in your blue dress."

"I've saved it just for special occasions. I decided to have my hair cut for graduation so it would look more like what they wear in college. Dale wanted me to have my picture taken, but right now I'm annoyed with him."

"What's he done now, other than not being here for your banquet?"

"Besides asking him to come to my graduation, I also wanted to find out how he felt about side dates. I was totally confused by his response."

"Why? What did he say?"

"He doesn't feel he needs to be looking. He enjoys my friend-ship, and doesn't want anyone stealing me."

"He's trying to protect his interests, and of course he doesn't want anyone to take you away."

"He also said it wasn't good to have side dates, but then said it was all right if I cared to. I wondered if he were just stringing me along so he'd feel less lonely. I'm so confused."

"I agree. That *is* confusing. Personally, I think if he's a long distance away, it's all right to have side dates. For now, you don't have any opportunities, but you can count on it, that will change when you're in Bloomington."

"I hope so."

"It will. And, I can understand why he couldn't come for your graduation. I'm sure he wanted to be here. It would be expensive for him to come for such a short visit for your graduation."

I did have my picture taken in my blue dress just to show Dale what he missed by not being with me at the dance. I enjoyed myself at my graduation and the banquet was nice, but I was disappointed to attend the celebration without my beau by my side.

❦

While Dale was still on the East Coast, I prepared to move on to a summer job awaiting me in Indianapolis. One of my former teachers at Vallonia High had given me the name of a relative who was looking for live-in summer help. I immediately wrote to Mrs. Sanders that I was most interested in the position. She responded that she could use me as soon as I could get there. I'd be living with them to care for their two small children, along with attending to domestic duties while the parents worked.

That same day, I received notice of a scholarship, a diary from Dale as a graduation present, and a letter from my oldest brother, Roy. As I started reading it, I immediately had a horrible memory of my childhood when I had malaria. The whole family paid so much attention to me that I became spoiled, but eventually all of that attention was difficult for Roy to accept. When he was a teenager he resented how the family doted on me, and often showed his aggression when no one was around. I recall, Mother yelling from another part of the house when she heard me crying.

"Anna, for heaven sakes! What are you crying about now?"

"Roy keeps punching me. He grabbed my neck, and I couldn't breathe. Then, he tripped me and pushed me down on the floor, real hard."

In a harsh whisper and putting his hand over my mouth to silence me he said, "Shut up, tattletale, or I'll punch you again. You dirty, little squealer. You're always getting me in trouble."

Usually Mother would yell back, "Roy, stop teasing Anna and leave her alone. I can't stand her crying." Then he'd squint his beady little gray-green eyes, purse his lips, and give me his devil stare, along with another knuckle punch as he ran out of the room.

Roy seemed to enjoy making me cry. Sometimes he really hurt me. For many years, Roy and I didn't get along, so I politely avoided him until I started high school. However, after he graduated college, Roy surprised me when he said I always had, in fact, been his favorite.

It left me completely confused when I received a graduation letter from him congratulating me on working for myself, but criticizing me for my personal shortcomings. It seemed Roy could still make me cry, but with words instead of fists.

Wabash, Indiana
June 5, 1928

Dear Anna,

Am glad to see you working for yourself. You'll more quickly learn the advantage of a dollar that way. I think you'll be doing fine to earn and save $100.00 this summer. If you can save $100.00 I'll sure make you a nice present to help you along at school this fall, especially if you get the scholarship. I do so want you to get it. Anna, be careful of your fingernails, hair, and teeth. If you brush your teeth often, keep your hair and finger nails looking nice, it'll help a lot. Pick up all the nice manners you can. Don't even laugh loudly, or talk unbecoming. A well-bred girl. Do not permit yourself to slump into such sloppy posture as our sister Truly does. Boys and girls notice those things, and I don't want you to be like Truly. Have some pride.

The reason Truly and I never got along was because she always jabbered way down in her throat and slumped over on one foot like our old neighbor, Mr. Richards. You can see what a poor figure she has now. Don't get the blues. Just think what a wonderful time you'll have at college. Anna you're lucky to have a job. Anything is better than to grow up in old dusty, stinky Vallonia. Grit your teeth, brush them often, keep yourself clean, stand on both feet, use your sense of humor, and you'll make good. I'm for you.

Love,

Roy

After I read Roy's letter over a few times, I was so hurt, I let Laura read it.

"Anna, that's awful. Roy can be the meanest person on earth sometimes. Why does he say those things? Doesn't he know how those words hurt people?"

"I don't know. Sometimes I think it's just intentional to see if it'll cause tension between Truly and me. I don't understand how he could think I'd appreciate hearing how he doesn't like or get along with her. He knows I look up to her."

"But, what he said about you was just plain mean."

"I guess he thought I didn't take pride in my appearance or he wouldn't have mentioned it; it certainly was hard to read."

"Just forget him. He's always had a problem getting along. He thinks because he's the oldest, we should all look up to him and take his advice. Try to forget that letter."

I hated how cruel and outspoken he often was, especially with his sisters. Knowing how desperately I needed that money for college, I wrote Roy thanking him for his brotherly advice. I told him how grateful I was to him for his offer to help toward my college expenses. But, I was still so upset, I sent the letter from Roy to Dale for him to read also.

June 7, 1928
Orange, New Jersey

Dear Kiddo,

I did get quite a kick out of Roy's letter. In a way, the advice is good especially about your appearance, though on that you could hardly improve. Truly certainly can't expect to accomplish much more in the way of social standing. I disagree with him about being lucky in having a job, because you have all your life ahead to do hard work.

Seems as though you're getting plenty of advice, but I'm sure Roy is more qualified to give advice than I am. Too much reserve, study, and hard work prepares you for a disagreeable old age. Don't you think?

Dale

I was upset by Dale's unfavorable response about my summer job because I was lucky to have it and be able to save money for school. The same day, I received a second letter from Dale telling me he was sorry I was going to work. He couldn't understand why I ever took such a notion to take that job. He was sure I didn't have to, and it could injure my health.

I was thoroughly annoyed at him for telling me I shouldn't be working, that it could jeopardize my health, and especially since I didn't have to do that anyway. I began to see that he was trying to influence my decisions. I didn't like what he said about dating others along with his remarks about going off to college. With that, I was deeply hurt and wrote back in retaliation, telling him I'd received a letter from his dad saying "Dale lost twenty-five dollars of his money in the woods." I felt certain he wouldn't want me to know that—and he didn't.

He responded immediately. "I didn't aim to tell you because, well, you see, I didn't want you to think I was creating an excuse to come back home. I've had a hell of a time getting by without money, but you wouldn't have known if it hadn't been for Dad. I lost it in the woods; probably the rope worked it out of my pocket. I lost all of the pictures of you, my 'Y' card, a book of stamps, and five weeks' pay of twenty-five dollars. It had me so upset, almost to the point of wanting to give up entirely if it hadn't been for what I knew you'd think, even if you were too polite to say anything. It's over now as I received my first big pay of four weeks' straight time, five dollars a day. I don't know what to do with all of it. Someone ought to take care of my money for me. I can't. Ha!"

Dale complained he couldn't save any money, then would write about how he'd spent his money on shows, canoe rides, magazines, amusement parks, books, or whatever there was available to amuse himself. Saving money wasn't a priority for him, but then he shared his dreams of having a family and building a home. I let him know, not taking care of his money was causing me concern. I suggested we talk about it when we were together the next time. Clearly, our values as well as upbringings couldn't have been more opposite.

Chapter Ten

June 9th, I moved in with the Sanders in Indianapolis to start my summer job. It felt good to be on my own and earning money for college. The Sanders welcomed me into their home and I liked my private room at the end of the hall, where I found it to be quiet and comfortable.

The first week in July, I received an upsetting letter from Dale while he was still in Orange, New Jersey. He said he was having a hard time warding off the loneliness because now he was unable to work. He felt a burning sensation and soon realized he had poison ivy. He was unaware he'd scratched his arm with dirty nails while trimming and it caused the poison to spread rapidly. The rash and the pain became progressively more intense. He had developed blood poisoning in his left arm which was so painful he couldn't sleep.

I was just about beside myself after I read Dale's letter describing what he'd been experiencing. I realized I had become fretful and fidgety, but I couldn't help it. I imagined the worst and began pacing, wringing my hands, thinking—what if it were so serious that the blood poisoning was fatal? It horrified me that his arm had turned black. What if they had to amputate his arm? I was scared. My eyes filled with tears and I wished I could talk to Mother. I grabbed a handkerchief from my dresser and went to the kitchen where I found the Sanders eating lunch.

"I hate to bother you with this, but I just received this letter from Dale. I don't know what to do. He's so far away."

My throat tightened and again my eyes filled with tears. I held the letter out to show them, but couldn't stop shaking. Mrs. Sanders reached for my hand and motioned for me to sit down beside her. I couldn't hold it in any longer and began to cry.

"What's wrong? What's happened to Dale?"

"He was trimming trees and apparently touched poison ivy. He said his hands and nails were dirty, and it wasn't long before he noticed the poison had spread over his entire arm. First, his arm turned purple then black, and he had oozing blisters from the armpit to his wrist. He's scared what might happen to his arm, but I'm scared what might happen to *him*. Could he die?"

"Oh, no! That sounds awful. The black part, I mean," Mr. Sanders said.

"That's what has me so upset too."

"It *does* sound like it could be serious. I've had poison ivy before but it never turned black. Does he have a good doctor?"

"I don't know, Mr. Sanders. I don't know anything about the conditions there. He said his arm started burning and there was a constant throbbing like his heart was in his arm."

"Kinda sounds like infection, don't you think?" Mrs. Sanders said patting the back of my hand.

"I do. He said he hadn't slept in days because of the intense pain and he was burning up with fever. He had chills off and on, along with wild and crazy dreams. He was afraid it could be dangerous, but didn't write much more because he couldn't concentrate."

"I wish we could do something to help."

"I don't think any of us can help."

"He's so far away. That's the hard part," she said.

"It worries me that he's alone and feels so miserable."

"Maybe they'll send him home. Let us know if there's anything we can do."

"I will. I'm terribly worried about him and I needed someone to talk to. I'll be in my room, if you need me."

Orange, New Jersey
July 2, 1928

Dear Anna,

I went to the doctor again, and Kid, you ought to have seen my arm. My entire arm from my armpit to my wrist was black. I watched the doctor while he cut away all the black skin from my arm. Oh, boy, I didn't think I'd survive the intense pain which almost brought me to my knees.

The rest of the day, I lay in a big cane chair on the porch, with the bandages covering my entire arm and watched the people go by. I finally fell asleep, which was the first in the last four days. I am worried about my arm and what is going to happen to me. It is the most frightening thing I have ever been through. I sure appreciate your letters.

Love,
Dale

This was someone who had been through horribly tough times all his life, but I could tell from the tone of his letter, he was struggling not only with the pain, but the fear about his future.

The extensive damage from the infection would take a long time to heal completely, and there he was, so far away from home and unable to work. I couldn't stop thinking about the difficult situation he was in, and I most likely wouldn't see him before I started college. I encouraged him to think about getting some college courses underway in the future, suggesting he might be able to make more money once he had completed some years in college. He might be able to have a less risky position and wouldn't have to work so hard.

Indianapolis
July 7, 1928

Dear Dale,

I'm sitting here in a blue flowered, over-stuffed chair in the living room beside the large picture window at the Sanders' home. I'm so enjoying the lifestyle they have created and hope someday to live just like this. They've gone to visit friends for a few hours and have taken the children with them. I put a roast with potatoes, carrots, onions, and celery in the oven. The house is fragrant and quiet. It's raining, and I'm listening to soft classical music on the radio. I have my writing tablet on my lap, composing some heartfelt wishes and prayers for your arm to heal. I know it's been depressing and hard on you, especially when all of the men go off to work. I imagine you're left there all alone, wondering if your arm will heal enough to continue working. I'm so sorry this has happened to you and hope this letter finds you doing much better.

I'm getting anxious about starting college and excited about what opportunities lie

ahead. I can hardly wait to be part of not just the academics, but the social part too.
As Ever,
Anna

Orange, New Jersey
July 10, 1928
Dearest Anna,
Thank you for your letter and inspiration. I'm doing a little better, but my arm still isn't healed. I've been trying to work, which has only made things worse for me because I tend to re-injure it.
I know you're getting anxious, but by all means, don't let anything stop you from going to college, for you can have most anything you want after you are through with it. I'll be sending applications, with my terrible grades to Bloomington and Kent to see if I can get into college. Thank you for your encouragement about furthering my education. I'm seriously considering it if I can get accepted.
I miss you too and wish I could hold you in my arms and kiss you into forever.
Love Always,
Dale

In his letters, Dale had a way of making me feel special, and I longed to be with him, to see his face and hear his voice. But, no matter how special he could make me feel in his letters, I was excited about making new friends at IU and living an adult social life away from the confines of Vallonia, and even my relationship with him. I'd read so much about the roaring twenties, the parties, the clothes, the music, and dancing. I wanted to at least experience some part of it. I wanted to go to the football games and yell at the top of my lungs for IU's team. I wanted to dance at the parties after the games. I wanted friends who were as excited as I was about our future lives after college.

It seemed when I last wrote him about it, he wasn't totally in favor of either of us dating another. In fact, he objected to it. Although I thought I'd have a fun social life, maybe join a sorority and live in a sorority house, I wanted the freedom to date college men. After all, I'd never had any other boyfriend or even been on any "real" dates. Opportunities in Vallonia were almost nonexistent, and Dale had never taken me out.

Orange, New Jersey
July 25, 1928

Dearest Anna,

It's miserably hot tonight. I saw my first dirigible today. "The Los Angeles" is here for the opening of the Newark Municipal Airport. Another new scene for me.

Now kid, I will devote the rest of this note to quarreling with you. First of all, it doesn't make any difference to me as to whether you think I should have dates or not. I am not acquainted with any girls for the simple reason that one is enough. Don't you worry about me. I am certain how I feel about us and don't want to date. I must get some sleep.

Yours Ever,
Dale

His response left no question in my mind regarding his feelings about my dating others. Dale was satisfied with his situation and wasn't interested in dating anyone else. He knew what his life would be like when he accepted the job with the tree service. He would be traveling, but he enjoyed experiencing new places. It appeared he wasn't concerned he was unfairly confining me to his wishes without considering mine.

I thought a lot about us during the summer and felt it was self-ish that Dale was so determined our relationship should be "his" way. In the beginning, he drew me in with his romantic attention, but now I wondered how much of our relationship was based on my own desire to feel special to someone. I realized he had me on a string . . . and that string had become the tourniquet threatening my future. I found my feelings for him had begun to wax and wane, and I was having second thoughts.

Chapter Eleven

*A*fter caring for the Sanders girls for many weeks, I realized that while I enjoyed watching them, they were so active they sometimes wore me out. I not only managed them, but cleaned house, washed, ironed, and prepared the meals. I began to appreciate my mother's own hard day-in and day-out responsibilities. It was a full day, each day, but I was grateful to have the work. It would help with my school expenses, and I'd saved every penny. I planned to finish the summer with my usual job at the canning factory in August. I hoped to see Dale sometime during the summer, but from what he'd written, it seemed nearly impossible.

Later that August, Dale arrived back in Hamilton and dropped me a note. He said he didn't write sooner because he'd complained so much in his letters already and didn't want to send me more letters filled with more complaints. His doctor had lanced his arm six times which was excruciatingly painful and he was all bandaged up, with a promise of staying that way for a while. I was disappointed to read that his doctor probably wouldn't consent to letting him make the trip down to see me before I left for college.

As soon as I completed my summer job at the Sanders', I began my two-week position at the cannery in Vallonia, where I'd make a dollar a day. This would leave a few weeks before going to Bloomington, and more than anything I hoped Dale could visit me during that time, but it didn't seem likely. I began organizing and packing my belongings so I'd be ready on September 11th, to leave my hometown and start my new, adult life.

My wardrobe had looked pretty sad for a college freshman, but Truly, my talented seamstress, came to the rescue. She made several dresses for me. My favorite was a navy-blue dress with pleats on the bodice and a white linen collar, along which she tatted a lace edging. I put on the dress, then pulling the long sleeves down and adjusting the collar, I performed a turn for Truly to admire her handiwork. The skirt flowed gracefully around my mid-calf as I gave the turn and I felt like the grown-up I'd soon pretend to be.

"The dress fits you perfectly. It makes you look sophisticated and even more slender. That navy brings out the blue in your eyes. You look just beautiful."

"I *feel* beautiful! Do you think the girls at Chi Omega will invite me to pledge? I'm so nervous about it."

"Of course. With your outgoing personality, you quickly make friends, and you're always helping others. I know they'll gladly accept you. Besides, you're family. Remember the legacy?"

"Yes, I just hope I won't get homesick."

"You won't get homesick. You'll be too busy having fun and studying."

⚭

To my surprise, Dale did get to Vallonia for a quick visit before I left for college. I greeted him at the door with a huge heartfelt smile.

"Hello, my darling. I'm so glad to finally get to see you."

"Come on in," I said excitedly.

"I wasn't sure I'd be able to make it here before you left for Bloomington. I hope it's all right I came unannounced."

"Of course, it's all right."

"May I kiss you before we go inside? I've missed you something awful."

I flashed Dale a wink and another huge smile as I bit my lip, wrinkled up my nose, and briefly squinted my eyes. Then I stepped out onto the porch pulling the door closed behind me.

"Certainly, I'd love a kiss. Even two, for that matter."

It had been such a long time since I'd been kissed that I almost forgot how his kisses affected me. Suddenly, that euphoric feeling was present and my entire body felt tickled inside. I was thrilled to see him and realized Dale still had a profound effect on me.

"Wow, Dale, that was delicious," I said rolling my eyes.

"My darling, that's what's referred to as an understatement. Ha! I think I just felt the earth move."

"Are you feeling better? I mean, your arm, is it healed?"

"It's better—much better. It's pretty discolored, but the pain is gone," he said rolling up his sleeve to show me his scars.

Holding the door open, I motioned for him to come in. "You know Mother always puts on a huge spread—there's plenty. We were just sitting down to supper, so it's perfect timing."

Dale stepped inside waving a hello to everyone and was greeted with a warm welcome in return. Mother had prepared a German supper of bratwurst, sauerkraut, boiled potatoes, mashed carrots, and biscuits with butter and honey.

During supper, my brother Doc was all ears about my college plans. From the time when he was just a little tyke, he always wanted to be a doctor like our neighbor across the street. He spent so much time over there, we started calling *him* Doc. He hoped to go to medical school in Indianapolis in two more years. Most of the family, including Dale, sat around the dining room table engaged in a discussion about the courses I'd be taking. They agreed it seemed to be a heavy schedule and even suggested I not take all the planned courses at the same time.

"If anyone can do it, you can," Dad said blotting his forehead with his handkerchief.

"Anna, have you lost weight?" Dale asked.

"Yes, I guess, maybe a few pounds because I've been so nervous. All I think about lately is going to IU and being so far away from home."

⁂

Wanting to be alone with Dale, I changed the subject and asked him to take a walk with me. When we stepped out on the porch, we exchanged a few more memorable and passionate kisses, then he took my hand as we began our walk.

"I'm so happy you could come to see me before I had to leave for school. I was beginning to think it was hopeless."

"It's been far too long since we've been together. When I first got here, I felt weird, like it was my first date or something." Dale leaned in and gave me a quick peck on the cheek. "Did you feel the same way?"

"Yes, I did at first, but your kiss on the porch made it seem like old times. We just needed some time to ourselves and privacy to talk. I've been wondering what you'll do for work."

"I'm not sure. I'll need a bit more time to completely heal, then I'll see if the company can use me around home. If not, I'll try to find something else around that area. One thing I do know for sure, I'm going to miss being able to come here to see you. I don't know how visiting you in Bloomington will work out.

⁂

The next morning, my brother Ken drove Mother and me to Bloomington to move me into the red brick, two-story, all-girl dorm.

We met my roommate, Dorothy, who also would be attending her first year at IU. Dorothy had already settled into our spacious room and helped us move my belongings in from the car. A twin bed lined each side of the room, and at the foot of each bed, a small desk sat against the wall. Closet space was limited, but we shared a dresser, allowing each of us two drawers. Two large windows filled the room with sunlight. I had no difficulty accepting this as my new home, at least for a semester.

After they helped settle me in, Ken drove Mother back to Vallonia. Dorothy and I decided to check out the campus. Even though I'd been there several times, it seemed strange to be in the midst of those who would have such an impact on my life. This is where my future would begin, and I had to make a go of it and not give up—ever.

We walked around campus, and I couldn't help but notice the men. Men of all ages and some were quite good looking. Some dressed casually, but many wore suits or dress pants with a shirt, and tie. The women were also well dressed. Noticing the details of their clothing, I was grateful Truly had made me such lovely grown-up dresses. This farm girl would now have a little bit of class.

◈

My first day at college was so exciting. I was relieved to have such a nice roommate. Dorothy and I hit it off right away, and I felt we'd always be good college friends. I didn't think of Dale once all afternoon, but after supper, I remembered to send him my address and told him how foreign everything seemed. I was finally living my dream.

Chapter Twelve

Many of the girls in the dorm stopped by to introduce themselves and Dorothy and I spent most of the week-end getting better acquainted. We laughed a lot and slept little. My stomach felt queer much of the time. The first two days were hectic, and finding my way around campus to get to my classes on time wasn't as easy as I'd expected.

It was a nice surprise to receive a letter from Dale so soon after moving to Bloomington.

Hamilton, Ohio
September 13, 1928

Dearest Anna,

It was wonderful to see you over the week-end, but I was sorta disappointed about the visit. It was too short, even though I realized it couldn't be helped. The little girl I'd known before has suddenly grown up into a more charming lady. Honest, the change in you is wonderful, and you looked so beautiful. At first, I hardly knew what to say or how to act. I had so much I wanted to say, but when I was around you I couldn't think of everything. I'd counted on having more time to spend with you alone.

Your mother asked what we are planning to do with the cabin property, and she asked Dad the same thing. I think it is a great place, and would take a lot of fixing up, but that would be something to work for. It has such natural beauty.

Love,
Dale

I began to read between the lines and wondered if Dale felt we'd be living on his property in our future. I'd seen it at a distance years ago while riding Spiffy, and it was certainly not what I considered "natural beauty." Maybe it was a great getaway spot, but I couldn't envision spending the rest of my life out there. What a scary thought. I just couldn't imagine what life would be like. I wanted a normal life, a little house in town, children that we could raise, keep them safe, and teach them well. I admit, I wanted more. A lot more.

Hamilton, Ohio
September 29, 1928

Dearest Anna,

I've had but one letter from you in over two weeks, which is a new record, but also can be easily broken. I wonder how you are and if everything's still so exciting. After all, do you find your work and studies to be worth it? I don't see how you stand the strain of it, though

*part of college life is terribly interesting. The
social part, I mean. I hardly know how to, or
whether to, write at all when you don't answer
my letters. It's barely possible that you haven't
time, but maybe you don't care to continue? It
isn't that, is it? I'd rather most anything else
would happen than that.*

*I started back to work but wanted to know
when is the next time I can see you? Please let
me hear from you.*

Love,
Dale

I couldn't tell if Dale was jealous, angry, or just feeling neglected.
I decided to at least refresh his memory about the real me and my
ethics when it came to academics. I reminded him that studying
was a priority for me and it consumed most of my time. I thought,
by now, he should know me well enough to understand my classes
and studies come first. I wanted him to know that I was studying for
tests and realized I owed letters to many, but needed to stay on top
of things and I liked it just fine at IU.

Dale was having problems with the car and wasn't sure when
we could meet. I sent another short note letting him know I was
disappointed, but I understood. I also told him of my deep concerns
about the upcoming Presidential election and was afraid it might
turn out badly. We often talked about our differences with regards
to politics, and he seldom passed up the chance to try to persuade
me toward his preferences as a Democrat.

I wasn't in favor of Hoover, but would never consider voting
for Al Smith, the Democrat from New York. The subject of politics
was always of great importance to me, and I often remembered the
time my dad ran for office in Vallonia on the Republican ticket.
He'd been the Postmaster for several years, so he felt he might have

a chance as "Trustee." Dad would have been a great Trustee, but he lost the election since the town was largely Democratic. He never ran again.

Hamilton, Ohio
November 8, 1928

Dear Anna,

You needn't be afraid about the election; it is all over now. Of course, I am sorry it had to turn out as it did, but here is hoping Hoover will prove better than the last few Republican presidents. I cast my vote for a now defeated man. It was a perfect landslide and all on account of religion. I believe I could be a good Republican, but I would have a hard time being a good Methodist. At best that would be halfway, wouldn't it? I couldn't tell whether you were serious or not about my conversions. I hope to see you for Thanksgiving.

Love,
Dale

Dale didn't come for Thanksgiving because he had to work the Saturday after, but he certainly hoped to come for Christmas. Later he wrote he "made a flying trip to New York with the boys" to go hunting. When I received his letter, I was as mad as an old wet hen. I tore it up in little pieces and put it back in the envelope. Something about his "trip with the boys to hunt in New York" and spending three days there didn't sit well with me, especially since he kept missing connections to be with me, and we hardly ever had any time together. Maybe it was partly the sarcastic way he said "he was glad I'd had such a marvelous time at Thanksgiving, so his being with me wouldn't have added a thing to my perfect day." Then I wondered if he ever went on hunting trips or other excursions he didn't tell me about. This set me to questioning myself—was this just another little imperfection in our relationship?

I was still seething about Dale's adventure to New York with the boys when I returned to campus late Saturday afternoon. When I arrived at the dorm, Dorothy was getting ready for a date with her boyfriend Charles to go to a dance at the hall.

"Anna, I didn't expect you back today."

"Me either, but I changed my mind at the last minute."

"How was Thanksgiving? Was Dale able to come?"

"No, and actually I'm disgusted about it."

"Why? What happened?"

"He didn't come, but instead went with his friends to New York on a hunting trip."

"What? A hunting trip?"

"Yup. A hunting trip. And was I ever mad when I got his letter."

"I thought he was always complaining he didn't get enough time to be with you."

"Ha! So much for that. Wonder what they were hunting."

"Why don't you join Charles and me and go to the dance? Come on, it's going to be fun, and it'll cheer you up."

"Are many students back from the holiday?"

"Yes, quite a few. The "After Thanksgiving Dance" is usually crowded. Charles said his friend Frank was looking for a good dance partner, and you'd be a great one to meet up with him."

I didn't even hesitate and surprised myself when I agreed so quickly to go along. After all, why should I pass up the chance to have a little fun? It would be my first dance at the college and I couldn't wait to meet Frank. He was a second-year mathematics student, and Charles told me all about him on the way to the hall.

"Frank, meet Anna. She's a great dancer and agreed to be your partner tonight," Charles said shaking hands with Frank.

"Fantastic. Anna, I'm glad you could come. I've been looking for a girl who can dance."

"I hope you won't be disappointed. This is actually my first big dance party, so I'll try to keep up with you."

"Don't worry. You'll catch on. I'll lead. Just follow me and you'll do fine. I've been dancing a long time."

I thought he seemed a bit conceited and a little outspoken, but it was too late now. I definitely didn't want to look like a fool out on the dance floor.

Frank loved to dance and was an interesting partner. He threw himself into the music and was all over the floor performing as if he were Fred Astaire himself. He seemed to enjoy the attention from the sidelines as he performed his smooth moves, but he also seemed to have been born with more than two hands. I felt certain he had eight, and they appeared everywhere—in the air, at his knees, on my shoulders, around my waist. I don't know how I endured the evening dancing with him, but I did. Dorothy didn't know him well at all, but I soon realized he wasn't my type.

It was a fun and different night out for me. I didn't hear from Frank after that evening, and that was just fine, but it gave me confidence knowing I could keep up with such a good dancer. And, at least, the music and the dancing made me forget my anger toward Dale that night.

Chapter Thirteen

I returned home for Christmas break and looked forward to getting reacquainted with my family while indulging in special holiday baking and decorating. My brothers and sisters looked forward to experiencing all of those loving times together every year with my parents, and we all tried our best to make it home safely, even in the worst weather. I've always thought of Mother's special traditional German coffee cakes as the smell of Christmas holiday. Mother let the round yeast dough rise in pans on the table, then she'd poke her thumb deep down into the dough to make a well for the melted butter and cinnamon sugar before baking. The lingering smell of the sweet baked cinnamon bread permeated our entire home.

Dale sent word he'd arrive in town Monday, Christmas Eve, and would join us for Christmas morning breakfast around eight. I was so excited to see him again. I kept looking out the window then I heard his signature three knocks on the door.

"I got it," I called out as I opened the front door and stepped outside.

"Good morning, my pretty lady. Merry Christmas."

"Good morning, handsome. Merry Christmas to you. I'm glad you were able to make it."

My old feelings for Dale returned instantly and I was thrilled to finally see him. Greeting me on the front porch, he quickly removed his black wool gloves and gave me a long and loving embrace. Holding my face in his hands, he kissed me passionately as though it came straight from his heart to my lips and I felt every bit of his love.

Once inside, the wonderful aroma lured Dale to step into the kitchen and check out the breakfast goods. The table was set, and Laura was helping Mother prepare the food while Dad was tending to the stoves in the house. Over the weekend, Kay, Laura, and I had made pine wreaths and garlands tied with red ribbons, which we placed around the house. The Christmas tree was beautifully adorned with a collection of homemade decorations, and the smell of pine welcomed everyone.

By eight-thirty, most of my brothers and sisters who were married or away at school had arrived home. Roy commanded everyone's attention so Mother could say grace, which she always said in German. After we finished breakfast, Dad stood at Mother's back, putting his hand on her shoulder as he always did, and he said, "Merry Christmas, Dora. That was a beautiful meal." I don't ever remember them kissing in front of us, but they shared a special bond witnessed by everyone who knew them.

While enjoying a festive day together, for me, the best part, other than the gift exchange, was singing Christmas carols with my family and Dale. He loved the scarf and the photo of me that I gave him. I loved the stationery he gave me, but thought the gift a little self-serving. Later that morning we saddled the horses, and rode through freshly fallen snow to Grandpa's house to complete our mission of getting mistletoe. We thought it gave us a perfect excuse to playfully steal a few kisses publicly.

Before we parted from my family, we walked down the lane with the excuse we needed to walk off some of our indulgences of the day. I grabbed my new navy wool cloche and long navy knit scarf. Even though we were wrapped in heavy woolen coats, the dampness in the cold air greeted us with a crisp chill.

"Anna, you look so cute in your new hat." Then, after giving a long sigh, Dale said, "And by the way, I think I'm falling in love with you. I find I'm obsessed with thoughts of you to the point I sometimes think I'll go crazy because I think of nothing else."

"I wish we had more time to spend together, but I'm not so sure if we lived closer, we'd have more time together, given my crazy class schedules."

"I'd love to have your drive to be successful, but I never thought much of being a college graduate."

"But why not?" I said wrapping my arm snuggly around his and continuing on our walk.

"It always seemed to be too much of a stretch for me."

"You're so smart. You read everything, and you write beautifully."

"I think in my mind, since I've always had so little, I never felt driven to reach for more. I think I merely accepted life as it is."

"Why don't you see what you can do to get started by sending your records to IU or Kent? I do think you'd enjoy college life, and we could be together if you'd come to IU."

"You know, I told you I went a few months to Columbia College, but didn't feel at all connected. Then, I quickly ran out of money. I do like psychology, and I've given some thought to studying it."

"I think psychology might be a good choice for you. It would be a long hard road to graduate with a PhD, but I know you can do it."

"I don't know, I think maybe I'm afraid of failure, again."

"You need to get that notion out of your head."

I was encouraged that Dale was considering college again in spite of his experience at Columbia.

"Right now, all I want to do is hold you and kiss you."

"You're so cute, Dale. But, you do have a one-track mind. I love it when you wrinkle up your nose and squint your eyes at me, making that funny little face."

"What? Like this?" he said making a face. "I won't head back, my darling, until you kiss me."

"Do you want me to give it to you, or throw it to you?"

We returned to the house to say good-bye and thank everyone for their gifts, then hurried to pack our belongings for my return to campus. Dale offered to drive me back to Bloomington, which gave us the opportunity to talk at length. On the trip back, Dale reminisced about the wonderful time he had spending the day with my family.

"You know, the celebrations at your house are so different than at mine. Everyone is so happy, talking and laughing, and the decorations and food are so festive. At our house, the day is usually much quieter. The presents are mostly for the children and often secondhand. Dad and I sometimes paint the toys so they look new. Later in the day, relatives stop by to share cake and coffee. But our celebration is nothing like it is at your house."

"I do love the holidays at home. My brothers and sisters always make a fuss over our parents and each other. Mother's responsible for that."

As we drove, I began to tell Dale more about my life at college. I confided in him that I felt I didn't always fit in because some of the girls in the dorm just wanted to socialize. I didn't feel I could afford the time to do that.

"It would be hard to find many students who *are* as dedicated as you." Dale said.

"There's a girl named Stella, and she prides herself as the leader in the dorm and is always stirring things up."

"So, what is it she does that irritates you?"

"Well, one Saturday evening she wanted some of the girls to walk over to the boys' dorm to see if they could meet up. They were cheering and giggling so loud I couldn't concentrate. When I asked them to lower the noise so I could study, she turned toward me, rolled her eyes and said, "Anna, you're such a blue-nose."

"A blue-nose? Are you joking?" Dale said.

As we drove along he took my hand, kissing it a few times and said, "I assure you, you are phenomenal. They know it and are just jealous."

"I know I could've handled it better, and I didn't want you to side with me. But, I don't like conflict, and Stella still isn't nice. Some of the girls kind of stick together, and I don't feel I'm in their social class."

"Are you kidding me? I'm sure you're more beautiful and charming than any of them. I feel quite certain about that. What about Dorothy? Is she still there? How does she feel about them?"

"Yes, and she feels the same as I do. Thank goodness."

"Thank you for a beautiful Christmas," Dale said leaning over to kiss my cheek.

"Please be careful going back to Vallonia. I'm going to miss you. It has been wonderful finally being together."

Dale helped me take my belongings to the dorm and as he turned to head back to his car, I saw him make a fist with his right hand, tap it gently over his heart, and then look back at me. He flashed a wink and sweetly threw me a kiss good-bye.

⊙≫

Dale wrote that he arrived home in Hamilton safely after the holidays. He advised me to "discard that little complex" of mine because there's no room for it. He thinks everyone has some sort of a complex, but I was "lucky because most people have more than one." He closed his letter by saying, "Just don't let the girls in the dorm get to you."

With papers to write, a book to finish reading, and personal finances to recalculate, I found contentment in the quiet and solitude of the dorm. I was happy to be back on track —both with Dale and with my studies.

Chapter Fourteen

*M*y contentment didn't last long after discovering my expenses were greater than expected. I'd hoped to have the promised money from Roy but, so far, he hadn't come through. I dreaded the possibility that I might have to drop out and certainly didn't want to be in the same boat as Dale when he went to Columbia.

I was down in the dumps and glad to see Dorothy who had just returned from Christmas break.

"Anna, Charlie and I are going over to the Book Nook for a soda. Why don't you come along?"

"I'd love to. I need to get out for a while," I said.

"There's a band forming on the street over there, and it looks like fun."

"That does sound like fun. Let me grab my jacket."

We walked to the Book Nook, and everyone appeared to still be in a celebratory mood after New Year's. Many of the students were singing and dancing in the street. One of Charlie's friends came over and introduced himself as "Big John." I was immediately taken with the tall, blond-haired fellow's good looks.

"And, who is this young lady?" he said extending his hand to me.

"She's Anna, my roommate," Dorothy said.

"I'm glad to meet you. Should I call you Big John or just John?"

"You can call me John. That's good enough. So, how are all of you anyway, and what's everyone doing later this afternoon? Anyone want to take in a show?"

I thought, *He seems like a nice guy. And, so friendly. I'd love to go to a show with him.* Dorothy and Charlie had already made plans, but I jumped at the chance. Later, John and I strolled over to the cinema to see *Street Angel.* It felt so good to be out on "a real date." I enjoyed the show, and I had an especially nice time with John. I found him to be a good conversationalist, so we had no difficulty keeping the conversation moving along.

"Where are you from, and what are you studying?" I asked.

"I'm from Front Royal, Virginia, and taking second-year English. How about you?"

"I'm a freshman and also studying English. I'm from Vallonia, about fifty miles south of here."

The day turned out so pleasantly and was just what I needed. I enjoyed John's company immensely. I found him to be both charming and handsome. I wondered if I'd be seeing him again sometime.

> *Bloomington, Indiana*
> *January 1, 1929*

> *Dear Dale,*
>
> *We have much to talk about when we meet the next time. I'm not sure I'll be able to stay here at IU. I'm in turmoil over my situation, studying, finals, and the possibility of lacking the funds I need. It seems my future here may be coming to an end. I'm sorry,*

but for the first time in my life, I'm feeling down-hearted. Even though I spoke to Roy about it Christmas day, he never made good on his promise to help me financially. So, I desperately need to earn money to finish my courses. I hope you understand and am sorry if I burdened you with my troubles.

Always,
Anna

Hamilton, Ohio
January 3, 1929

Dearest Anna,

Well, I expected a letter from you, Kiddo, but you sure floored me this time. Dearest, it is surely fine when one can brave all odds and come out a winner. The stress of study is bad enough, let alone the stress over finances. I think after a good cry and some sleep you will then be able to concentrate to figure out a plan that will make a difference in the path for your future. I want to offer advice, but I would never forgive myself if you afterwards resented an action you had taken upon my recommendation.

Dearest, I love you. I desire to give you my best and don't know how. Don't stop to wonder what other people may think. If they mind their work, they haven't time to think of yours. I must close now. Get some sleep and quit worrying.

With Undying Love,
Dale

When I read Dale's letter, I appreciated his concern and knew he wanted to help, but my problem was something I needed to resolve in my own way. I'd been studying for tests and doing research in the library on a required presentation for English when Dorothy stopped by. We began to explore my financial situation to come up with ideas on how to stay in college. Suddenly, it came to me that I could change direction and still reach my goal. If I left IU and went to business school to become a secretary, it would take a little longer, but I was certain it was manageable. I just needed to think it through over the next few days and see if it still seemed to be the right thing to do.

A few days later, I sent Dale a letter to update him on my progress. I was feeling better about my future and it had helped me to write down my frustrations. I was back on track once again and determined to make it through. I could clearly see how to attain my goals and was eager about an opportunity to become a secretary.

Hamilton, Ohio
January 8, 1929

Dearest Anna,

I want you to know my feelings for you are strengthened, and I want you to believe me. I realize you have never said you love me, but I want to be a real friend until you feel differently. I wanted to tell you I was afraid you hadn't understood me when I told you that I love you. I don't know when I first began to love you, but the change from friendship took place long ago, in fact it seems ages. Sometimes I think I shouldn't have told you. I am not sorry though. I would never have told you had I thought it would have made a change in our friendship. Please don't let it do that. I would be forever sorry if it did.

I wanted you to know that I love you most dearly and with the purest and most noble thoughts. I have pledged myself to you and that love. Let us continue as we have always done, and I am sure in time it will bring a richer and better friendship than we have ever known. I hope this doesn't sound foolish, if it does, forget it. In the future, I will pledge my letters solely to the daily news. I wish I could have written it better. I wrote all this so you'd understand and I hope you will. Christmas, I had such an enjoyable time with you even if I didn't hold my fork right. I will work on that and try to do better the next time.

With Deepest Love,

Dale

Dale mentioned in his letter that he wanted to work on his table manners. At times, I tried to overlook it and it didn't bother me, but other times it was a biting irritation. At least, he acknowledged an awareness and continues to try to improve. I thought back to our grade school days when our classmates commented on his poor manners and how he often talked with his mouth full. Now, at least, there were signs he was making progress.

Although I hadn't told Dale I loved him, I wasn't surprised he signed his letter "With Deepest Love." There were many things I loved about him and was attracted to him, but wasn't in love with him—at least not yet. When I thought about our relationship, it concerned me that he had little interest in setting goals for himself. Many times, I wondered whether we were even right for each other. He was definitely a dreamer but had little ambition to make his dreams a reality. I was concentrating on how to stay in school and had a long way to go before I could commit to any man, especially one with an uncertain future.

It lifted my spirits when I received a letter from Truly. She'd been the past president of the Chi Omega sorority, and was invited to give a presentation to the new inductees here at IU. I was excited to be able to talk to her about my change in plans. As a social worker, Truly always seemed down to earth and practical with her advice, and I valued her opinion.

With a warm sisterly hug and kiss, I welcomed her at my dorm.

"You couldn't have come at a better time, as far as I'm concerned."

"Oh, what's been happening?" She said removing her gloves and coat.

"I've hit a roadblock about my future here."

"How so? What kind of a roadblock?

"I'm about to run out of money, but I'm working out a new approach to get back on track."

"Wait a minute. How much do you need?"

"I don't know just yet, I'm still working on it."

"I can front you some money to help you out. And what about Roy? Has he made good on his offer to help? Didn't he tell you he'd send you money if you received a scholarship?"

"Yes, he did say that, but when I approached him at Christmas, he never answered back. He seemed as though he was avoiding me the entire day."

"Don't worry. I'll get after him to make good on his promise."

"I've given a great deal of thought about going to business school in Seymour to become a secretary."

"Anna, that's a great idea. You'll then come back to IU, won't you?"

"Yes, I figure there are probably many secretarial positions here in Bloomington, and I might be able to work during the day and take courses in the evenings until I graduate."

"You can live at home and take the bus to Seymour."

"Yes, that's what I've been thinking."

"I wouldn't think it would take long to get a secretarial certificate. What a great plan. Now, let's eat dinner and talk about you pledging Chi Omega."

Truly gave me an advance so I could continue at IU and promised she'd make certain Roy kept his promise of one hundred dollars toward my education.

Chapter Fifteen

*L*ate January, Dale wrote he'd started working at the Ford Auto Factory. He'd make the same amount of money, but the work was much easier. I asked if he could come to see me at IU, but he said he wouldn't be able to make it to Bloomington. The train schedule was too complex and required several changes each way. He wouldn't get back in time for work, and his old Ford wasn't in good enough shape to make the trip.

※

Friday after school, Dorothy and I stopped over at the sorority house to visit with some of the girls we'd just met. When we walked in, they were all huddled together in one room, giggling and whispering. We were curious, and knew right away something was up.

I lowered my voice and asked, "What's going on with you girls?"

They began motioning to us, "Anna, Dorothy, come over here. Want a drink? We have a bottle of giggle water and some Coca-Cola."

"Wow, where'd you get that stuff?" Dorothy said in a whisper.

One of the girls said, "We had Big John get it for us. Have some. It tastes pretty good."

I wondered if she meant the Big John I'd met. Of course, we all had to try it. I'd never had alcohol before and thought it wasn't too bad. No one in my family ever drank alcohol. Well, no one I ever found out about. Maybe some of my brothers tried it. I'd imagine Roy probably had. Maybe even Ken. I didn't feel any different after I drank it, but maybe I hadn't had enough.

I wrote Dale that some of the girls at the sorority house indulged in alcohol on occasion and that I'd tried it. He wrote back saying, "So you've taken to drinking, have you? Is that what goes on at the sorority houses? I'm sure you're aware we still have prohibition, so don't get caught with that stuff. It sounds as if things are turning out pretty well for you. I'll bet you're tickled pink just to get to room with the girls. Please don't leave these letters lying around for someone else to read."

❦

We were again trying to match times when we could see each other, but found it difficult with our schedules. Dale hinted that he had something special for me which "has strings attached." I wondered if he were preparing to give me an engagement ring or a promise ring. After all, he *had* professed his love for me. He asked me to try to guess what that special something could be. I wasn't going to suggest to him that I wondered if it might be a ring, just in case that wasn't what he had in mind. I knew eventually time would tell, but I thought it was too soon for thoughts of engagement. I doubt I'd ever finish college if I married, because it would be a financial strain on both of us. I realized he was pressing for a commitment, but I wasn't ready. Besides, I didn't even know how Mom and Dad felt about him.

February 15th, the day after Valentine's Day, our Chi Omega chapter was to hostess the Valentine-themed Sorority State Dance. Many of the other Chi Omega Sorority house members from around the state would also attend. I bumped into Big John on campus a week before the dance and asked him if he'd attend with me. He reluctantly agreed. He told me he didn't like to dance, but accepted anyway since his friend Charlie would be there with Dorothy.

It was a big celebration, so everyone wore their best gowns. Dorothy loaned me a beautiful ivory-colored dress with a lace bodice which fit me perfectly. We styled each other's hair, securing our curls on top with hairpins, and giggled about the glamorous styles we'd created. It was great fun getting ready for the dance.

John sat on the sidelines most of the evening, but since several other fellas asked me to dance, I enjoyed myself. After the dance was over, John escorted me to his car. When he got in, he offered me a drink straight from a bottle.

"Try this, Anna. It'll make you feel relaxed."

"No, John. No thanks, I don't drink."

I realized he reeked of liquor, so I guessed he was probably in his car while I was inside dancing. I began to feel uneasy and was certain he shouldn't drive. I wondered how I could graciously abandon his company—when, suddenly, he grabbed me in a strong hold, pulling me toward him and began kissing me hard.

"Stop, John! Let go. You're hurting me."

"Come on, Anna. There's something I want to show you."

"I have to get back to the dorm. I told Dorothy I'd be there in fifteen minutes. She'll be wondering where I am."

I struggled to push him away, but he restrained my arms and began kissing me even harder. Pulling away and fighting him off, all I could think was, *Please, get me out of here and don't let him tear Dorothy's dress.* I scratched his cheek, unintentionally, when I thrashed around trying to protect my face while struggling to get away. Then, thankfully, a surge of strength came from nowhere, and I shoved him off of me and bolted out of the car. Hairpins fell to the ground in every direction around me and my coiffure hung on the side of my head. I pushed it back, pulled off my shoes, and took off running.

"Stop, Anna. Get back here right now," he demanded.

When I looked back over my shoulder, I saw he was out of the car and running after me. Then, when I looked back again, I saw him suddenly fall to his knees in his drunken state, then attempt to stand up. I continued running across campus until I reached the dorm. Breathless and scared, I closed the door and was relieved to be safe inside. I prayed no one would see me in this embarrassing state and quietly tip-toed to my room.

I had a hard time falling asleep and when I awoke the next morning, I recalled that awful scene with John. It sent chills down my spine to think what could've happened. I told Dorothy what actually *did happen* and how grateful I was to have gotten away unscathed. She said later that John came back into the hall looking disheveled with dirt on his trousers and had a scratch on his face. He told Charlie that I became fresh with him and refused a ride home. Because we knew each other so well, she wasn't surprised to hear the truth.

❦

I sent a note to Dale to let him know I'd pledged Chi Omega and would be getting my pin soon. It was a lot of preparation and study, but I think all of it was worth it. Now I had such a sense of belonging and enjoyed living with my sorority sisters. I hoped Laura and Kay would follow Truly and me, and also be our Chi Omega sisters one day.

Hamilton, Ohio
February 22, 1929

Dearest Love,

I finally received a letter from you last night after I came in from work. I thought you had deserted me. It seems as though all else comes first and then finally you remember, vaguely, that your boyfriend might be in need of solace, so you decide to write.

Most everything is closed in observance of Washington's Birthday, even some of the shops. Ford, though, doesn't respect holidays much. In fact, he can't afford to. At present, Ford is over-producing. I imagine you'd be interested in seeing his factory. He manufactures a little more than five new cars per minute! An average of seventy-five hundred a day. None of the work is hard, but it's very tedious. I'd give anything if you could visit the plant. It is pretty astonishing.

On the ground floor the punch presses and die setters are located. Outside of being mighty noisy, there isn't much interest there, except that everything is clean. On one side of this floor, they start a piece of sheet steel, which goes through many different punch machines, until it reaches the opposite side where it becomes a finished product. Fenders start in a sheet of raw steel and in ten minutes, it's a bright new fender. On the upper floor is the wheel plant. Pieces of steel start on one side in an endless chain, and each man does something to it until it finally ends as a finished wheel. They turn out about two thousand wheels every eight hours. One can't talk, for you can't hear anything. There *are three eight-hour shifts which uses the whole twenty-four-hour day. The machinery never stops for the entire work week.*

So, you attended the Chi Omega State dance? I'm sure you had a good time. Dad wants to go to the cabin for a few weeks so my brother-in-law LeRoy will take him there since I can't get off from work. I wish I could see you, my darling. Take care of yourself.

Lovingly,
Dale

I wondered why Dale hadn't responded to my letter or commented about my Chi Omega pledge, but then realized when I received another letter the next day.

February 23, 1929

Dearest Anna,

From the contents of your letter, you surely must have enjoyed your initiation into the sorority.

I received a little note from Laura today. She says Clint has a new Roadster. I can just see them in it. Those Roadsters are quite some car. So, I guess Laura and Clint are a pretty good match. Wish I had his money.

I forgot to tell you, I've helped to make 100,000 brakes already and Ford put its millionth car on the road last Thursday.

The picture you gave me at Christmas is admired by everyone. Some think you look just like that film star, Ann Harding, and I think there is something to that. I do enjoy your picture so much and look at it often.

Lovingly,
Dale

Hamilton, Ohio
March 26, 1929

Dearest Anna,

I wish you would write more often. I've sent way more than I've received. Do you save all of my letters? If so, I hope you are careful where you keep them, as I wouldn't want anyone to get a hold of them. They're not for anyone's eyes but yours.

I'll be driving down to Vallonia in LeRoy's Ford Friday night around 10 p.m. to be with you over Easter. I should be at your home early Saturday morning for breakfast. Thank you for the invitation.

Lovingly,
Dale

I was enjoying myself at college and loved the freedom to do pretty much as I pleased. I felt like I'd matured so much since I arrived as a nervous small-town girl last September. I experienced some social problems and financial setbacks, but I knew even then I would succeed in my plan to finish college.

As Dale's Easter visit drew nearer, I grew increasingly uneasy. I had mixed feelings about what Dale had been writing in some of his letters and hoped Truly would be at home when I got there for Easter break. I hoped we could talk privately about my concerns and I could have her honest opinion about some of his comments and the disturbing developments in our relationship.

Chapter Sixteen

I was excited to see Truly at the house when I arrived home. We loved taking walks together, so I asked her to join me after supper.

"It's been a while since we were together and I'm so glad you're here."

"I'm glad to see you, too. What's been happening in your life since we were together?"

"I wanted to talk to you about some concerns I have about my relationship with Dale."

"Well, let's hear it."

"First of all, getting right to the point, it's a growing concern to me that Dale has no interest in moving above the level of a day-laborer. He went to college for less than a semester, gave up, and left. He said he ran out of money, and he didn't think he was cut out for it. He worked as a tree-trimmer and only made wages enough to cover his living expenses, then twice gave up and left his job. He's working at Ford Auto Plant now, but they are always having layoffs.

I've encouraged him to try college again, but he's never able to save any money to go back because he squanders it away."

"Those seem to be some pretty legitimate concerns, I think."

"Don't get me wrong. Dale's real smart, and he's a good person. He reads everything, and we do have a lot in common. But, another problem is that he's become possessive and makes comments such as he's afraid he'll lose me. He's so loving and I know he loves me more than I love him. He pays a lot of attention to me—sometimes maybe too much. I wonder if I'll ever love him as much as he loves me."

"It appears you're in a tough situation. It's always difficult in a relationship when one person has more intense feelings."

"I find, even though I'm discouraged that he isn't at all interested in college, he does make me feel special. He's supportive and encouraging about my accomplishments, and writes beautiful heartfelt letters expressing his love. That's pretty hard for me to ignore. When he's around me, I always feel happy."

"You'll have to weigh out the good and the bad and figure out what's important for you. What you can and cannot live with. Not what's important for him, but for you. Once you figure that out, you'll know what's best. Telling him what it will take for the two of you to stay together, will, I'm afraid, be difficult."

"I'm sure, to some degree, you've probably already noticed some of these flaws in our relationship. But, I'm not perfect, either. I do care about him, and we've come a long way, so I'm not ready to give up on a future with him."

❦

I was anxious to see Dale and was up early to help Mother bake our favorite Easter breads. Peering out the window, I saw Dale step toward the door and rap three times. I immediately opened the door and couldn't help but laugh when I saw how it startled him.

"Anna, my darling, good morning. You look so adorable. Did you just wake up?"

Still chuckling, I said, "No, I've been up about an hour. Come on in. I've been waiting for you." His face was red and he appeared embarrassed but brushed it off quickly.

"Good morning, Mrs. Fosbrink. Happy Easter."

"Happy Easter to you, Dale. You should've brought your dad along for breakfast."

"We were up late, so he was still sleeping. Smells good in here. You'll probably see him tomorrow morning at Sunrise Service."

"Good morning, Hezekiah."

"Good morning, my daughter. Good morning all."

"Mrs. Fosbrink, you've made a delicious-looking spread again this morning. I'm always amazed at the food you prepare."

"Go ahead, Dale. Have some sausage and eggs. There are some home fries in that blue bowl. How about coffee?"

"Yes, please, Mr. Fosbrink. Are you planning on working in the field today?"

"I'll just hitch up the horses and plow it under. It's not a big job, but has to be done. Should'a done it before today, I reckon."

"We'll all be looking forward to those melons come July," Dale said.

⁂

After breakfast, Dale saddled the horses for our ride to the hills. A slight breeze and the cool overnight rain left the air smelling fresh, emitting a pleasant aroma from new growth. I always enjoyed riding through the woods in the morning and watching the sunlight flicker through the branches.

When we reached the edge of the woods, we dismounted and began to embrace and kiss more passionately than ever before. In spite of my recent misgivings, I felt certain of the direction of our growing romantic love.

Nearly a hundred feet into the thick of the woods, we held hands and continued walking the horses. We reached the fallen log where I often come when I need to get away. While Dale was carving our initials inside a heart on a huge sycamore tree, he confided in me something I was surprised to hear.

"Anna, do you realize we went to school together for almost seven years? Lying in bed the other night, I recalled how I'd watched you growing up. When I thought back on it, I saw how I was becoming more and more interested in you as time went on. Then I realized you've been in my mind for as long as I can remember."

"I have? I guess I've always had my mind on other things and never paid much attention to the boys."

"I noticed all the girls, and you're absolutely the prettiest of them all. Do you know, you have the reputation of being the prettiest girl in Jackson County?"

"Dale, will you stop making stuff up?"

"I'm not making anything up. It's true. And, yes, I've had my eye on you for a long time now."

"So, you have, eh? You've been watching me out of the corner of your eye all this time?"

"Certainly, that's what guys do. We're always looking at the girls. I love how charming and innocent you are."

"Oh, I wouldn't say I'm innocent," I said with a wink and feeling the surge of a blush.

"Well, I think you are," Dale swayed to the side giving my shoulder a nudge. "You know, this morning, I woke up early and as I drove to your house, I rolled down the windows to breathe the fresh clean morning air. Taking in the beauty of the clear, blue sky and huge fluffy white clouds, I stopped to listen to the birds singing in the distance. I thought, *Oh God, you've truly blessed me; how could my heart be any happier?* I was so excited. I could hardly wait to be with you again."

"I looked forward to this also and I loved watching you carve a forever heart on this sycamore for everyone to see."

"Pretty nice artwork, if I do say so myself."

"Yes, it'll probably be there for a thousand years."

"No, my darling, I want it to be there for an eternity. I want everyone to wonder who those initials belonged to. Just who were those lovers?"

"No one will ever know."

"Do you think we should be getting back to the house?"

"Probably so, we've been gone a good long while. I don't want Mother to worry."

"Just one more kiss, then we'll head back."

❦

Before Dale drove to the cabin after supper, we arranged to meet at the Methodist Church for Sunrise Service. Easter morning brought to mind the time when Dale arrived late last year. I'd left my place during the service to go to the back of the congregation and stand beside him. He felt I was acknowledging him for who he was deep inside, and today he confided that he loved me even more for that acceptance. How much our lifestyles differed was always on his mind, yet he appreciated how I shielded him from the criticism of those in our town who were more prosperous and socially refined.

After services, Dale the storyteller, spent the better part of the day with my family telling some pretty wild stories. One of his stories was about a time when he was ten and found a little boy around three years old wandering in the woods near his cabin. He took the child to his dad and asked if he could keep him. Dale thought it would be fun to have a little brother, but his dad said they already had enough mouths to feed, so he took the child to the sheriff's office to locate his family. Apparently, the boy couldn't speak clearly and had wandered away from home without anyone in his family noticing. I thought it was sweet that Dale was so concerned about the child that he wanted to keep him, but I was never certain if it was a true story or not.

It had been a pleasant day and Dale loved gathering gossip from the residents in Vallonia as we meandered around town. Later in the evening, he drove me to the station so I could return to school.

"I had a fun weekend with you and your family, but I wish you'd marry me so we could be together every day."

"You know we can't do that. Don't you?"

"I know, but if I could get a better job and save some money, we might be able to manage it."

"Let's get back down from those air castles and face reality."

"It makes me crazy sometimes when I think of how long it'll take for us to reach our goals and I get so darn frustrated. Can't you think of some way we can do this?"

"Stop, Dale. Stop! We keep going over this. There's no way we can get married. Not for a long, long time."

Then, while still in his car, Dale suddenly grabbed my face and kissed me hard and forcefully. It was so abrupt that it startled me. Maybe because it was the same sort of experience I'd had with Big John becoming so aggressive, that it instantly angered me. I pushed him back and turned my head, wondering *Why would he think that was okay?* When I looked back at him I saw his reddened face and tight fists. He was visibly agitated with my rejection. It was uncomfortable and awkward, and I didn't want it to end this way. We'd had a good time and I didn't want either of us to leave with feelings of hurt and anger.

"Come on, Dale. Look. It would be easy to quit, but I'd be letting myself down, and the disappointment would probably make me depressed in the end."

"I'm sorry, my love. I admit, I'm depressed much of the time."

Wanting to lighten the conversation as we approached the station, I said, "Kiss me, sweetheart. I have to hurry. Thanks for the ride. Be safe driving home."

"Please don't be upset with me. I love you."

"I'm tossing you ten kisses to remember me on your way home." I wondered if he noticed I didn't say "I love you" back.

Suddenly, as I turned to board the train, out of the corner of my eye I saw Liz headed toward the bus stop. *What was she doing here? Had she just gotten off the train? Where had she been? Hamilton? Certainly, Dale must have seen her also. What a perfect opportunity for her to hail him down and ask for a ride home. My heart sank.* I boarded the train and teetered down the aisle while struggling to see his car from the window, but my view was blocked by a lady in front of me. I hoped he'd just go to the cabin and ignore Liz completely. Darn it. What was it about her that made me so suspicious and distrusting?

⚬⚬⚬

On Monday, after Easter break, it was back to the routine of preparing for a week of tests. I thought back on my visit and how nice it was to have had some free time to talk with Truly. I wanted to pay attention to the situations we discussed to see if some of it might be resolved by talking with Dale. I enjoyed the visit with my family, but I especially enjoyed the good times Dale and I shared and the closeness I felt when we were alone riding. However, the thought of his rough kiss flashed back in my mind several times. It puzzled me why he'd done that and why it had irritated me as much as it had. The thought of Liz at the train station kept entering my mind. Was she still after him? Dale said she'd gotten chummy with his sister to try to find out information about him. Had she just returned from Hamilton? Was she ever at his house when he was there?

I wanted to put all of those concerns to rest. It was hard to leave everyone in Vallonia, but it would only be a few more weeks until I'd be back home for the summer. I knew I needed to concentrate on doing the best I possibly could and complete my courses.

Chapter Seventeen

At the beginning of May, Dale sent a postcard asking if he could come to Bloomington on Sunday, May 12th. I met him at the church and after the service, we walked to the Chi Omega sorority house. He stepped inside the front entrance to take a brief look around. I wanted him to see where I lived so he could picture my life in Bloomington.

"Isn't the sorority house nice?"

"Looks good to me. Guess I know now why they won't let me be a Chi Omega. All I see are females in there."

"You were just teasing about wanting to be a Chi Omega, and you knew you couldn't be anyway, didn't you?"

"Come on now. Are you kidding me? At least now when I think of you, I can place you in the right spot."

"I'm starving. Let's go over to Cauble Coffee Shop and get something to eat. It's just around the corner over there on Kirkwood Avenue," I said pointing in the direction of the shop.

As we rounded the corner, I suddenly felt sick. Who else but Big John was coming out of the restaurant?

"Hello, Anna, so nice to see you again. I haven't seen you since the—"

"Hi, John," I quickly interrupted. "I want you to meet my friend, Dale."

"Nice to meet you, Dale. Are you a student here also?"

"No, not yet. Maybe soon."

"You two have a nice afternoon," John said as he hastily continued walking up Kirkwood Avenue.

As soon as John was out of view, Dale started the interrogation. One question after the other. Who was John? How did I know him? What was John referring to when he said he hadn't seen me "since the . . . ." Since the what? He asked everything except what John was wearing the last time I saw him. Smoothing it over wasn't easy, but I wanted him know I'd be making friends here, and, of course, not all of them would be female. He seemed to accept it, but I could tell he didn't like it.

After lunch, we walked back to his car to say our good-byes. We sat for a while until the windows became fogged from the dampness outside, creating within a shield for us to steal a few kisses. It was a humid day with hovering dark clouds threatening to pour any minute, but it didn't start to rain until late afternoon just as Dale was leaving.

We had such a pleasant time together—short, but we both enjoyed the entire day with one exception—the interrogation about John. I didn't want him to question me every time I bumped into a male friend or mentioned a male classmate in my letters.

⚬⚭⚬

I was in my room studying when Dorothy came in, obviously upset. She went over and sank into the middle of her bed and began crying. I started over to console her when I noticed she had a large purple bruise on her right cheek. It looked swollen and painful.

"Dorothy, what on earth happened? Did Charlie do this to you?"

"We had a horrible fight. He's been seeing another girl. She's a 'Deltie,' and I found out he's been with her almost every night since last month. He always said he had to study so he couldn't see me, but he was actually out with her."

"Oh, my, I'm so sorry. Did he hit you? Your cheek looks awful."

"Yes, and he cracked me a good one on my back when I tried to jump out of his car. I slapped his face, and called him a bastard. He became enraged and started yelling. He floored the gas, driving faster and faster like a crazy person, then he grabbed the steering wheel and rocked it back and forth screeching the tires. He lost control of the car, went up on the sidewalk and hit a tree on Smith Avenue. When his car got stuck in the mud and started smoking, I jumped out and ran. I was so upset. I shocked myself when I called him a bastard. I think I lost my mind, I was so angry."

"You mean you tried to jump out of the car while it was moving?"

"Yes, I know that was stupid, but I think I was so stunned I went a little crazy."

"Had he ever treated you that way before?"

"No, we were serious about each other—I thought. We talked about getting married someday. I love him with all my heart. How could he start seeing someone else?"

"I don't know, but thank God you didn't jump. You could've been killed. You almost were anyway."

"I realize that now. But, honestly, I don't think I was able to make any sense of it when he was telling me about her. I was so hurt."

"Listen to me, Dorothy. I know it isn't going to be easy, but I hope you won't give another serious thought about seeing him again. Not even if he wants you back."

"After today, he's never going to ever want me back. I'm sure it's over."

"Oh, I predict he'll want to get in touch with you again."

"It's over for me. I'm finished. I know I'll never forget this."

"Give yourself time. Time happens to be what we need to help us heal."

"I can't believe this. I'd never trust him again. I feel so betrayed."

"When he realizes he lost such a beautiful person, he'll likely try to see you again. Don't be surprised if he tries to get you back."

I made a cool compress to put on Dorothy's cheek and sat up with her most of the night to let her cry and talk it out. I knew it would take her a long time to get over the assault, but hopefully she'd see it for what it was. Betrayal. Poor dear Dorothy, what a horrible thing to happen to such a nice person. She didn't deserve that, but it was better she learned it now rather than later. I wondered what I'd do if I were in Dorothy's situation and Dale turned on me.

Chapter Eighteen

It was embarrassing for Dorothy to sport that bruised cheek because it was so obvious. She started to come around about two weeks later when her appearance improved, but she was still a different person emotionally. Our sympathetic sisters in the house were concerned about her and chimed in on many good talks we had about men, dating, and college life. We covered just about everything, including what we wanted and didn't want out of our years at IU. But, above all, we talked about what we didn't want in a man.

Dorothy was disappointed that I'd be leaving soon to start business school, but understood why I had to. Her parents were financially well off, so she planned to stay on campus most of the summer, do some writing, and line up her courses for September. I had mixed feelings about leaving but hopefully we'd room together again when I returned. I looked forward to seeing my family and friends and in two weeks, Ken would be coming to take me back to Vallonia.

Hamilton, Ohio
May 28, 1929

Heart o' Mine,

I've been dreaming and thinking of you as you reluctantly take leave of your studies. I've been reading Socrates and some of Pascal:.

"O let me steal one liquid kiss, for Oh! My soul is parched with Love."

No need for me to try to explain this verse, or else it need not have been written! I learned from Pascal, not to ask if what you have read has bored you, because he says the reader doesn't entertain that idea until it is suggested by the writer. Is that so? I can't take much of Pascal at a time, but I do like Socrates. If what he says is true, this earth won't be our happiest place, after all. Now, just think, if this is so, and we have reasons to believe it to be that way, you and I will always love each other and know it even after death. Which, according to him, is just freeing our souls of the earthly body and burdens, and affording us more time to form our higher selves.

Beautiful thoughts. Do they seem so to you or am I crazy? If so, I'm also ignorant of it, therefore perfectly happy in the thought of it. I must close and get some rest.

I love you,
Dale

I asked Dale to bring both of those books the next time he comes to Vallonia because I knew so little about Socrates or Pascal. I was especially interested in Socrates and his philosophy of life, especially the part where Dale had written, "If what Socrates says is true, this earth won't be our happiest place, after all. Now, just think, if this is so, and we have reasons to believe it to be that way, you and I will always love each other and know it even after death." That had never occurred to me and it intrigued me so much, I found I'd memorized it.

Hamilton, Ohio
June 2, 1929

Dearest Anna,

I just finished reading the rest of Socrates, and I do believe, as he says, that God is omnipotent and life is evermore. That our souls live forever and that Truth is the only thing in life worthwhile. I believe when you've completed his works you'd do as I did and agree with him. But though I know him to be right, will I give up everything and follow Truth? As surely as I sit here, I will not! And therefore, I will never be great, but I know I shall be better. But I like this saying best, "A friend is a gift of God and He only who made hearts can unite them." God seemingly has offered you and me friendship, and I sincerely hope that He will do the rest.

It has been a long time since you've taught me to do something better, and I used to get those lessons quite often. You might write me your solution for our church problem. There is a solution and though my creed and faith are iron-bound, can I hold out against you forever? I'll try to be faithful to the new.

Forever yours,
Dale

In his last two letters, Dale appeared to have been into some pretty heavy reading material and was caught up in the philosophizing himself. I wanted to learn more about the teachings of Pascal and Socrates, but I thought it was more important to explore the comment of his solution for our church problem. I don't know if there's a solution to it, but it did concern me that he was Catholic, and I was Methodist. I had no intention of converting to Catholicism.

※

On June 10th, Ken came to IU to help me move back home. He was the strong protective kind of brother every girl dreamed of having in her life. He was always there to help and nothing was too much trouble. It didn't take long to load my belongings into the car and I looked forward to the ride home. I didn't realize how sad it would feel to be leaving the sorority house until I closed the car door, and we started to drive away. Many of the girls had already checked out, so it had begun to seem more like a skeleton, with emptiness so evident. I surely was going to miss all of it. It had been a lot of work but it had also been great fun. I hoped my plan to earn and save money would work out. If I could get into business school this summer, I could return to IU in September.

Vallonia, Indiana
June 15, 1929

Dear Dale,
I'm home now for the summer and just trying to get everything back in order here. I miss you and hope you'll be able to plan a trip down sometime soon. I had a dream of you last night and woke up crying, but now I can't remember what it was all about. I tried to write you a little poem, but it was so trite I didn't send it. I think it probably was worse

than the one I read to you Easter weekend.

What's wrong that you're broke again? Are you able to work? When will I see you? I'm sending you ten kisses in this letter, so I hope you can find them. Please give my regards to your family.

Always, I Love You,
Anna

Hamilton, Ohio
June 18, 1929

Beloved,

You must have dreamed something horrible about me for it to have made you cry in your sleep. Nothing's wrong with me, except that right this minute I'm flat broke, not a penny except a book of stamps, and won't have any money until next payday. I thank you for the kisses, although what I long for is your own sweet lips on mine. For now, I must be content with the written ones, visioning a future bliss.

There's one thing, Sweetheart, that I'd take upon myself to admonish you to do, and that's to devote more of your time to literary work. Going back to the verse you read to me Easter, I could feel the meaning in your verse because I know you, but it lacked expression from choice of words. It was a nice thought, but you can do better if you devote more time to it because haste was plainly written in it.

You're to be congratulated for the accomplishment you've made in the successful closing of your first year in college. I sent you a bouquet of red roses, and hope you enjoy them.

Until the end of time, I remain always in love
with you,
Dale

So now, Dale, my perpetually penniless boyfriend, admonished me to my writing table to devote more time to literary work. I almost felt as though I'd been spanked when he critiqued the verse I'd read to him at Easter. I wished I'd never read it. But, as for the flowers, they were beautiful and it was thoughtful of him to send them. That must have taken his last red cent.

Vallonia, Indiana
June 20, 1929

Dear Dale,

I remembered what made me cry in my sleep. I had a dream about you and Liz. She wanted you to come to her house because she had baked you a cake. When you got to her house, there was no cake, just a love letter with a red heart on the front. She told you she wanted to be your girl and that she was still deeply in love with you. Then you looked into her eyes and kissed her. That's why I woke up crying. She has intruded and disrupted my thoughts too often. I question if there is anything I should be concerned about with regards to her. I saw her at the bus stop when you dropped me at the train station Easter weekend, and wondered if you talked to her, or maybe gave her a ride home. I hope that wasn't the case.

Love,
Anna

Mother and I had planned to spend the day in the kitchen canning, and I welcomed the opportunity to be with her to catch up on what had recently been going on in my life.

"My dear, I can see you've grown up while you've been away. I expected you to become more independent and I believe that's good for a girl today."

"I feel so lucky to be able to go to school, and I'm determined to finish what I've started. Are we canning string beans or okra?"

"Okra. I have no doubt you'll finish what you started. What are your plans for this fall?" Mother asked while washing the canning jars.

"I definitely plan to stay home until I save enough to get into business school in Seymour and become a secretary. So, I'll be here at home for a while longer."

"Please don't give up your dream of getting your degree from IU?"

"That's still the plan. It's just a little side step for me to go to business school."

"What about Dale? What are his plans?"

"We're still writing each other, but don't get a lot of time together. I think it's hard to have a relationship with someone who lives so far away. How do you feel about him?"

"I like him all right, but have some uneasiness about the way he was raised, and I think he lacks ambition. Certainly, he's not like you."

She said there were many things she felt Dale and I needed to straighten out if we planned to stay together. She wondered how strong his faith was, and if our political differences could be a future problem between us. She also said she sensed he was already deeply in love with me and she wanted me to stick to my goals, no matter what. I knew she was right about that.

Chapter Nineteen

*D*ale wrote that he was excited I was home for the summer because it would be easier for him to take the train to Vallonia to see me. He looked forward to being with me more often on weekends, but also hoped to see more of my family as well. He was especially anxious to go horseback riding once again so we could ride and talk privately. He also planned to check on the cabin and replenish the cupboards and asked if I'd like to go along.

Dale arrived at his cabin early Saturday morning and only slept a few hours. I felt he'd be here early, no matter what time he arrived because he wouldn't want to miss Mother's breakfast. I saw him coming up the lane and waved to him from the porch.

"Good morning, honey! I'm so happy to finally see you. I'm here to collect a few real kisses, if my lady doesn't mind. The ones in the letters don't nearly satisfy."

I loved listening to his endearing words and was so happy to finally see him. I slowly nodded my head "yes" then he pressed his lips on mine with a passionate wet impression of a kiss. Such a welcomed request, I gave him what he asked for and loved it.

Entering the foyer, Dale looked at me and admiringly said, "You look so cute with your hair pulled up like that." Then as we were walking toward the kitchen, he leaned in as if he were going to give me a kiss on the cheek, but pulled back when he realized my parents were sitting at the table looking at us.

"Good morning, Mr. and Mrs. Fosbrink. It sure smells good in here."

"Dad, what are you planning for today?" I blurted out when I noticed his raised brows and smirk when he caught Dale just about to give me a peck.

"I'll be working in the sand fields after bit. Goodness, Dora, that platter of sausage and eggs looks and smells great. Dale, help yourself."

"Thank you, don't mind if I do. Want some help in the field, Mr. Fosbrink?

"No, I do it all the time and I imagine you kids have plans. You're going riding after you finish eat'n, aren't ya?"

"That's our plan, but Dad, we can help out if you like," I said.

After breakfast, while on our way to the barn, Dale reassured me he had absolutely no interest in Liz. He wanted to put my mind at rest, that there never was anything between them, as far as he was concerned. He realized her fantasy and that she'd made her wishes known among her friends, but she definitely wasn't his kind of girl. He felt I'd had that dream because I still wasn't convinced she meant nothing to him.

Dale saddled Nellie and Spiffy, and we took off in a race to the edge of the hills. We continued farther into the woods to see who'd be the first to reach the tree where he'd carved our initials inside a heart. We tied the horses and sat on the fallen sycamore log to talk. Raising his eyebrows and smiling as though giving his approval, he slowly looked around nodding as if he hadn't actually noticed the surroundings.

"We didn't have much time when we were here before. I guess I was too intent on creating my artwork on the tree and missed all the beauty. This is truly amazing!"

"Welcome to *my* spot."

"What do you mean *your spot?*"

"This is Arcada."

"I don't understand what you mean. Is that what you named it?"

"Arcada is this place—the archway. I feel such happiness here. It's where I come to meditate and pray. It's the place where I feel peace and my prayers for prosperity, health, and love are heard. When I'm finished meditating, I feel complete, both mentally and spiritually, and have a greater awareness of my own inner strength and independence. I love to spend quiet time here."

"I never heard you mention this before. Why didn't you tell me about this?"

"I'm telling you now. I come here every chance I get. Especially in the morning or early evening when I'm home on a break or I'm upset about something."

"It's so peaceful here. I'd love to stay all night and see what it's like under the stars in the quiet away from everyone. Wouldn't that be great?" he said leaning over and softly kissing my forehead.

"I never thought about spending the night, but I love to sit here on this log and quietly think. It's my own personal space in the entire world. My oneness. My own sanctuary with God. Don't you feel there's something mystical about this place?"

"I do. Have you read much about the spiritual movement going on in different parts of the country? Does anyone else know about this place?"

"I've never told anyone but Dad about it. Not even you, when we were here the last time and I watched you carve our initials on the tree. And, yes, I've read a little about the movement, but I've never been to a meeting. I heard there's a tabernacle where they hold spiritual meetings, but I don't know anyone who ever went."

"My dear, sweet girl, you're even more of a mystery than I've ever known or expected to know."

"I'm simply a spiritual girl with a loving heart who wants to be loved purely and completely."

"You're certainly all of that. Please, I hope you can see that loving person in me too. I want to be the better person you want me to be."

"I *do* see how you are. You're a kind and loving man."

"You're my teacher. I know how to love, but I need you to teach me how to be a better man. Teach me manners. Teach me how to dress. Teach me how to dance. Teach me who I need to be to become your lifetime partner. I want it all. I want you."

We embraced and kissed for what seemed both an instant and an eternity, then we lay on the ground on piles of leaves and moss. Dale started a conversation about marriage and having a home and children. We agreed we'd like three children, teased and laughed that they'd probably all have red hair. He expressed his desire to have a son so he could teach him everything his father taught him—to value reading, to hunt, to be kind and generous, to possess a strong faith and a loving soul.

"You know, Dale, I'd love to someday have a house just like my parents'. But it isn't just the house, it's the home. It's the wonderful feeling of love and joy that fills the house when you're with a contented family inside. Don't you think?"

"There's no question about it. I think the credit goes to your mother. If I'd had the love and guidance of my mother, I'd have known so much better how to live."

"You're making progress, actually great progress. I'll help you . . . always."

"You're a kind teacher, and I'm truly grateful. I love you even more for so patiently helping me to know the right way to do things."

"I know you get annoyed at times with my persistence about going to school, but that's what my parents have instilled in us for as long as I can remember. We need to meet each other on a more common ground so we can be stronger if we do get married. My parents are so wise about their money. Maybe it's their German upbringing."

"You're right about the money part. I know in my heart you're right. It's just that we've come from such different social classes. I've never wanted for higher ideals, at least not until you came into my life. We've lived worlds apart."

"Yes, but that doesn't mean it has to stay that way. We've such a great future ahead of us if we stay on track."

⁘

We talked about our political and religious differences and what we could do to meet each other in a more comfortable and compatible manner of respect. We talked about our dreams to have a home together and what it might look like. What our deepest desires were and how we'd guide our children to grow up to be strong and independent. Thinking back about it later, I realized I was caught up in the intimacy of our conversation. We were sharing our innermost selves in Arcada, my own private paradise—a sacred and safe world. I believe Dale was surprised when I shared my ethereal Arcada with him. He loved knowing there was a mystical part of me he'd never known before, and it intrigued him.

We mounted the horses and slowly rode through the hills. Cantering side-by-side through the woods, we were transported to heaven on earth as the rays of sunlight danced through the branches exposing our blissful state. When we came to a clearing, we dismounted and paused to enjoy a spectacular cloud formation. There was an intriguing challenge for a seemingly spirited game of "see the character in the cloud?" Dale teasingly insisted he saw a lion, but I teasingly insisted right back—for certain that it was a bear. As we started to leave, I leaned toward Dale offering a kiss, but he turned and wrapped me tightly in his arms. My desire was fulfilled by his passionate response.

We felt we'd only been away for a couple of hours when we reached home and found Mother preparing supper, but we both felt transformed by our deepening bond. We hadn't even missed not having lunch. Dale cared for the horses while I helped Mother complete the meal for the seven of us. She'd made her famous fried chicken, boiled potatoes, biscuits and gravy, accompanied by thick sliced tomatoes, mashed carrots, and string beans from her garden. We ended the meal with her sweet cinnamon apple pie.

After supper, Dale walked back to his cabin. It felt good to have talked through my concerns in our relationship that had been worrying me. Dale had been so open to suggestions on everything we discussed, that I felt we may have truly resolved some of our differences about life, love, and our relationship. Now, I was excited and looked forward to his next visit and hoped it would be soon. I was beginning to feel I could have a future with Dale. I was falling in love.

Chapter Twenty

That summer Dale worked hard on the Ford assembly line as they were behind in production. They couldn't make enough new cars to meet the demand. He hadn't been there long enough to get a pay raise, but was offered a new position, which he felt was more like play than work. However, there'd been talk of possible layoffs for a week, since Ford would be making a change in the wheels, which meant a change in machinery.

With each letter that summer, our bond became stronger as we shared a deeper desire to be with one another. In our letters, we hoped our next visit would be July 4th weekend but Dale wasn't sure he'd be able to get off. If that were possible, he'd like to go horseback riding if the weather was cooperative. Dale wrote he imagined there'd never come a time when he wouldn't want to ride through the hills by my side. Riding together made us both feel so alive.

I was pleasantly surprised when Decoration Day came and Dale arrived unannounced.

"Anna, Dale's here," Dude said bringing Dale to the kitchen.

"Hey, I didn't think you'd be able to get off work."

"I didn't either, but production was a little slower this week, so the boss asked if anyone wanted off. He didn't have to ask twice, so here I am."

"We're going to the river for a swim and a picnic. I suppose you'll want to join us."

"I've wanted to go for a swim, but up our way it's been raining and the river's muddy. Has it been raining here?"

"Just a little, day before yesterday, so the river should have cleared."

"Will we be able to ride the horses later?"

"I think we should be fine for a ride tomorrow. Say, Dude, could you round up something for Dale to swim in? I have to finish the rest of the food, then we'll be on our way." I said giving the fried chicken another turn in the pan.

"How many of us are going?"

"Kay, Dude, you, and me. Mom and Dad left over an hour ago to start setting things up. There's been so much talk about it this year, I imagine most of the town will be at the river for the celebration. The chicken's fried and the tomatoes sliced. Mom made German potato salad and took it with her already. Dad took ears of corn, so I'm sure there's going to be plenty to eat. Um, he took a few melons too."

"Dude, grab the chicken and the swimsuits. Kay, bring the tomatoes and blankets. I'll get the bread and towels, then we're off to the river!"

⁂

We tried to pack as much into our time together as possible that weekend. The weather was perfect for a swim in the river, and the picnic dinner with my family and Dale, so pleasant. We finally had enough time together to ride the horses to the hills. During those two days, and finally alone, we spent many hours engaging in long conversations about our lives.

"Anna, when we spend time together, I feel so much closer to you. I think our feelings are mutual for one another, and we've shared so much. Sometimes it's hard for me because it's been so long since I've had anyone to share my innermost thoughts with."

"Don't worry. You have my absolute trust. Whatever we tell each other is strictly between the two of us."

"I hope you'll help me to tell you of my own self by simply asking. I think you know I must, for my own happiness, tell you nothing but truths. Feel free to ask me anything about my life, my experiences, my family—anything."

This seemed foreboding, and I wasn't sure why he'd make these statements. I shook the feeling and reassured him.

"I will, and I hope you'll ask me also. I think I'm an open book, but we should expect complete honesty with one another," I said.

"I'd never betray your trust. And as time goes on, and our relationship deepens, we'll probably confide in each other even more. Don't you think?"

⁂

When he returned to Hamilton, it was back to writing each other letters. Dale expressed his concern several times that he didn't want his letters to fall into the wrong hands and hoped I kept them safe. He told me I'd sent him 140 letters, and I recall him writing, "Someday I expect to re-read all of these letters of yours. How rich I shall be then." He said he cherished my last letter above all he possessed because I wrote, "Always I love you," which left him longing to be with me again, forever. He never imagined such happiness existed. Finally, he realized the necessity of money which he'd never desired so much before. He felt a year in college wasn't impossible, although improbable, but knew it would bring the culture and opportunity he lacked. Even though we were falling in love, and becoming more honest with each other, I hoped he'd reconsider pursuing an education. I felt he at least was making progress about money, our future, and even the possibility of some college.

※

In a major turn in our relationship, Dale invited me to visit him in Hamilton. He thought I should see his folks just as they live every day, but warned me to prepare myself to dine simply on common food. Teasingly, he suggested it might be better if I brought my own. He reminded me frequently his family lived differently than my family. He confided he hadn't taken me to the cabin because he couldn't get up the courage to show me how rough he used to live. He painted a dreadful picture of a life scarred by death and poverty, and if he hadn't loved me, he would've let me find these things out for myself because he saw his poverty and living conditions as major obstacles in our relationship. At least now, he trusted me enough to accept him, in spite of how his family lived.

※

Mother was in the kitchen preparing lunch when Dad came in with one of his prize watermelons. It was only the three of us at home when Dad began the conversation about my relationship with Dale. He wanted to know if we were getting serious about each other because it seemed he was visiting more and more often.

"I'd like to know what you see in Dale. He seems like a nice fella, but I wondered why he never has any interest in school. You know, getting an education gives one a huge advantage in life."

"I know, Dad. I'm working on him about it, and he knows exactly how I feel. He seems as though he's starting to get the picture as to how life would be so much better if he did. I see such good in Dale, and he appreciates everything I do to encourage him. He's real smart and a good worker. I enjoy his company and care a great deal about him. Even so, I think if he continues to be opposed to getting an education, I'll have to make some serious choices."

"What do you know about his family? Do they all live together, or is his dad living elsewhere?"

"Dale seems to be close with his sisters and his dad. His sister is married and has two children. They all live together in Hamilton and want me to come for a visit."

"Oh, I don't know about that. Mother and I'll have to talk it over. I'm not so sure it's the best thing for you to go there."

Chapter Twenty-One

I was hoping to find a summer job, but wasn't sure of anything except that I was struggling with finances. The business school in Seymour seemed to be the best option, but I learned I wouldn't be able to start a summer program. I was hopeful to enroll in September. The school had a good reputation from what I'd found out, and I planned on making a visit to see for myself.

After several talks with Mother and Dad about my going to see Dale, with their hesitant approval, I let Dale know I'd visit him in Hamilton. I told my parents that Dale couldn't get off work, but he'd assured me his sisters would be there with me until he returned home. He planned that we'd go swimming, have picnics, and take in some shows. I was glad to have the time to visit his family and see where he lived, but admittedly, I was a little anxious.

Dale's sister picked me up at the train station, which was only a short distance from their home. I only knew her casually and struggled to keep her engaged in the conversation until we reached the house. As we entered, I guess I hadn't expected their home to look so gloomy and the furnishings to be in such poor condition. There were only three bedrooms and his sister apologized that I'd be sleeping on the sofa in the living room. I wondered, *had it even occurred to anyone before I arrived that I'd have no privacy?* Already, I felt uneasy.

Thank goodness, it wasn't long before Dale arrived home from work, and I was relieved to see him. I offered to help with supper, but he and his sister assured me they could manage. The meal, as he had warned, was plain, but I also found it unappealing. The mashed potatoes were gray, thin, and fairly tasteless, the beets were hard and tasted scorched, the rice was undercooked but the carrots were fine. They made no apologies about their cooking, which made me wonder how it must've been to regularly look forward to that kind of a meal. I did eat some of it, but wished I could close my eyes until it was over. I knew if I *did* close my eyes, they'd wonder what was wrong with me, so I said I was trying to stick to my diet and ate mostly the carrots.

After supper, we went to the backyard and sat on the swing in the dark.

"Anna, do you remember when you gave me the book to read on the train the last time we met and I wrote to you after I arrived back home?"

"Yes, of course. Not sure what you're getting at, though."

"Do you remember when I wrote I hoped you'd help me to tell you of my own self by just simply asking, as I must—for my own happiness—tell you nothing but the truth?"

"Yes, I remember. I wondered what you meant."

"I said I wanted you to ask me if there's anything about my life or my family that you want to know. I want you to feel certain about us and there's nothing in the future that could cause us unhappiness."

"I'm not sure what you are getting at."

"I've been worried for a long time about something in my past that might cause you to break away from me, and I want to get it off my chest."

"This sounds serious. Is it bad? Tell me."

"Oh, it's bad, all right. It isn't going to be easy for me to tell you, but we're serious in our relationship now, and I don't want you to think I'm hiding anything from you. It's something that might come up at some time in our lives together, and I'd rather you hear it from me now."

"Dale, what is it? Tell me."

"It's something that happened when I was in high school. The story was covered in the papers, and the town was all a-buzz about it."

Then, he paused in deep silence, leaning forward with his hands clasped and elbows on his knees. He gazed into space as though he may have had second thoughts of what he was about to divulge.

I asked, "What are you talking about? Tell me."

"It's . . . um, well it's that my dad blackmailed our neighbor— the next farm over."

"Are you sure about that?"

"Oh, I'm dead sure."

"What do you mean, blackmailed? Blackmailed him for what?"

"Dad was envious because the man had a lot of money, and he was desperate because my family had no money or food. Dad wrote a threatening letter and tacked it onto a tree in front of the man's house. He wrote he'd burn down his house, his corn cribs and kill all of his animals if he didn't pay Dad five hundred dollars. In the note, Dad told him to put the money in a jar and put it in a certain place. Even worse, Dad threatened to kill him if he told anyone about it. Dad said in the note he'd pay it all back with interest. Clearly, he was not in his right mind."

"So, what happened?"

"The man went to the sheriff and showed him the note Dad wrote. They set a trap to be at the place Dad had specified for the man to put the money along with the note in a jar. When Dad showed up there, they caught him red-handed, and he was arrested. Dad admitted he wrote the note, but insisted it was just a joke."

"Is this another one of your tall tales?"

"No, it's the absolute truth. I hate it, but I'm telling you the truth."

"Did he have to go to jail?"

"Worse than that. He was put in jail awaiting trial for a few weeks. Bail was two thousand dollars, which of course we didn't have. My grandparents were living with us at the time, and my grandmother about went crazy with worry. She said Dad had been acting strangely at times, which scared her. When he went out that night, she saw he had put his pistol in his pocket. He told her he was going to the home of a neighbor and would be out late."

"So then, what happened after he was arrested? Did the sheriff tell your family where he was?"

"No, when he didn't come back by morning, they were afraid he may have taken his life or had left town. They called my uncle in Hamilton who drove to Brownstown to see if Dad had bought a train ticket, thinking he might have gone to Hamilton. He was shocked when he was told about the serious situation Dad was in and that it could result in a prison sentence."

"I can't believe all of this. This is dreadful."

"It *is* dreadful. It's going to be with him—us, for life."

"What would make him do such a thing anyway?"

"Periodically, our poverty and desperate situation affected his mind. Once, he even served a term for burglary in Ohio before this happened."

"What? Burglary? Did you say *burglary*? I can't imagine this of your dad. He seems so kind. Like he'd never do anything to hurt anyone."

"I know. He's a good man and a good father, but he seems to suffer bouts of illogical thinking at times. Many of the townspeople at the trial said our family had always been held in high esteem by everyone who knew us. They said our family was good, smart, and even mentioned the younger ones being talented musicians. They thought well of him and spoke up for him at the trial, but it didn't make any difference in the end. I hate this. I hate what happened to us. I hate what happened to Dad. I hate that people will have doubt about us forever."

"What happened at the trial?"

"Well, he admitted to writing the note. But, they didn't believe he meant it to be a joke. He was sentenced to a year and a week in state prison in Michigan City."

"I just never would've believed he could do such a thing."

"We're better about it now, but it was hard on the whole family when it happened and for a long time after."

"I never heard a hint of any of this, but of course, I was only eleven or twelve. I wonder if my parents know about it."

"Oh, I'm sure they do. I guess they must have reconciled Dad's past as the result of his desperation because they invited us to take meals with your family. I think if they had a problem with it, they wouldn't have wanted him in your home. Or even for me to be with you."

"Maybe they never heard about it." I didn't say it at the time, but I didn't think my parents could overlook such a crime. I planned to ask them about it when I returned home.

"I'll bet they did. There were articles in the newspaper and interest about it all over town. Well, my darling, how are you feeling about the entire story I've told you? You know how I feel about trust. I wanted everything out in the open between us."

"I feel badly that you've suffered something so senseless. You had no part in it yourself. You were just a young boy. But it's affected you. There's no question about it."

"I think that's why Dad is so quiet now. He wonders what people remember."

"Do people treat him differently?"

"No, but that's why we moved here. People in Hamilton don't seem to know anything about his past. We weren't allowed to talk about it or tell anyone about what happened. However, he loves the cabin and the property back in Starve Hollow. He doesn't ever want to have to give that up, no matter what the townspeople might say behind his back."

"I'm glad you told me about this, even though it's still hard to believe. I can see how difficult it is for you to even relive the whole thing as you're telling me the story."

"Yes, it's difficult, but I'm finally beginning to trust again. Trust is such a hard thing to get back when something like that happens in your life. Dad told me many times how hard it was for him while he was in prison. He missed us all and had many regrets. I know my grandparents took it extremely hard. Now he realizes how much he hurt everyone in the family. Sadly, I don't think Grandpa will ever be the same."

At that point, Dale and I sat quietly for a few moments. Finally, he broke the silence and asked, "Do you still love me?"

"Of course, I do, silly. You think I could fall out of love that quickly?"

⋘⋙

I felt sorry for Dale and his family and wanted to reassure him, but this news worried me deeply. If our relationship progressed and we had children, how could we explain their grandfather's behavior?

⋘⋙

Dale took all of us to a show and swimming in the river both afternoons. Everyone sunburned terribly, but Dale's was the worst because of his red hair and fair skin. He had such a bad burn, his entire back was one huge blister, so he had to sleep facedown. Even though terribly miserable, he did have to work. He'd hoped it would be wonderful for me to be there with him and his sisters.

As I gathered my belongings to leave for the train station, I looked around and thought how differently we lived from one another. I returned home after just three days and knew he'd most likely feel hurt. He probably thought I left because I was uncomfortable there.

He would be right. I liked his sisters, but we had little in common to talk about. I felt out of place and wanted to leave.

On the ride home, I had a lot of time to reflect on my visit. Dale's life in Hamilton was considerably better than it was in the cabin where he'd spent most of his childhood. If we ever were to marry, how would I feel sharing holidays with his family and leaving mine? And, I gave a lot of thought to the story he told about his dad blackmailing his neighbor. Being honest with myself, I knew the revelation about Dale's father's criminal behavior was weighing on my mind. I'd never known anyone who had been incarcerated and it bothered me to think he could possibly be part of my family at some point. Would my family accept him? Would he be forgiven by them?

I'd never heard any of that before and wondered why my parents hadn't said anything about it. Maybe this was one of the reasons they didn't feel good about me going to visit him in the first place. Surely, they must've known about it.

Chapter Twenty-Two

$\mathcal{A}$ few days after I returned home, Dale sent a card to wish me a wonderful nineteenth birthday. He hoped I'd received his gift, even though it wasn't exactly what he had in mind. He had six notions to get on the train to come down to see me, but seven notions why he couldn't. His letter inside the birthday card said, "Sweetheart, you wanted a love letter, and I thought I'd send you one. As for making you feel loved, I think I've always tried. I'd do anything to have you come back to me to stay. I'll continue to work on the car and hope to come to see you as soon as it's repaired. I love you always."

✦

Dale wrote that he went uptown earlier that morning to get some taps and washers for the car and, of course, he chose to stop at the Ford Sales Company to buy them. A new convertible coupe caught his attention, and he could scarcely get his eyes off it. It sure was snappy, and he'd love to have it, but it cost seven hundred dollars he didn't have. He dreamed of owning a car like that one, so he could drive down to see me whenever he wanted. He could daydream all he wanted, but I wondered what he'd do to make it happen.

⁂

When Dale arrived at my house the next Saturday afternoon, he appeared short-tempered, irritable, and fidgety. We were sitting on the porch swing, and I began talking about having gone to Seymour to check out the school. He abruptly sat erect on the edge of the swing, turned to face me, and put his hand over my mouth. I pushed him away. I could see he was seething. His expression had suddenly changed. His jaw tightened, his teeth clenched, and his face was red. His widened eyes appeared blazed with anger as he drew in a breath between his teeth. He closed his fist, then yelled as he pounded his fist on his leg.

"What the heck is wrong with you? All you talk about is school, school, and more school!"

"Stop yelling at me. What's *wrong* with *you?*" His extremely hostile outburst caught me off guard. I couldn't imagine what had outraged him and made him suddenly act like that. It scared me. This was not the man I knew and had come to love.

"I'm sick of it. Real sick of it."

"Sick of what? What are you sick of?"

"I'm sick of you putting everything in life before me. It's always about you and what you want. It's never about me. Never. I write you more letters than I ever receive in return. And I'm sick of hearing that you don't have money to get through school. You're more interested in good grades than you are in me."

"That's not true. And you know it's not. And what is it with you, that you keep such a close count on the number of letters? Is there a scorecard you're keeping or something?"

The visit, obviously, didn't go well. Clearly, he was steaming mad, and with heavy footsteps, he stomped off the porch. We were both upset and when he left I didn't try to stop him. I was horribly shaken inside and glad mom and dad weren't around to hear him yelling. They certainly wouldn't have approved. I didn't know what had provoked him, but he seemed upset about the letters. I didn't understand why he kept track of how many he wrote and it puzzled me why he addressed them differently each time . . . "Beloved, Hearts Mine, Peaches, Sweetheart, Dearest" and so on. How could he remember how he addressed me in the previous letter? I didn't understand if he was compulsive about the letters or obsessed with me. He claimed he'd "read them in his old age and become ambitious again." What was that about? Was he losing his ambition?

When he returned home, he wrote that he was sorry our time together ended so badly. He thought at first, he'd write me a letter full of feeling and remorse, but knew that wasn't what I wanted to hear. He felt he hurt me more than he thought he could hurt anyone. After all, he knew I'd given so much to him and he wondered how he could behave like that. How could he be so mean? Even after we sat on the porch and I promised him again that I someday would be his.

❦

After he left, I thought back over his visit and how odd it was that he so abruptly changed. Dale's outburst was a shock, especially since I'd never witnessed that kind of behavior before. Not from anyone. He'd been so emotional, it left me feeling uncomfortable and unsure of him. It brought to mind, what he told me his grandmother had said about his dad's illogical thinking and acting strangely before he carried out his threats against their neighbor. I wondered if there was something he and his father shared in common that caused them to become unbalanced. I contrasted his hostility with his loving, but pleading, letter and I wondered how emotionally sound he was.

When Mother and Dad came home from Grandpa's, I wanted to ask some questions about what Dale had told me when I was at his house.

"Did either of you ever know anything about Dale's father attempting to blackmail one of their neighbors back in the early twenties?

"Goodness, child, that's going back a good bit," Dad said.

At first, I could see they both looked puzzled. Mother didn't read English and only knew what Dad told or read to her, but she was certainly all ears.

"I vaguely remember something in the papers about it, but heaven sakes, that was a long time ago. Let me think a minute." Then he said, "It seems there were some unanswered problems about it. Mr. Stevens said he only intended it to be a joke, as I recall."

"Yes, but did you know there was a trial and he served time?"

"I heard that, but we didn't get the *Banner* here in Vallonia. People in town talked about it some and were upset because they felt he was railroaded. They were sympathetic to his desperate situation because his family, although poor, was well-regarded. Most townspeople admired Dale's father as a fine music teacher, so how could he have intended the threat as more than a joke?"

"I know, but he *did* admit to writing the note. Joke or no joke, the jury didn't accept it. I feel bad for Dale. He had nothing to do with it, but he said it was such a disgrace for the family, they moved to Hamilton."

If I interpreted Dad's response correctly, my parents didn't seem to be profoundly upset about the situation or label Dale's dad as the "outlaw." I needed to decide if it mattered to me and whether the incident had left such deep scars on Dale that it would penetrate the foundation of our relationship or marriage in a negative way. Already, I could see Dale's past had caused him to be insecure. I thought he often exaggerated his feelings for me to compensate for the fact he thought he wasn't good enough. As much as I loved Dale, his extreme emotions and lack of ambition were concerns that kept coming up, no matter how much I wanted to forgive and forget.

Chapter Twenty-Three

$\mathcal{D}$ale returned to Vallonia the next Friday night to spend part of Labor Day weekend with me. Saturday morning, while dusting in the living room, I saw him when I peered out the window. I hurriedly opened the door to welcome him.

"How's my beautiful Peaches this morning?"

"I'm good. It looks like you're dressed to ride."

"I thought it best to come prepared this time. Is anyone else up yet?"

"Sure, the folks are in the kitchen having coffee."

"Something smells delicious," he said heading toward the kitchen.

"Let's eat breakfast before we leave. It's biscuits and gravy this morning."

"You can't imagine how good that sounds."

Placing a large bowl of gravy on the table, Dad looked up and said, "Come, sit down and join us Dale."

"Good morning, Mr. and Mrs. Fosbrink."

"*Guten morgen,*" Mother said.

"Help yourself. Want a cup of coffee?" Dad offered.

"Yes, please," Boy, these biscuits are delicious. They're like pillows—the biggest and fluffiest I've ever seen." Dale dabbed his lips with his napkin and replaced it on his lap. He turned and winked as if to say, *You see, I listened to you. I'm learning.*

After we finished eating, I told Mother I was taking a picnic since we were planning a long ride and not to expect us back until late afternoon.

"Well, be careful and have fun," she said pouring another cup of coffee for Dad.

⁂

Dale saddled the horses, and we took off in a chase to the hills. When we almost reached the edge of the woods, Dale slowed down, "Anna, how would you like to see where I grew up?"

"That's fine with me. I'll race ya' til we get to the lake!"

We turned around and raced toward the south of town. As we came closer to the property, I saw it wasn't at all what I'd expected. The sight left me with a cold, lonesome feeling—even somewhat frightened. I recalled when we met, Dale had said he lived just out of town in a log cabin, but this was hardly what I'd imagined. I expected it would at least look inhabitable. He said it had been there since late in the seventeen-hundreds and had obviously seen better days.

As we reached the cabin, I couldn't see anything through the clouded six-pane window on the back wall. The fireplace on the outside was still standing, but the mortar was crumbling. The porch had rotted and partially fallen away where the deteriorated roof had caused the posts and logs to collapse. Now, because of the decay, the room at the north end looked as if it could possibly cave-in, as it was separating from the structure. Dale said it once had been a bedroom for his sisters and grandparents, but was now closed off, due to its deteriorated condition.

We dismounted the horses and walked past the front porch. Dale pointed out where there were portions of a split-rail fence, which at one time encompassed the entire property. The thick overgrown field of tall weeds had grown close to the cabin, and the fence was mostly hidden in the brush with only a small portion of it still standing around the back. A few dried flower stems stood choked by the weeds on the side of the cabin. A number of red rose bushes in full bloom were nestled in the back near the rain barrel.

"You know, I've always loved flowers," he said.

"I've noticed you often talk about their beauty."

"Red gladiolas and red roses have always been my favorites."

"I sense your enthusiasm and how special and meaningful this place is for you."

"Yes, probably because of the way I was raised. Most of my childhood, I cared for chickens, pigs, sheep, goats. I had a little of everything when we lived here."

"So, this was your little farm?"

"It was, but as you can see, not now."

"Do you miss it?"

"After we moved, I'd still come back here and attend to the garden so the next time, we'd have flowers."

"Hum, looks like something's missing here," I said with a chuckle.

"Well, since you came into my life, my garden has been badly neglected."

"Oh, so now it's my fault.?"

"Not hardly, my darling." He kissed my hand and said, "are you ready to go inside?"

"Uh, better now than never," I said hesitantly.

When he took me inside, I tried not to gasp. It flashed through my mind that he'd actually grown up here. I couldn't help but feel sorry for the existence he'd experienced, considering how crude the place was. To say it was shabby was an understatement. It was run-down, musty, and dirty. I stood wondering how could anyone live in these conditions for so many years. Maybe he'd accepted it better because he was so young when they originally moved here. A young boy might have thought it an adventure to live in this kind of place. As I looked around, I noticed how they'd tried to make it livable, but I'd never seen anything quite like it. The furnishings were so awful, they resembled trash that may have been found dumped along the roadside.

A crudely built table with an oil lamp and two benches served as their eating space. Pans were scattered about the floor and on counters to collect the rain from the leaky roof. The beds were pallets which were padded with thick feather comforters, hand-sewn by his sisters. The bed frames consisted of four-inch-thick logs laced with rope to support the padding. In contrast, the neatly folded sheets and towels appeared clean, lying on top of the beds. Dale laughed when I moved toward the fireplace and screamed when a mouse ran out and hid under a chair. I noticed a clock sitting on the mantel stopped at 4:30. A framed picture of an attractive young woman was propped next to it.

"Is this a picture of your mother?" I asked.

"Yes. She was twenty-seven."

"What a nice-looking woman. She's most attractive."

"Yes, she *was* pretty. All my life I've wished I'd known her."

"I'm sure you must always feel her loss."

"I do. I'm certain, though, she and God are constantly watching over me."

Instinctively, I began to straighten up the place, but soon realized there wasn't much I could do to improve the appearance.

"Well, is it what you expected?"

"No, not exactly. I can't imagine how cold it must get here in the winter. It seems so, uh, primitive."

"I guess one could say it is."

"It's hard to imagine how you stay busy all day out here."

"We keep the fire going much of the time."

"But, what do you do when it's so cold outside? There can't be much to do out there."

"Well, Dad and I read a lot, sometimes all day until it gets dark. Then we talk about what we've read. I tell him about my fantasies, which amuses him because he thinks I'm such a dreamer. We make up all kinds of stories to tell each other, always trying to outdo one another. Sometimes at night, our stories become way too graphic and horrific—we even frighten ourselves."

Suddenly, he stopped talking, walked over, and gently pulled me toward him. He took me in his arms and held me in a lustful embrace. In boundless time we stood in silence, enjoying the sensual touching. I loved being wrapped in his strong arms and feeling him so close to my body. He began kissing my forehead and cheeks, then gently slid his hands down my arms while kissing my neck, my breasts, then passionately again on my mouth. He picked me up and carried me to the bed, gently laying me down. He smiled sweetly, while gazing into my eyes and, as if in slow motion, began kissing me again. Whispering softly, he told me how beautiful I was and began slowly removing my clothing, then his. He lay beside me, touching me ever so lightly as if his fingers were simply feathers so softly tickling my body. He whispered how much he loved me and would forever be in love with me. He then confided he'd loved me far longer than I'd ever known—and for a moment, I was puzzled by what he'd just said.

"Sweetheart, I want to make love to you," he said softly, then tenderly kissed my neck and brushed his lips across my shoulder.

I whispered, "No, I can't do this. I'm afraid."

I tried to resist giving in to his gentle kisses down my neck, then briefly raised my shoulders and inhaled a long deep breath. I tensed up momentarily, nestled my head back onto the pillow, then gave a slow quiet exhale and relaxed.

"Don't be afraid, my darling. We are one. We are one, and we're alone."

Dale knew the temptation of sharing our passionate love for each other while quietly hidden away from everyone had excited me. I found myself caught up in the thrill of the moment and unable to turn back. I knew then, these were more than just sexual feelings for each other. I felt what we shared was true love, and afterwards— joy and contentment.

Lying face to face, staring into each other's eyes, we softly spoke to one another with such deep emotion, each word so full of love and meaning, each seeking to make the other happy and once again to extract the greatest part for ourselves. We told each other we felt fulfilled. We reminisced, recalling that it was nearly two years prior when we began our journey. Little did we know where it would lead us, but now that journey had given us immense joy as if by magic.

"Anna, you know, a change came over my heart the night you left for Lake Geneva? Our first kiss did for me what nothing else could."

"Our first kiss did that to you?"

"It absolutely did. And, now I know to truly make you happy I have much to accomplish to bring myself to better ideals. I don't know what there is in my makeup that commanded your love, but I adore you for it."

<hr>

Our laughter seemed to echo throughout the old cabin while we ate our picnic lunch and told each other funny stories. All the way while riding to the hills before returning home, I wondered if anyone would ever know what we'd done. What would people think of us? What would my parents think if they found out? I prayed to God no one would ever know. I hoped he'd spare me from disgrace.

Mother was busy in the kitchen canning tomatoes, and Dad was gathering the remainder of the melons in the sand fields. Dale and I sat on the porch swing, and softly told each other how deeply in love we were and how our experience earlier in the day had more deeply bound our love to one another. He told me he was happy to know that we had a spirit in common, for after all, my body responded to his even though he was aware I willed against it. For him, that proved I love him. He only hoped that wouldn't change.

Dale wanted to go for a walk before he had to return to his cabin. He held my hand while we slowly walked down the lane. He hated to leave and wanted reassurance about our love.

"Dale, what's wrong? Do you think I don't love you?"

"I feel uncertain as to whether my soul is good or bad."

"Why would you say that?"

"I've wondered if I'll ever be noble enough to be your companion."

"Apparently, you must have serious doubts, or you wouldn't have brought it up."

"I often wonder if I can make you happy. I sometimes question if I love you enough to give you up, rather than keep you and crush your happiness."

"I don't understand why you would say that."

"I do think you love me. I cherish all that you've given, even though it caused you pain to give it."

"Then what is it that's bothering you?"

"I worry that God might punish me by taking you as payment for my blindness. I love you as no one else can, and know that I always will."

"I'm not going to leave you. We're going to be fine."

Sunday, we went to church together and I silently prayed for forgiveness. We attended a picnic and ice cream social later in the afternoon. Several of my friends were there and wanted to know if I still planned to live at home and go to school in Seymour. All day I kept having flashbacks of my secret and spellbinding experience with Dale on Saturday, but now it was time to get back to reality and move forward with my plans. Hopefully, there would be a space for me next month in business school.

Chapter Twenty-Four

After Labor Day, I returned to my job at the canning factory for another two weeks. Dale was persistent in wanting to get married. He didn't want to wait, at least not for three or four more years. He wanted me to go to business college in Hamilton, thinking maybe he could buy a piece of property there, but I discouraged him from those ideas. Realistically, how could that happen when he had no money? I'd be entering into poverty along with him. Didn't he see that? By living at home and graduating from business school, hopefully I could reach my goal of landing a secretarial position at the university. I think Dale considered the consummation of our romance a signal I was ready to get married. I wasn't. Nothing would keep me from the future I was planning.

The next time Dale came to Vallonia, we sat on the swing, and he told me about the problems he'd had on his way back to Hamilton.

"You wouldn't believe what happened on my last two trips home. The first trip, I had nothing but tire trouble, which delayed me getting back. Then, I overslept and arrived at work two hours late."

"What did your boss say? Was he mad?"

"No, he just thought I forgot to clock in, but the next time was even worse. I was so late I was frantic and didn't know what I'd do, because I knew I'd be fired. My sister called work and said I was sick. It was the only excuse they would take, but I had to have a doctor's certificate or even that excuse wouldn't be good. I couldn't afford to be let go."

"Well, I guess so. Why didn't you ever write me of this? You know now you can't ever be late again. That would be the end."

"Yes, and I knew you'd be upset if I lost my job. I made up a story about something personal that ailed me, and the doctor ordered me not to work on the cyanide furnace for a few days and gave me the certificate."

"So, now is everything settled with your job?"

"I think so. But that last time as I drove home, I was totally consumed with worry about the thing that was threatening our love. That we'd once again forget ourselves with that overpowering desire. My beloved Anna, over and over, I prayed so hard. I begged God to watch over you and not let me harm you. To guide you safely through these next few years until you can come to me. To help you with your temptations, as you help me, but let us always have this in mind as His lesson to us, and that we're careful not to let that happen again. Let us lose ourselves in our work, so this will not trouble us so."

I was relieved to learn he hadn't been fired. It would only have complicated his life even more and would be harder for us to be together. He'd have to make certain he allowed plenty of time to get back to Hamilton and not ever be late again, because jobs were just too scarce. I treasured my time with Dale, but once again, I questioned his priorities, if only to myself. And, it did concern me, that because he was late getting back to Hamilton again, he involved his sister, his doctor, and himself in an excuse for his boss which was basically a lie.

Chapter Twenty-Five

There I was, all alone in my world and scared out of my mind. There'd been no monthly sign, and I felt certain I'd been cursed. For the second time in my life, there were no clear thoughts in my head. I was terrified that I could be pregnant. What on earth would I do? With my thoughts so clouded, I felt I had to warn Dale I could be in serious trouble. I needed to keep calm, so Mother wouldn't suspect something was wrong.

On October 3rd, I sent Dale a note telling him I was beside myself with worry, and I felt awful even telling him that I thought I might be in a bad way. Nothing had happened since we were in the cabin, and I was constantly praying to God to not let anything happen to me. I told Dale I was so fearful I couldn't sleep, and asked that he burn my letter after he read it.

I spent more time alone in my room reading, and praying. I hoped Mother wouldn't ask me any questions or think I was avoiding the family. Finally, I asked Dad to saddle Spiffy so I could ride to Arcada. Riding to the hills always lifted my spirits and more than anything, I wanted to pray and ask for forgiveness. I needed time alone to think.

> *Hamilton, Ohio*
> *October 7, 1929*
>
> *Dear Love Girl,*
>
> *I should be in bed instead of writing to you, but am concerned about the fear you have, which must not be held in your heart long. Every time you write, it makes me wish with all my heart, that I could have known the things I know without so much sacrifice on your part. I believe now, no matter how much you love me, you'd not entrust that lesson again for the first time. I mean, if you knew the unrest it would bring to you afterwards. The act was mine. Dear Heart, settle in your own soul whether it was right or wrong, since you know how I've devoted myself to you.*
>
> *Let's help each other along, for we are following a dangerous road in our search for happiness. You must read some of these letters again someday and know then, if anything should happen, how I still will be loving you.*
>
> *Love me, Sweetheart.*
>
> *Dale*

I wrote back letting him know I was still living in constant fear about my awful predicament. I hadn't been able to sleep and my mind was such a mess I couldn't think straight. How could I have been so careless? I didn't want anyone to know about us, and prayed it would soon be resolved. I needed Dale to hold me and tell me how much he loved me. I tried my hardest to keep my composure and appear as if I had no concerns other than to enjoy the rest of the summer at home with my family. I couldn't count how many times a day I thought of what I'd do if I *were* pregnant, and had to admit it to my family and friends. My stomach was in knots and my nerves were frazzled. What a horrifying situation.

Hamilton, Ohio
October 13,1929

Dearest Beloved,

You are constantly on my mind and I wish I were there to hold you and give you the reassurance you need to get through this. It's been hard for me to be so far away from you, but I promise you that my love for you will never change. I am, and always will be, devoted to you.

Would Dad and Mother understand and forgive or condemn? People would be only too willing to condemn, but they've forgotten love, or more likely they never knew it as we have. I do hope you are well. You are free to do as you think best, otherwise I'd feel as though I'd swayed your whole life. I don't know how to give back that which I've taken from you. I only hope that you don't want it back too badly. Truly, I didn't know, and don't know yet, except there's a strange warmth in my heart with your touch and your kiss. I loved you before, I adore you now, for did you not against your own will, blindly trust yourself to me? I'll trust and confide in you since we must wait.

I love you,
Dale

Finally, the day came that I'd been praying for, and although I felt awful, I was happy at last. I couldn't wait to get a letter sent to Dale to tell him about my joyous celebration.

> *Vallonia, Ind*
> *October 15, 1929*
>
> *Dearest Dale,*
>
> *All clear! God is in his Heaven. All is right with the world once again after nearly eight weeks of torture! I'm well and feeling more content and happy. I'm counting on your help from this day forward. We need to be strong for each other. I think everything is fine and should know for sure by next month.*
> *I love you,*
> *Anna*

> *Hamilton, Ohio*
> *October 20, 1929*
>
> *Dearest Beloved,*
>
> *That was brief and to the point. However, I feel like I want to hold you tight in my arms. I'm in love with you. Do you see? It's only when we misunderstand each other that we become estranged, so please if ever there's anything I do or say that's not clear to you, just ask me. I'll tell you the truth, even if it turns my soul wrong side out.*
> *"God's in his Heaven, all is right with the world." Did you mean to say that God has taught us our lesson and spared you of disgrace? Honest, Sweetheart, was it wrong? I*

do hope you're well, but to comfort you, I truly think you can consider yourself so now because the natural condition rarely carries on so long after you become otherwise.

I'm afraid to use the right words for if anyone ever read these letters, they'd know. Yours are safe with me. Do you keep mine the same?

I love you always and forever,

Dale

I was sure I'd eventually look back on this scare as one of the most worrisome experiences in my life, but was also sure it was the harshest lesson learned. I had the good fortune to escape the disgrace and embarrassment so many before and after me have not. This one misstep could've cost me everything I'd been working so hard to accomplish. Hopefully, in time, the circumstances surrounding this entire affair would become a mere, thin, silver thread in this chapter of my life, and I would not dwell on it ever again.

Chapter Twenty-Six

I had hoped to be back in school again in September, but it hadn't worked out for me financially. I stayed at home to work on some writing and began reviewing courses for secretarial school that would begin after Christmas. Thanksgiving came and went, but I enjoyed every day with my parents. Several of my brothers and sisters were planning to be home for Christmas, and my parents, as usual, were excited. Mother was in her glory cooking for the holidays ahead, especially since so many of her children loved to come home for their favorites.

Dale took the train home Christmas Eve, but I was disappointed his visit would be brief since he had to return the next day for evening shift. At least we'd have a few hours to celebrate.

Entering the front door, he greeted us with a wave and a, "Merry Christmas, everyone."

"How was your trip getting here last night?" Ken asked.

"Good, Ken. It's been awhile. Nice to see you again."

"Yup, it's been a long time since we were working the timbers together."

"Can't say I miss that kind of work, but it seems like things slowed down all over the country since the stock market crash. It has me worried. There's over a million unemployed now," Dale said.

"It has everyone worried. What're you doing now?"

"I work at Ford's Auto Plant. It's an easy job, but they're always having layoffs."

"That's what I heard. Surely keeps one's life stirred up," Ken said shaking his head.

"I'm just hoping I can stay employed there until next fall. Anna wants me to join her at IU next year if I can."

"Oh, nice. What's your interest in a degree?"

"I'm not sure, but psychology stands out in my mind. I'm not certain I can even get accepted. My grades are a major concern."

"Good luck with that one."

"Dora, it looks like everyone's here. Let's have you say grace and feed this gang," Dad said.

The family was still sitting around the table after finishing breakfast when Dale stood up and pushed his chair back. He knelt down on one knee, turned to me and gently stroked my hair.

"My Beloved Anna, I'm asking you to marry me. Will you accept this ring, which will be my lifetime gift to you?"

I gasped and let out a little squeal. I truly was unexpectedly surprised. My heart raced and a surge of pressure pounded my temples.

"Yes, I will," I said. Even though I wanted to say, *It's too soon!*

Dale stood up and bent over to kiss me after placing the ring on my finger. Then looking at my hand, I noticed the center diamond had two smaller diamonds on each side and was mounted in yellow gold. While everyone was examining my ring, I realized why he'd made a long trip for a short stay. He'd traveled just for the purpose of asking me to marry him. Dale commented that he'd visited the jeweler every payday until it belonged to him and this was the happiest Christmas of his entire life.

After he left to return to Hamilton, I couldn't wait to share the news of my engagement and show off my ring to my girlfriends. Delores said she wasn't surprised he gave me the ring, but Carolyn just raised her brows and said "Hum, nice. When's the wedding?"

*

January, 1930, Dad loaned me money to start school in Seymour. I was so happy to be back in a classroom and working toward my secretarial certificate. Dale returned to Ford, but he reported yet another rumor of a layoff for single men, explaining that married men would not be laid off from their jobs. Even though Dale was lucky enough to keep his job, he constantly faced financial burdens, largely because he couldn't hang onto his money. At times, he had less than a quarter left only a few days after payday. He was considering using some of his reserve to get started in business school himself and hoped I could help him with his coursework. I reassured him I'd help as much as I could, but wondered why he might need that kind of help, since he was obviously smart. I was even more curious as to why he dropped out of Columbia. Could it have been academic as well as financial?

*

The winter proved to be harsh with persistent snowstorms and bitter cold temperatures. I rode the bus back and forth to Seymour, which was difficult at best, but it allowed me time to study. Dale was laid off from Ford again and became so discouraged with the auto industry he started business school in the evenings not far from his home. He wanted more than ever to stay focused on work so he could make a life for us—one I would be proud of.

Dale was called back to work at Ford praying every day that his job would last until fall. The workdays weren't dependable, mostly hit or miss. He continued to go to business school and hoped he would find a better job as a male secretary when he finished his courses. He couldn't stop dreaming of having me with him and found it depressing to calculate how many years it would take to achieve our financial goals before we could marry. I didn't dwell on getting married. I just wanted to complete school, then fulfill my dream of reaching my goal at IU.

❦

I remember how Dale raved about my cake when he and his dad came to dinner the first time. Mother would send birthday cakes to my brothers and sisters when they were away from home, and they always arrived fresh, usually by the next day. Trains from Vallonia ran many times a day, so mail delivery was prompt to many cities. Mother taught me how to wrap a cake in wax paper, and place it in a perfect size box, which my uncle always saved for us at his store. In March, I baked a cake early one morning, let it cool and mailed it to Dale, along with a new photo of me for his twenty-third birthday. I apologized to Dale for the meager gifts, feeling they weren't enough. He wrote a thank you note telling me that he didn't ever want me to feel what I sent him was "so little," as all his life he'd had "little." Monetary value meant nothing to him, anyway. I'd noticed that many times, but if Dale and I were going to have a future together, he'd need to see money differently.

Chapter Twenty-Seven

*W*ith my nose in the books, the weeks moved along more quickly and I found school to be pretty easy. Dale was in Hamilton and continued in business school there, but asked for some coaching. Lessons by mail were time-consuming and it was difficult for both of us. Our dreary weather made the loneliness worse and I missed him more than ever, but I found my thoughts often turning to how I felt about my relationship with him—my engagement to someone I rarely saw. I wondered which commitments were the most important to my future . . . my life. I needed more than a once-in-a-while visit from Dale, and doubts entered my mind more than I cared to admit. Then, I'd receive a letter from him and instantly I was reminded of how charming he could be.

> Hamilton, Ohio
> April 10, 1930
>
> *Dearest Love,*
>   *Out of the three hundred odd letters I've*
> *written you, this like the others is that dreaming*

kind. I noticed your last two had a tendency to be that way also. I'm glad, for I want you to dream of me when you write.

You know I like to read short fiction in my magazines and have often wondered how a story of our romance and dreams, well written, would sound. I should love some future day, not too long hence, to write our beautiful love story. Could you have known what would happen? I still thrill to that indefinable charm which exists when we're building our air castles together. It's the same sweetness, like I remember at the old home place, when all the honeysuckle and tube-roses were in bloom. The sweet-scented flowers especially at night, when life is still with misty shadows all around. How can I tell you more than that, just knowing my soul is rapt in your dearness and mystery? I miss you and would give anything to be able to see you and hold you in my arms.

I love you forever,
Dale

Vallonia, Ind.
April 13th 1930

Dearest Dale,

Your letter hit a home run with me. I'm so interested in your comment about how a story of our romance and dreams, well written, would sound. You suggested you'd love some future day to write our love story. I, too, have thought many times of doing that myself because the letters you write to me are *so beautiful. I was thinking we could write it together someday while we're in college. Perhaps it could be published. I love to write stories and with your talent, I know it could turn out quite well.*

I'm wondering if you'll be coming home for Easter this year. Easter's on the 20ᵗʰ, so I hope to see you soon.

Love,

Anna

On Easter Sunday, Dale arrived in Vallonia to celebrate the holiday. Watching from the window, I was so excited to see him in the distance, I took off running down the lane to meet him. I wanted him to wrap me in his arms and smother me with kisses, but I knew Mother was in the garden and probably watching.

"I'm thrilled you were able to make it down here. I know it isn't easy, especially with your fragile work situation."

"Can we go for a walk? I want to talk and have you all to myself."

"Sure, is anything wrong?"

"No, I am just feeling lonely. It's been over four months since I've seen you. I want you so bad sometimes I can hardly stand it. Sometimes, I just want to take you away." Pulling me nearer, he leaned over and whispered in my ear, "I want to take you away and make love to you."

Holding him at arm's length while slowly shaking my head, I said in a whisper, "Hey, we both know a harsh lesson was learned, and we can't put ourselves in that position ever again. It was the worst time in my life when I thought I might be pregnant."

"I know, my darling. I hated that you were here alone and I'm so sorry I couldn't come to be with you."

"I desperately wanted you here with me. I couldn't talk to anyone and I needed you. That was a horrible experience for me."

"Please don't feel I'm pressuring you to make love. I just want you to know, I want you. You're forgiving my error; your faith and trust fills my heart and I love you for it."

"Everything will work out for us. I feel sure it will."

He held me in his arms so tenderly, so lovingly, so quietly. As I leaned my cheek on his chest, he ever so gently ran his fingers through my hair. He drew my face up toward his and began softly kissing my forehead, cheeks, and lips, leaving warm impressions of his tenderness. I was reassured of his love in the deepest part of my soul.

"Spending time with you makes me feel more hopeful and excited about our future, but I still feel uncertain about so many things. More than anything, I want to find a better job and begin to put some money aside for us."

"With the way things are going, I also have a lot of anxiety about finding work myself," I said.

"Believe me, you won't have any trouble getting a job. You always seem to come out on top, no matter what you go after."

After supper, we sat on the swing and talked about our dream of writing our love story. We reminisced about our times together and how our love had grown. At first, we thought we could write our story for one of the magazines he was fond of, but there was so much in the beautiful letters he'd written, I wanted to include some of them. It was exciting for me to think of possibly writing something for a magazine or even a romance novel, especially if we were together at IU.

After he returned to Hamilton, he wrote that he was back in school in the evenings with his usual day job at Ford, but he'd been reprimanded by his boss because he'd either missed days or arrived late to work too many times. The thought of him being reprimanded and possibly losing his job hit like a lightning bolt. He'd never be able to afford anything if he lost his job.

Now Dale was working harder than ever to succeed in business school, but he felt his typing skills were lacking and his "wooden fingers" wouldn't cooperate. At first, he didn't like receiving a typed letter from me, but after taking the business courses, he praised me for my progress since he himself had experienced how difficult it was. Only after his own struggle in typing, was he able to give a little credit for my accomplishment, and it pleased me that he'd not only recognized it, but more-so that he'd openly offered the compliment.

Chapter Twenty-Eight

I loved the challenges of business school and excelled in my courses. I thought this would put me ahead when it came to getting a good job later. After I graduated my course work with honors, I remained at home for the summer, confident that my plan to return to Bloomington in the fall was the right path for me. I could begin to see my future. My parents were happy I'd finished and could move on to reaching my goals at IU while supporting myself.

"Anna, your father and I are so proud of you. You stuck to your guns, and it didn't take long to finish what you set out to do," Mother said slicing a freshly baked coffee cake.

"I'm glad it's over, and I feel good about it because I'll always have that to fall back on. Now I can look for a secretarial job, hopefully on campus."

"What's going on with Dale these days?" Dad asked taking a slice of cake.

"I just heard from him yesterday. Bad news. He was fired from Ford, so he's now without a job."

"Fired? How'd he get himself fired?" Mother asked.

"He was late getting back to Hamilton a few times after leaving here, then he said he lost his badge. His boss was upset over his losing the badge, so he fired him."

"Do you think that's what actually happened? It seems odd that losing his badge was that critical," Dad said wiping his mouth with his napkin.

"I don't know. Anyway, that's what he said happened. I can't imagine how he's going to find work that will pay anything decent." I could see by the look on their faces, my parents were beginning to doubt Dale would ever be able to keep a job.

It was hard for me to believe also. When I read his letter revealing the bad news I thought, *What the heck? I can't believe this. His irresponsibility has caught up with him again.* Although he claimed to have another job possibility, I wondered if he was just trying to cover his embarrassment about losing the best job he'd had so far.

◈

Since I had more free time, I offered to help the decorating committee with flower arrangements for our yearly Vallonia High alumni banquet held each May. Early Saturday morning, I rode out to Starve Hollow to pick flowers at Dale's property. As I approached the cabin, I again recalled the bittersweet memories and the intense desire we shared for one another, which often repeated in my mind. I picked many dozens of roses and gladiolas, sprinkled the stems with water from the rain barrel, and wrapped them in newspaper. I placed them in a large tin Dad had fashioned into a container with a handle and rode home with a glorious bundle of flowers.

Delores and I arranged many bouquets that made a spectacular spray of color for the dining tables and school hall. It turned out to be the talk of the evening, and I knew Dale would have loved the compliments on his gladiolas. The fragrance from the roses lingered in the air, but nestled sweetly inside me were the loving thoughts and memories of our day together in the cabin as it replayed in my mind. Feeling sad and lonely after the banquet, I wrote Dale about the evening to let him know how much I missed him. Being so far apart was hard on both of us, but now even more so since he didn't have a job. I prayed that something would come his way soon.

> *May 17, 1930*
>
> *Dearest Dale,*
>
>   *Earlier today, I rode Spiffy out to the cabin to pick flowers for the banquet and brought bundles of them home for table arrangements in the hall. This morning, when I reached the cabin, I suddenly felt the thrill as I recalled the bittersweet memories of our romantic experience. I pressed one of the red roses from your yard to send in this letter so you too will recall the loving day we spent together. I know you wished you could be with me for the dance this year, and I think I felt even more lonely being surrounded by your flowers in your absence. Please look for the forty kisses I put in the envelope with the rose.*
>
>   *Lovingly,*
>
>   *Anna*

Our letters became less frequent since Dale had little news to write. He hadn't found work and was becoming more depressed about the difficult situation he was in, and never able to afford a train ticket to come to Vallonia. We hadn't seen each other since Easter and it was beginning to take a toll on our relationship.

CHAPTER TWENTY-EIGHT

August 4, 1930

Dearest Anna,

I'm sorry you will be celebrating your 20th birthday August 6th without me. I won't be sending a present or a card, but hope you receive many pretty gifts. I wish that you have many, many happier birthdays with much happiness growing old with me.

It has been a few months since my interview for the job with the company that promised me a position. I feel certain now that I won't be getting the job I hoped for after all. I have had so many failures that I feel surely I must have good luck sometime soon. I know my life is dull and am certain my letters are likewise because of my lack of activity. I'm more than aware I gather little to write about and am becoming more and more depressed.

I love you always,
Dale

I realized Dale had only been to see me once during the entire year. More than anything in the world, he wanted to visit me if at all possible. He made a little money working for his uncle to help make ends meet, but there was nothing left to save. At least, that's what he said.

In spite of his own situation, Dale encouraged my business career aspirations and was certain I would succeed. He said he knew I'd do just fine because of "my wonderful mind and spirit." Besides, at least in his view, I always seemed to get whatever I went after.

However, Dale himself hadn't been successful in securing a job during the past three months since he was fired. He turned down a railroad position waiting for another he thought was going to pan out for him, but nothing became of it. It had become even harder to find a job, although he said he went on interviews almost daily. His depression progressively worsened, but he kept busy in the meantime with his studies and passion for reading. He read anything and everything. Even though he didn't have a spare nickel, he regularly bought and read magazines like *The American, Collier's, Saturday Evening Post, The Liberty, Good Housekeeping, Pictorial, Ladies Home Companion* and *Review of Reviews*. Always the philosopher, he also read many others—Homer's *Odyssey*, Freeman's *Race and Language*, and Herodotus's *Egypt*.

Dale tried to keep busy at home with the garden, which had produced many vegetables for canning to provide food for the family over the next winter. However, his lack of work was ever on his mind, and it tormented him. I could understand his frustration, but at times I couldn't feel sorry for him. After all, it was his irresponsibility that placed him at risk in the first place.

⁂

Now that I had my secretarial certificate, I searched for open positions at IU and businesses around the town of Bloomington. It occurred to me that available positions might need to be filled before school resumed. With fall classes approaching, I hoped to get an interview in one of the departments on campus and began to focus my efforts in that direction.

Chapter Twenty-Nine

It didn't take long to find a part-time secretarial position on campus. I interviewed in Bloomington and was hired on the spot. I wanted to share the good news with Dale, but didn't want him to feel even worse, since he'd not had luck in getting work of any kind.

Mid-August and not long after my good fortune of getting a job, Truly stopped by the house and asked if I'd like to join her on a trip to Canada for a week.

"Count me in! I don't have to start my job at IU for about three more weeks."

"I thought we could swing down to check out New York City, then stop to see Dale on our way back home if you want."

"We haven't had much luck in getting together since he lost his job. I think he'll probably jump at the chance."

Truly and I had a wonderful time in Canada and New York. We shopped, toured museums and churches, and enjoyed all the sights. I was impressed by the women in town who appeared so well dressed and sophisticated. I liked many of the hairstyles and thought I might even consider a change when I returned to college. While we sat on a bench in town and watched the women stroll by, Truly sketched a few dresses and nifty hairstyles to help us recall them when we returned home.

Dale was thrilled we stopped to visit with him since his family had recently moved to a larger home. He hoped that his home wouldn't be a huge disappointment to us, because he knew it was nowhere near what we were accustomed to. I already knew the meals were plain compared to the food my family prepared. He wanted me to stay a week with him and let Truly go on home, but we only stayed little more than a day. We both were worried about our sister Laura who was sick at home when we left for Canada.

Laura suffered from nervous spells and appeared to have greater than usual difficulty coping during her teenage years. Apparently, she'd been staying in her darkened room nearly two weeks with the drapes pulled most of the time. Too thin already, she was severely depressed and barely eating. Mother said she'd had a nervous breakdown and had been in a seriously fragile state for some time. It appeared to be centered on a fellow, Clint, whom she'd been dating. Mother was worried because she could hear Laura crying uncontrollably and asked our family doctor who had treated her before, to stop by to see her.

My parents felt helpless and unable to deal with Laura's deep depression. Many times, Truly and I tried to console her, but were disappointed we couldn't lift her spirits. We felt her relationship with Clint was purely a physical attraction, as any pretty girl like Laura would surely be sought after. Even though she didn't admit to it, we felt she may have given more to Clint than she should have.

The next day on my way home from visiting my cousin, Clint happened to drive by with his friend Ritchie. He was hanging out of the window, smoking a cigarette, and honking his horn as he slowly cruised closer. I was uncertain of his intentions, and dreaded the encounter.

"Hey, Anna, how's your jazzy family doin'?"

"Just fine, Clint. Everyone's doing just fine."

"Good, Anna, good. How's Laura doin'?"

"She's nifty, just nifty as always. Well, gotta scoot home. Toodle-oo."

I hated that I'd been trapped in that exchange and wanted to be on my way. I had absolutely no interest in talking to that skunk since he was apparently the reason my poor sister Laura was having such a difficult time.

⁂

I heard from Dale that he was working on the possibility of coming to Vallonia and thought he might be able to stay a couple of weeks. As it turned out, his friend Jesse brought him early the next morning and I met them as they stopped at the end of our lane.

"What a nice surprise. I can't believe you're finally here. I have a big hug and kiss for you, if you want them," I said motioning with open arms.

"Of course, I want them. I've missed you more than you can possibly imagine."

He took me in his arms and hugged me so tightly I could hardly breathe, but I didn't want him to let go. I'd dreamt of this moment so many nights as I lay in bed wanting to see his face and feel his touch.

"I've missed you too. It's been far too long since we've had any alone time to be together."

"I've actually felt the pain of loneliness within me. It's been hard to endure this stretch waiting to be with you again. Sometimes, I felt as though I was completely coming apart and my mind began to play tricks on me."

"When I try to put myself in your place, I can't even begin to feel what it must be like to get turned down time after time. You've put in so many applications with nothing coming your way."

"I'm not kidding. My life is so monotonous and boring, I hate to wake up because I know it will be the same thing all over again. I wake up thinking, today's the day I'll get called to work. But nothing. Nothing happens, and I go to bed discouraged and depressed all over again. I want to put the pillow over my head and scream and scream as loud as I can."

I began to see that Dale's mental state wasn't that different from Laura's. It worried me because it seemed as though he'd become even closer to a complete breakdown too.

"My life has become so dull at home, sometimes I think I'll go crazy. I walk for miles and miles, but can't turn off my mind. I think and think, rolling the same things backwards and forwards in my brain. The same old thing, day in and day out. Going over every application wondering why they didn't want me. Why? Every job? It's beyond frustrating. If it weren't for the few small jobs around home, I think I'd go nuts."

"How awful it must be to face that every day. I can see how tough the rejection is and hard to understand, but I don't think it's personal, just that there isn't anything out there."

"I'd like to stay here with you, at least for a little while, but I don't want to be a lot of trouble. I need to get rid of some of this depression if I can."

"Oh, you won't be any trouble. It's fine for you to stay. Don't worry about it. The change in scenery and getting out with the horses will be good for you. And for me, too, for that matter."

After supper, Mother asked Dale if he'd like to be the sofa guest, and he jumped at the chance to spend the night for the first time with my family. Of course, Kay, who was ten, was happy to have him stay at our house because he teased her and she loved it.

Dude, Laura, and Kay, were still around home for the summer. After breakfast the next day, Laura who seemingly was doing a bit better, came to the dining room, but was downright mean and irritable.

"With a forced smile and a glare, she sarcastically said, "Good morning, Anna dear. You seem awfully happy with yourself this morning."

"What are you saying, Laura? I don't understand what you mean by your tone of voice."

"Oh. You don't? I heard you've been asking around about me. You're always getting into everyone's business. Why don't you just stay out of my personal problems?"

"I don't know what you're talking about?"

"Oh, yeah. I think you do. You just act like you don't. I don't like that you're checking around town trying to find out from Clint what happened to break us up. You need to leave us alone."

I was not only shocked, but hurt because I didn't understand the accusations, and she refused to tell me what was bothering her. She was clearly angry, and that was unusual. I was upset and puzzled by her actions. I pulled Dale aside and asked him to come to the barn and saddle the horses. Then, as soon as he had Spiffy saddled, I took off on one of the fastest rides I'd ever taken. I was raging mad, forcing Spiffy to gallop faster and faster, racing like I was the devil possessed.

When Dale caught up with me, he yelled, "Anna, *what's wrong with you?*"

"Just stop it!" I yelled. "Leave me *the hell* alone."

"I want to know why you're behaving this way!"

Shrieking at him and pounding my sweaty fist on my thigh, I blurted out, "I'm just ANGRY, that's all. Can't you see that?"

"Yes, I see that, but I don't understand why."

I broke away with Spiffy again, racing even harder and faster. I almost reached the fence, but Spiffy wouldn't follow my command to jump. He was snorting and prancing back and forth as if he knew he'd failed me for the first time ever. I'd never commanded Spiffy like that or ever commanded him to jump that high. I began to cry hysterically, all the while knowing I was out of control. I'd never used profanity before and knew it probably surprised Dale as well. It wasn't like me to exhibit that kind of behavior. I wondered if it was the culmination of the enormous pressure and conflict within me, worrying about Laura's fragile situation, Dale's joblessness and penniless existence, or the self-imposed pressure to be successful with my new job and school. Maybe all of that set me off. I was wrong and thought Dale may have been angry with me.

"What's wrong? What's wrong with you?"

I was sobbing hysterically and realized I needed to calm down. Dale pulled me off of Spiffy, forcing me to dismount, and held me tightly in his arms. I struggled to get away, while he coaxed me to tell him what had made me so upset.

"I don't know why Laura was accusing me of interfering with her relationship with Clint. I'd never, ever do that."

"Why? What did she say?"

"I guess she thinks I talked to Clint about her, but I didn't. I saw him and Ritchie when I was on my way home from Delores's house a couple of days ago. It was merely a brief exchange. He asked how Laura was and I told him she was *fine*. That was it. That's all I said."

"Maybe she heard something about it from someone who added a little something to it. The best thing is to tell her you're sorry for the misunderstanding. Reassure her you'd never stand in the way of any relationship of hers and you love her."

"I'm certain you're right. I know she's been taking the breakup extremely hard. I want her to be happy again so she can do well at IU. I want to be with her there. It'll be good for both of us."

"And, it will be fun. She just needs some time to get over Clint."

"It hurt me to think she had so little trust in me. Why would I talk to Clint anyway? I know I have a lot on my mind and let everything get to me."

"I think that's probably it. You've been under a lot of pressure and me losing my job hasn't helped. Still, more than anything in the world, I want to be with you in Bloomington. Come on, sweetheart, let's head back to the house."

I wanted Dale to be at college with me, too, and if he could have a decent-paying job, it would ease my mind. I wondered if he were still putting forth the effort, or if he'd become so discouraged that his negative attitude hindered his success in securing employment.

We had a great time together for those two weeks. Every day we built air castles with our hopes and dreams for our future. We rode the horses whenever it didn't rain and swam every warm day that came our way. Our daily walks often set Dale to dreaming while softly composing poetry which seemed to flow so simply and naturally from his lips. I often wondered how he thought of such beautiful things to say. One evening, I gave him a pencil and tablet to write. I curled up in the swing, laid my head on his lap, and listened to music on the radio coming from the open living room window, while he wrote a few verses.

"So, my love, here's one for you," he said

Sentiment is a cherished thought
So loving and so true
I would not think of being taught
To love another—than you.

A kiss, a smile, with dear embrace
I'll await, for 'tis my goal;
To see your happy gentle face
Fills with joy my soul.

Perchance another one might see
What beauty that I've held so dear;
But if it's love you've given me
You will not pause to hear.

Yet unexpected this might be
Full well we know it can
I've faith you'll judge twixt he and me
And find the better man!

For when once a heart you've taught
That high ideals are better aims
You did to me with patience bind
My life to yours and I proclaim, my love.

"And, just like that, you wrote that poem for me?" I asked.
"Just like that. You inspire me with your love."
This time it was harder than ever to leave one another. But we both felt we finally had the time we needed to create a deeper love and our relationship had become even stronger.

⁂

I was excited about my new job and looked forward to returning to campus at IU. Mostly, I looked forward to returning to an environment with motivated and educated people. Truly created several dresses for me to wear to my new job, using the sketches she'd made while we were in Montreal. They all were beautiful and fit perfectly. I felt I was definitely in vogue with my stylish new clothes and couldn't wait to show them off.

Laura came to my room as I was finishing packing, and we talked about the morning she'd become upset, thinking I'd interfered in her relationship with Clint. I told her it hurt me to think she didn't trust me. I admitted to seeing him in his car when I was returning home a few days ago. I assured her that our encounter was brief, that he did ask about her, and I said she was fine. She apologized about her misunderstanding. Clint had played games with her mind, and she was shocked when he suddenly dropped her. We hugged, and she said she was happy I'd asked her to share an apartment in Bloomington. She felt it was probably just what she needed to get over her heartbreak. She promised to join me at IU in two weeks.

I was excited about what lay ahead and the people I'd meet, both on campus and in my new job. As I thought about the past two weeks, I couldn't have asked for a better time with the one I loved. However, I did wonder how our future would flourish with us being so far apart and my focus on my new job and studies. I re-read his poem again and sensed his insecurity to be more profound than I'd realized when I first read it. In the last two stanzas of his poem, his concern about losing me was obvious.

Chapter Thirty

$\mathscr{I}$ returned to IU in Bloomington at the end of the second week of September 1930. I began working as the secretary for Dr. W.W. Wright in the Bureau of Education four hours a day and the other four hours a day in the School of Education. Not only was I earning a good salary of thirty-five cents an hour, but everyone in the office eagerly welcomed me, making me feel at ease.

A fellow named Guy worked for Dean Henry Smith in the same office, but in the Bureau of Co-operative Research, writing speeches and annotating bibliographies for him. They told me about Guy, but I hadn't seen him my first day at the office. I wrote my name 'Anna Marie' on the blotter next to my typewriter. A few days later, Guy came in the office after returning from vacation. He walked over to the table where I was working, holding out his hand to greet me.

"Good morning, I'm Guy. I noticed you wrote your name on your workstation blotter. I always liked the name 'Marie.'"

"Well, good morning to you. I'm glad to meet you."

I instantly felt my stomach begin to whirl and my knees weaken.

I'd never experienced a sensation like that before. Standing right there, right by my desk was a tall, handsome man with kind brown eyes, and black wavy hair just beginning to gray at the temples. Wearing black suit pants, a white long-sleeved dress shirt with cuffs rolled up twice, and a steel-gray necktie, Guy looked like he'd just stepped out of the men's display window at L.S. Ayres in Indianapolis. Handsome and distinguished. I felt my heart skip, not one, but two beats, and I tried to catch my breath to respond. I thought, *Here, at last is the man of my dreams. Oh, why couldn't I have met him before this?*

I snapped out of my inner swoon when Guy noticed my hand and commented, "It looks like you might be engaged."

"Yes, I became engaged last Christmas. My boyfriend Dale lives in Ohio."

"I'd like to meet him sometime."

"You probably will have that chance," I said smoothing my hair back off my shoulder.

"Are you a local?" he asked.

"Yes, as of two weeks ago. I'm from Vallonia. I share an apartment with my sister Laura over on Smith Avenue."

Dorothy, my Chi Omega Sorority sister who was one of my best friends, also worked in the office. We'd roomed as freshman here at IU and had known each other for two years. At lunch break she approached me, and I softly asked her about Guy.

"So, Dorothy, what's with Guy?"

"What do you mean, what's with him?"

"Is he married?"

"No, I guess you could say he's sort of available."

"How sorta?"

"My roommate, Bea, the other girl in our office that you met, she's had romantic feelings for Guy for about a year, but they've only casually dated."

"That's what I was wondering. Thanks."

I was so happy. I had a good job, I liked the office where I was working, I liked the professors, and I was happy living with Laura in our own apartment. What more could a girl want?

Hamilton, Ohio
September 17, 1930

Dearest Anna,

Just a brief note to let you know I'm back in the full swing at business school and have at least two full days of work this week. It's good you've gotten to your work early, especially now with finding things are easier than expected. It's nice when you not only find your way, but also that you find more than you anticipated. I wish you much success, as you know, hoping that your work will be as pleasant as one could want.

I'm sure you and Laura are glad to be together there at the university, especially since she's feeling better. I'm certain she'll continue to improve as time goes on, and she begins to date again.

I can't tell yet if I'll be able to be with you for Thanksgiving. It's too early to know at this point. I'm just trying to stay positive and pray I'll be seeing you soon. Fighting depression is difficult.

I love you always and forever,
Dale

With the holidays approaching, it concerned me when Dale wrote he'd worked only a few days and was having more and more difficulty fighting his depression. His letters continued to concern me, and it was becoming harder to lift him up. Without work, Dale felt he wasn't worthy of me. He explained that he wouldn't live the life of a day-laborer, not that he was above that, but he knew I was and he thought I could choose nearly any man I wanted.

He was concerned that I was either preoccupied, was not well, or had taken on too much work, because he'd received fewer letters from me lately. My enthusiasm about our last visit was dwindling and I struggled to stay positive about Dale when his letters were shrouded with doubts and negativity.

Meanwhile, I continued to work in the office for the professors doing research, which I loved. I realized I'd rapidly developed a crush on Guy and looked forward to seeing him each day. Sometimes my attraction to him made it hard to keep my mind on my work. I even found myself daydreaming about him. I looked for every opportunity to be in Guy's company, but found myself off guard when I stopped in the break room at the office one day and found Guy was alone.

"Say, Anna, I was hoping you might show up here for lunch. Come join me."

"Thanks, I'd love to."

"So how do you like it so far?"

"To tell you the truth, I love this job. It's turned out to be so much more than I ever expected." I thought, *here comes that fluttery feeling in my stomach again. My heart is pounding. I wonder if he suspects I have feelings for him.*

"It looks like you immediately got a grip on the work, and that's certainly impressive. Personally, I find our work here to be quite satisfying, and my boss is such a fine man."

I sat with my elbow on the table and my hand supporting my head while gazing into his beautiful brown eyes. I was mesmerized by Guy's soft voice and almost forgot to pay attention to what he was actually saying. When I realized how entranced I had become just listening to the inflection in his voice, I felt my neck and face becoming warmer and wondered if I looked flushed. And, that fluttery feeling was right back again. As I jumped in to recover my end of the conversation, he said, "I hope I haven't bored you too much. You had a rather faraway look just now."

"Oh, no, Guy. I'm listening. I was just wondering how you stay so calm. Do you ever get excited or upset?" *Goodness gracious, this man is easy to look at.*

"I guess I never gave it much thought. I probably was born that way. I think it's important to be patient when you're looking toward a teaching job."

⌘

While talking to Guy over lunch, I learned the apartment he shared with his sisters and brother was also on Smith Avenue. A few days later we began to walk home together after office hours. Even after two months walking home together, each time we met, I was aware that the same fluttery sensation had returned in my stomach. In spite of the intense feelings I still had for Dale, I couldn't get Guy out of my mind. Unlike Dale, Guy was not given to exaggerating or to fluctuating emotions and I found his confidence refreshing. I never had to reassure him, and he always treated me like a woman. I hoped he'd ask me out on a date sometime, because I loved his great sense of humor. I was more like my true self around him and his teasing only drew me to become more infatuated. But he never made any comments, and whatever thoughts he had about me, he kept to himself.

Chapter Thirty-One

On Saturday, November 22, Indiana University and Purdue University held their annual rival football game. My friends Bea and Dorothy had gone with the gang to Lafayette to watch it and root for IU. Guy was a Mason and asked me to go with him to the Masonic Temple to listen to it on the radio. He said we could sit or even dance if we liked. I'd been to a few exciting IU games with my older brothers in the past, but I found being with Guy in the beautiful, comfortable lounge at the Masonic Temple was the next-best place to be.

When IU won, the whole town was in a state of ecstasy and celebration. Bonfires everywhere illuminated the campus and surrounding area. The Fox Theater even opened its doors, free to all college students. This set a joyous backdrop for Guy and me to celebrate with everyone else, and we did. Guy seemed more relaxed than I'd ever seen him, and I felt he even looked at me differently.

"Anna, I can't remember when I've ever had such a wonderful time. The game was exciting and so were all of the celebrations.

That was unbelievable fun."

"I feel the same way. It *was* great fun, and the best dance I ever went to."

Guy leaned toward me and whispered, "How do you feel about us seeing each other privately once in a while?"

"I think it would be just fine. I'm not sure it would go over well with Bea, and I wouldn't want her to be hurt. Some of the others in the office might object if we openly saw each other. But, I think it would be fine to be together on occasion, and to tell the truth, I'm looking forward to it."

That was exactly what I'd hoped for and I was jumping for joy now that Guy had finally asked. Although I felt guilty about wanting to be with Guy, it was hard to deny my feelings for him when I was around him every day. We worked so closely together that he was constantly on my mind. I realized he was everything I wanted in a man. Dale was hardly ever around, and I thought of him less and less because my mind was so preoccupied.

When we returned to work on Monday, Bea brought Guy a little souvenir from the game at Purdue, but neither Guy nor I mentioned that we'd listened to the game together on the radio. Guy continued to walk Bea home on occasion and ask her out for a brief "Coke" date at the Book Nook, so that she never suspected he was dating me.

My sister Laura highly disapproved of me dating anyone other than Dale. But when Truly visited me the previous weekend, I talked to her about Guy. She heartily approved after meeting him. She saw no reason for me to give up all college fun when Dale was a hundred miles away and not making progress toward joining me at IU. Still, I felt conflicted because Dale and I would be together over the coming holidays. I didn't want him to sense another man coming between us—even though there was some truth to it.

November 24, 1930

Dearest Beloved,

Dad and I've been working on the Ford to get it in shape to make the trip to Vallonia for Thanksgiving, and thank you for the invitation. I can pick you up in Bloomington, if you want us to drive you to Vallonia also. I may visit Bloomington anyway since I'll be free for about two weeks. I could see where you live, get a better feel of the campus and be introduced to some of your friends. I'll be so glad to see you I can hardly wait. Please let me know if you want me to pick you up.

I just read in the paper where Capone is feeding over a thousand men a day in Chicago. This, in itself, is something more than we can see as "goodness," since it's coming from a hand of the lawless. There have been so many robberies here in the past three weeks, but I suppose there are more to come as it gets closer to Christmas. The pressure of unemployment continues to take its toll on society.

> *Just a wild-rose*
> *And a little pearl*
> *God has put together*
> *So sweetly—my Girl!*

I love you,
Dale

Dale did arrive at his cabin Wednesday night, and we spent time with my family over the Thanksgiving holiday. We had plenty of time to talk privately, but I found some of our conversations uncomfortable.

"Anna, do you remember when you told me you went to the football game between IU and Purdue with that fella?"

"Yes. What about it?"

"I was wondering why you dated him. I thought we already discussed side dates."

"But, Dale, I don't understand what the problem is. I told you it was just a social engagement with someone from the office. We didn't go to the game, we merely listened to the game on the radio. I certainly didn't see anything wrong with that!"

"I guess there's a difference between a social engagement and a 'date,' and I'm sorry if I was seemingly impertinent about your affairs."

"Just drop it. I don't think we need to make any more of it than it was."

"Don't get mad at me. It's just that I feel my blood loves passionately and hates passionately, but I must understand how to better myself about those things, I guess."

We drove back to Bloomington Saturday afternoon and met my friend Alvin at his apartment where Dale spent the night. Before we knew it, the weekend was over, and I was back at work. Monday morning, I returned to the research department, bringing Dale along.

"Everyone, I'd like you to meet Dale Stevens, my fiancé. He decided he'd like to see where I worked before going back to Vallonia."

"Hello, Dale. Good that you could stop by. Are you planning to join Anna here at IU at some point?" Dorothy asked, even though she already knew his penniless situation.

"I'm not sure right now. I want to see how things turn out as far as work and how much I can put away."

"We surely do appreciate having Anna on board here in the Bureau. She's doing a fine job and is a big help to everyone," Guy said.

"Yes, we certainly do like having her here. She's taken a load off of my workday. I can tell you it certainly makes a difference for all of us," Dr. Wright said.

"Anna seems to fit in wherever she goes, and she's a hard worker. I hate to make this so short, but I'd better be heading out. Nice to meet you all," Dale said giving a wave.

After he left the office to return to Vallonia, Dorothy said, "I'm glad to finally have met Dale, but I have to say, he's not quite what I expected, even though you showed us his picture last week."

"How so? What do you mean?"

"I don't know. Just different than I expected. I mean, he seemed nice and all. Maybe I thought he'd have more to say or something. He seemed uncomfortable. Maybe he felt self-conscious?"

⚬⚭⚬

Dale returned to Vallonia to pick up his dad and return home to Hamilton. The next day he wrote a letter confiding in me that during the long ride home, he began daydreaming. His mind drifted to a discussion we'd had. I'd told him of a book by Judge B. Lindsey who wrote about couples living together to see if they were compatible before getting married. A couple of my friends had read it and thought it was an interesting concept. I thought it might be of interest to Dale and wanted his thoughts on it. If we were to try it, at least we'd know if we were suited for one another. He said he re-thought my offer to live together at Bloomington, but he feared it would come with many hard bumps. He explained he was eager to start life with me, but if he couldn't succeed, he didn't want to. And, he was afraid his financial problems would adversely affect me and our relationship—something I was concerned about myself.

After meeting Guy in the office Monday, Dale wondered if there were more to his compliments than I'd said. After all, he was obviously a good-looking single man, and seemed genuinely fond of me. I couldn't, of course, tell Dale how I felt about Guy. In fact, I didn't even admit to myself how intense my attraction to Guy was becoming.

Recalling our visit to the office and Dale's introduction to my co-workers, I wondered what they truly thought about him. He appeared uneasy when asked if he were going to attend IU since he still didn't have any money and what's more, still no job. Dorothy seemed hesitant to give her opinion, but I decided to take it up with her at a later time. We were good enough friends, and I was sure she'd give me her honest feelings about him. I also wondered what Guy thought about Dale and whether or not I starred in Guy's daydreams, as he did in mine.

Chapter Thirty-Two

I looked forward to being back in the office where so often my days were rewarding. I loved working not only with Dorothy and Guy, but the professors as well. Of course, there was no way I could know how important Dr. Wright was when I interviewed for the job. It certainly made me happy that he immediately thought so much of me to give me a chance to work in the Bureau of Education. I loved research work, and my schedule of working for two professors provided such variety, my days were never boring. And, to have a job making thirty-five cents an hour was nothing to quarrel about. Yet, the best part was that I saw Guy almost every day.

A few days after Dale left, I had an unpleasant encounter after work when everyone, including Guy, had already left the office. I remained to finish filing papers when I realized I wasn't alone. Before I could turn around to see who it was, I suddenly felt hands squeezing my shoulders then briskly drop them to my elbows with a gentle caress. Instantly I turned around, only to realize I was now face-to-face with and wrapped in the arms of J.D., the assistant professor.

"You startled me, J.D. What are you doing?" I was stunned when he leaned forward and tried to kiss me.

"I thought, since your boyfriend's never around, you might need a little sugar."

"Come on, now. This is just wrong," I pushed him back and he reluctantly released his grip.

"Anna, you must know what a curiosity you've become around the office."

"No, I wasn't aware I was a *curiosity*—as you put it."

"We all watch every move you make."

I attempted to gather my belongings, but J.D. stepped in front of me to block me from leaving. "Let me take you out for dinner tonight. I insist." he said.

"No, I need to be on my way home. I'm late already." My head was pounding and I knew my face must have been beet red.

"Aw, come on. Just this once? Or, we could go to your apartment if you prefer."

"I have classes tonight. I'll see you Monday. Enjoy your weekend." I gave a nervous half-chuckle hoping to lighten the tension after rejecting his offer.

"Yeah, you too," he said in a discouraged response.

I couldn't get out of the office quick enough and all the way to my apartment, I was shaking inside. I wondered what his wife would say if she knew. Even though it was awkward, I wanted to be professional, so I didn't say anything to anyone about the incident or let it affect my work. But, I did remain cautious and after that, I never stayed late in the office by myself again.

Within days of his departure, Dale wrote that he reached home safely in Hamilton with his dad. He said he was growing more deeply concerned about the terrible state the nation was in. Economic conditions worsened, and relief organizations could do little to help. After all, where would the money come from? The banks even sent out the Christmas savings checks, in hopes there'd be a much greater volume of buying. However, many of the larger stores dismissed all extra help, as shoppers' purchases didn't meet their expectations.

Newspapers reported that national unemployment included nearly three million men. Out of that number, about three hundred-fifty thousand men were destitute. Many companies had greatly reduced employee wages, but kept full-time hours just to stay afloat. Already, many more bread lines had formed, and people were stealing anything they could get their hands on. There were robberies everywhere, and it was dangerous to walk or drive after nightfall. As conditions worsened, Dale became even more worried and depressed because he still hadn't found work.

He was hopeful to see me over Christmas if he could get a ride to Vallonia, but warned me again he wouldn't have a present for me. I assured him that his gifts were perpetual, so he needn't be concerned about it.

⁂

I was glad to hear from Dale that he could come for the holiday, since it would be the first anniversary of our engagement. Most of my brothers and sisters had already arrived and finished eating by the time he showed up at the house. He saw me watching him from the window and blew a kiss on his way to the door.

"Merry Christmas, handsome. We weren't sure what time you'd arrive, so as you may have guessed, we ate earlier. Come in the kitchen, and I'll make you some breakfast."

"Merry Christmas, Mrs. Fosbrink."

"Merry Christmas to you, Dale. Anna, are you making something for Dale to eat?"

"Yes, I heated up the biscuits and gravy and put on a pot of coffee."

"And, the biscuits and gravy are out of this world, Mrs. Fosbrink."

"When you finish, let's move into the living room with the rest of the family," I said as I planted a kiss on his forehead. "Did you see I collected mistletoe from Grandpa's tree?"

"No, I didn't. But when I finish my coffee, I'll get to work on it," he said with a wink.

It was apparent Dale felt uncomfortable during the gift exchange, since he was unable to afford gifts, not even for me. I tried to pass over the uneasiness I knew he was feeling by recalling the previous Christmas when he put the ring on my finger and I was so giddy and nearly speechless.

Later in the day, I whispered and motioned for him to join me in the kitchen.

"What is it? Is anything wrong?" He asked.

"No, I just want to talk to you about something that happened at work a few weeks ago. One of the professors in the office made an advance toward me. It not only caught me off guard, but it truly upset me."

"Are you kidding? Who was there when he did that?"

I noticed Dale's expression change as his face reddened and nostrils flared while he grew increasingly upset when I described what happened.

"Everyone had left for the day and suddenly he was standing behind me and put both of his hands on my shoulders like he was caressing me. It startled me, and I spun around, not knowing who it was. He leaned in toward my face as if he intended to kiss me, and I backed away."

"What? What kind of a guy is he, anyway? That makes me sick, him putting his hands on you."

"Please, Dale, lower your voice and simmer down. Everything is under control."

"He had no right to do that. They should fire him!"

"The whole encounter shocked me, and I was still unsettled when I returned to the office on Monday. But you needn't worry, I think I handled it well and am prepared to discourage any further advances."

Again, before Dale left to go home, he needed reassurance that everything was fine. I tried to make light of it, not wanting to carry the discussion further. I wished I hadn't brought up the incident with the professor in the first place because all it did was make him feel more uncertain and pressure me for details.

Dale told me one of his greatest fears was that someone would steal my heart, which would leave him devastated. He said he worried about it often. In the back of my mind, the possibility had occurred to me also. Once in a while I've wondered about it, so much so, that I realized I'd memorized the last verse in Dale's poem which kept popping into my head—"yet unexpected this might be, full well we know it can, I've faith you'll judge twixt he and me, and find the better man!"

Chapter Thirty-Three

After Christmas, there was such excitement at my house while I was on hand to help with the live birth of my new nephew and my parents' first grandchild, Robert. The birth was uneventful, for both mother and baby, who were doing fine because of the many loving hands available to help care for them. What a beautiful, thrilling time for my family to share with Ken and his wife, Opal, and a maturing experience for me that I'll never forget.

I had plenty of time to reflect on my holiday with Dale and began to realize even more so that his unfortunate circumstances had become overwhelming. It appeared he was unable to move forward, but also, it seemed he didn't realize or acknowledge that he'd brought it all on himself. I began to wonder if there actually were no opportunities for him to earn a little money, or if he was just so depressed he couldn't put forth the effort to secure some kind of work even for a little pay. Did he just lay around reading all day to drown his worries?

Hamilton, Ohio
December 29, 1930

My Beloved,

I'm more than happy, for I think the first anniversary of our engagement was wonderful as a whole. Please allow for my faults until I may improve. I know I have great faults, but you're a wonderful teacher, and I want so much to learn how to be better.

You've always seemed so good, so pure, so lovely. It wasn't your shortcomings that caused what happened with the professor. It was the natural thing. You're a beautiful woman now, so I'm sure he's been taken with your wonderful spirit. If he'd been a fine man, his restraint would have triumphed over his impulses. I can admit what you told me was a great shock, but I also know you are dealing with a good stiff problem.

I'm hoping against hope, that I will be able to find work soon, so I can fulfill our dreams of my going to college. I'm pleased that you are encouraging me, because I want it more than anything and I'm especially interested in psychology. Have you ever studied psychology? I want to thank you for introducing me to your book by Judge B. Lindsey on the controversial trial marriage he advocates. Until I finish reading the book, my feeling is that the arrangements for a trial marriage are too risky, and I seriously doubt I could ever agree to it.

I had a wonderful time with your entire family over the Christmas holidays. I'm so pleased to have been able to meet Truly's

boyfriend, Earl, and hear him play the piano.
It still fills my soul with pleasant memories of
the beautiful arrangements he offered. He's a
most accomplished artist. I am so happy that
Truly has found a place for her love and trust.
With all my heart, I love you,
Dale

I received a postcard from Dale welcoming in the New Year, 1931. He hadn't started back to business school, but would resume his studies the following week. He was content to lose himself in reading to block the reality of his unemployment.

Hamilton, Ohio
January 2, 1931

Dearest Anna,

I finished reading Judge B. Lindsey's book
on trial marriage, but don't lay claim to any
of the judge's thoughts. It was not that the book
produced a chaos of thoughts in me, but I didn't
realize that the judge's thoughts would influence
you so strongly that you would actually consider
it. I feel there is danger in all new concepts such
as trial marriage. The thought of living together
as man and wife "in a trial" while not married
is difficult for me to accept. What happens to the
broken hearts if it doesn't work out for one or both
parties involved? I don't want to experiment. I
don't want to enter into marriage just to try it
out. I already know what marriage is.

I'll take the Civil Service exam next week,
but there are only eight positions with over
one hundred and fifteen men applying to take

the exam. I know special compensation will be
offered to ex-soldiers first, which is another dis-
couraging position for me, but I want to pursue
every opportunity.
      I love and miss you my darling,
        Dale

There was no doubt in my mind how he felt about living together in a trial marriage. I had suggested he read about the concept only because I felt there were problems we could work out if we spent more time together and saw each other at our best, as well as our worst moments. However, reconsidering the details of the experiment more thoroughly, I realized I could be entering into something greater than anticipated. Besides, I agreed with Dale. I already knew what marriage was, but unlike him, I was beginning to regret prematurely making a lifetime commitment. Examining my feelings more closely, I realized how much freedom I'd already given up, and knew it would dwindle even more when Dale arrived at IU.

After the Christmas holiday, I returned to work in Bloomington, but within a week, I developed an infection from a spider bite on my hand. The doctor feared it was blood poisoning. I used a germicide soap I purchased at the drugstore for a quarter, but the infection interfered with my work. I did my best to persevere with the pain, and tried to work around bandages while typing. Having been able to save money with a steady job, I enrolled in two evening classes at IU, which I attended after work. I was finding my days were quite long, but I was determined to pay back my debts to Dad and Truly while working toward completing my education.

During lunch break at the office one day, Dorothy stopped at my table to talk.

"Anna, what's going on with your long-distance relationship?"

"What do you mean?"

"I was just wondering about your boyfriend. Are you guys still solid?"

"Yes, we're engaged."

"I can see you are, but I was wondering why you would still be with him?"

"Why? What are you saying?"

"Didn't he get fired a while ago? I mean, he had a good job and couldn't keep it."

"Yes, but he's been constantly looking and has filled out loads of applications for any kind of job you could imagine."

"I just can't see it, myself. He's not at your social level, has no money, and you say he's depressed much of the time."

"I know. I'm always worried about him. Still he has such a brilliant mind, I truly think if he'd come to college, he'd definitely make something of himself."

"I don't know. Are you in love with him?"

"Yes, of course. I *think* I am. We do have a lot in common. We enjoy so many of the same things."

"From what you've told me, you also have a lot that's *not* in common."

"I'm concerned he's become a different person since the Depression's getting worse around the country. He's so unhappy all the time now. He's even more dependent on me for support. Not money. Just emotional."

"I've wondered if his depression is making him unbalanced."

"The whole thing is worrisome. I think about it all the time. I know he feels trapped, and now so do I, but for different reasons."

"Anna, you're such a special person. You need to take care of yourself and the bright future you have ahead of you. Don't you see that?"

"Please, Dorothy, don't say anything to anyone here in the office about it, and especially not to Bea. I'm having a hard-enough time without feeling my personal affairs are being discussed by everyone."

I was beginning to have greater doubts about my relationship with Dale. I hated to entertain the thought, but I wondered if I was just holding on to the hope he'd change. Was it that I wished to break off the engagement, but couldn't bear the pain I knew it would bring? So often I'd considered what he might do to himself if I were to break it off. After all, he seemed so much more emotionally fragile now that I was back at IU and his unemployment seemed never-ending. Maybe I was feeling increasingly guilty because of the fondness I'd already developed for Guy.

It seemed so long ago when Dale and I began our journey. In the beginning, when he first wrote, I was just a naïve girl happy for the attention of an older boy. After so many long separations, the beautiful letters over the years had become the story of our love. We yearned to hear from one another with intense anticipation and fell deeply in love through our written words. The separations and longing to be with each other only heightened our desires to express our love when we were finally alone.

As I reflected back over the past four years of our relationship, I tried to come to terms with what drew me to Dale in the first place. Had I felt sorry for him, how he lived, how he was accustomed to having so little that he didn't expect more out of life? I've now admitted to myself, in the beginning I *had* felt sorry for Dale and wanted to help guide him to become a better person. I began to realize he looked to me for the sweetness and comfort I could give him, but that was also what I looked for in return. Then as our relationship developed, it seemed as though the more I gave, the more he needed from me to make him happy and he became controlling—possessive. Now, I feel I've come to his defense so often to provide protection for him, I wonder, if our relationship continued, would this be my "forever" role as his partner? These questions seemed to have no answer, but raced through my mind, night after night as I lay in bed.

During the day, however, I found my thoughts shifting toward Guy. He stopped by my desk after work each day offering to walk me home. It thrilled me that he'd taken such an interest in me, and I didn't want it to stop. I learned from Dorothy that after I brought Dale to the office to meet everyone, she overheard Guy telling the assistant professor, "I'd be willing to bet you, she'll never marry that guy." I was surprised when Dorothy told me that. It only added to a multitude of doubts I was already experiencing about Dale. And, it seemed that Guy might have pretty good insight into character.

Chapter Thirty-Four

I knew in my heart, it was time to come to grips with my feelings about my relationship with Dale, and I needed to begin letting him know how I felt. I realized how fragile he was and was certain the news would be devastating, no matter when he received it. I expected he would view it as an ultimatum. Dreading this undertaking, I sat staring at a blank sheet of stationery struggling to begin such a difficult letter.

> Bloomington, Indiana
> February 3, 1931
>
> Dear Dale,
>
> I've been thinking a lot about us lately and have spent many sleepless nights while searching my mind about our relationship. It seems as though our life paths are separating farther and farther apart as we move forward with our goals in life. I have no doubt you are aware

just how strongly I feel about my education and I've never thought of giving that up.

For such a long time now, you've said you wanted better for yourself, but I question how serious you've been. You've made some unfortunate decisions with regards to your work. You've quit jobs, quit college, been fired, and now have started business school. Those choices placed you at an even greater disadvantage because of the Depression and I worry how this will turn out for you—and us—in the long run. I try to imagine our lives with only one of us being serious about a career and wonder how we'd support our family.

This is not the future I want. Unless your prospects/career take a turn for the better, I don't feel comfortable about our plans to get married. I thought I should share this with you, because you've always said our relationship needs to be built on trust. I trust you would want to know how I feel. I've not intended this letter to be in a mean spirit or in anger. I only felt I needed to share my concerns for our future.

Love,

Anna

After dropping the letter in the mail, I felt sick inside. It was the hardest letter I'd ever written because I was fully aware of Dale's deep love and admiration for me. I knew he'd be hurt and feel I'd betrayed him, but my conscience told me not to continue to drag it on any longer.

Hamilton, Ohio
February 7ᵗʰ 1931

Dearest Anna,

I had a pleasant day trimming trees, for which I was glad to have a day's work. I wasn't tired until I sat down, but I think it's because I'm so tired, that your letter hurt me. Why did you choose this time above all others to write this? Beloved, I want to be angry. Do you think I don't suffer when I know what your friends must be saying to you? Do you think I've forgotten how proud you want to be of me? I hate people! I hate those who know me as a friend, but then criticize my situation! I never had anything. They pity me because I've tried to climb, reaching for new and higher ideals, but Kiddo, who offers to help? I don't want their help, if they would just leave me alone! Don't you believe me when I say I can't even purchase a steady job? Anna, it's taken all the courage I have to go on.

I started business college, and the manager said I'm ready to be placed, but he hasn't even been able to place anyone in over ten months. Do you know what it means to be turned away day after day? I'm wondering if I'm in my right mind. I'm beginning to think my life is nothing but strange fantasies. I truly am facing a critical period.

Beloved, I know you've raised those air castles around me. You want to be proud of me. Oh, God, I have so little. I know that I

*can do it. I love you. Don't you know? Tell me
you haven't promised too soon? Oh, please not
that. I wish you could tell your friends some
good of me. Tell them—tell them I'm working
tomorrow, Sunday, do you hear? For money,
money, money. I hate it. But I must have it
to purchase my happiness, my friends, even a
place in heaven. Why didn't they let my mother
stay? She would have loved me, not pity, love.*

*I don't mean these horrible words. Yet, if I
get a good job, they'll all be my friends again.
I don't ask you to suffer humiliation because of
me, but you have my heart and soul. What will
become of them?*

*I think I've taken your last lesson the
hardest. That is, I must succeed or there's no
place for me. You have no cause to feel unwor-
thy. My devotion to you is the one thing that's
truly been like sunshine to my life. I've grown
wonderfully, I think, from the once ragged,
warped creature that I was. I can sacrifice for
you, Beloved, but first let me plead for just
a little more time. Please let's not write any
more of these. Tell me you love me! May I call
you Ann?*

I love you,
Dale

Dale seemed to be slipping even deeper into depression, and I
worried about him more than ever. Because he was so depressed,
most of his energy was trapped in negative thoughts. I felt so conflicted about our relationship. As Valentine's Day approached,
already I was feeling an even greater sadness for what we'd lost.

February 13th 1931

Dear Dale,

I hope you received my Valentine I sent yesterday and the box of candy. I know how you like my chocolate fudge. I've been missing you and feel you've had it pretty rough facing such hard times lately. It would be so different if we lived closer and could see each other more often to comfort one another in such difficult times. Please try to keep your spirits up. This can't go on forever. And yes, it's okay to call me Ann, if you like.

> I love you,
> Anna

Hamilton, Ohio
February 13, 1931

My Sweetheart Ann,

I've been sitting here listening to the radio and must tell you my fortunes have been all or nothing. I can't even send a miserable little card when I want to send roses, loads of them. It was nothing again at Christmas. It hurts less for me to know that you think I don't neglect. I just can't stand one's brave efforts to appreciate even those hard-earned little tokens. Even personal efforts more directed to these gifts, seem to make them no more dear. I can remember once, I made some Valentines by hand. I never attempted it again. I think I'm losing my dreams. Yet here is an effort . . .

St Valentine: I hear
You bring good cheer
To humble hearts as mine.
If this be true
I promise you
My debt is always thine!

Man's wants we know
On Earth below
Are little, so we hear
So with bold face
I ask your Grace
To whisper in your ear.

Please grant to me
But wishes three
More Joys I'll ne're possess
They are so dear
I breathe with fear
Their sound, a sweet caress.

In a far off land
My Dearest Ann
Lest slumbering fair
Oh, give her happiness
Just Peace and Blessedness
No sorrow and no care.

My first wish gone
The second not so long
Just tell her I am here
And lovin' day by day
As birds do love the May

And wishin' she was near.
In her fair heart
Lodge Cupid's dart
('Tis selfish, that I know.)
That she may grieve the time
Which parts her heart and mine
And shorter make it grow.

St. Valentine; I trust
These wishes not unjust
('Tis the heart that speaks in need.)
There's music sweet and low
My thoughts. They come and go
Come! Clasp my hand and lead!

I promise to love you forever,
Dale

I probably shouldn't have sent the letter and candy to Dale for Valentine's, and I admit it most likely was out of guilt, but unfairly it sent a mixed message. I might've been having more difficulty letting go than I realized. I told myself what I wanted for my future, and what I needed to do, but the feelings for Dale still tugged at my heart. His Valentine poem was so heartfelt and sad. And, when I re-read it, tears blurred my vision as I sat slowly twirling between my fingers, the pressed red rose that had fallen from his letter.

February 17, 1931
My Dear Ann,
*   I received your beautiful letter and Valentine's candy which I both enjoy and appreciate. Your letter was full of feeling, a cherished, lovely one. I know when this time is*

over, I'll be very much in debt to you, in many
ways. For a long time, I've been wondering how
my credit stands with you and even though my
gifts are small, I'm in hopes they'll last until I
can get back on my feet. How much I do love
you for your patience. Before many years have
passed, I'll come to you with my treasure ship.
Somehow the storms are too severe now for a
ship that needs repairs, is without a crew and
has a sick pilot. I dream of the day that will
come for us to be together, my beautiful.

TO MY BEAUTIFUL ANN

Sweet west-wind, blow gently my dreams to
her there
Of sweet, fragrant gladness, and fleet sad despair:
Yes, waft it away this night, if you can
To meet her in slumber, My beautiful Ann,
Pshaw— 'tis thoughts of the flowers that bloom
in the glen.
They're asleep now; with snowflakes piled high
on their fends.
Their souls shine so sweetly from the encir-
cling band
Of the ring on your finger, My Beautiful Ann
Oh stay! Please come back! Oh, God, it is gone!
Will she know whence it came, to whom it belongs?"
Will it rest there in peace, fairest dreams of
a man?
In her sweetest, white bosom? My beautiful Ann.
Believe me, of all those endearing young charms,
That I gaze on so fondly today, were to fade by
tomorrow and flee from my arms,

like a fairy gift fading away,
Thou would still be adored as this moment
thou art,
Let thy loveliness fade as it will. And around
the dear ruins
Each wish of my heart, would entwine itself
verdantly still!

I will love you forever. You own my heart.
Dale

I was wrapped in even more guilt, and feeling not only sorry for Dale, but sorry for myself. I'd never had so much difficulty expressing myself or knowing exactly what I wanted until this time in my life. I was so confused.

Chapter Thirty-Five

Dale wrote he was sorry he wouldn't be coming to Vallonia April 5th for Easter Sunday because he hadn't completed the work on his uncle's house. It was the first Easter we wouldn't see each other.

That spring, I continued my schedule of eight hours a day in the education department along with taking courses at night. Although I'd dated a few other classmates, I became more infatuated with Guy as we spent more time together. I couldn't tell if Guy returned my affection, but after months of friendship, he *finally* asked me on an actual date.

"I'd love it if you'd have dinner with me this evening after work."

"Of course, Guy, I'd love to. But, why don't you come to my apartment and let me cook for you?"

"I wasn't looking for an invitation. I thought I could take you out for dinner."

"I have plenty of food in the apartment. Just stop by, and we can chat while it's cooking."

When Guy came for dinner that night, he appeared oddly cheerful, and his expression conveyed a clever joke about to be revealed.

"I guess I should tell you, I just had a funeral at home."

"What did you say? A funeral?"

"Yes, I burned all the letters from my old girlfriend, Olive."

I chuckled and said, "You seem to be all right with it; at least you're smiling!"

"I am all right and have been for quite some time."

"I've never heard you talk about her. What happened?"

"I met Olive when I lived in Tucson while attending the University of Arizona. We were engaged, but broke it off when I needed to return to Indiana to recuperate after surgery. Olive came to see me and tried to persuade me to reconsider, but we both realized it was over."

"I think it's hard to keep the fire going in a relationship with someone who is so far away. I completely understand," I replied.

"We continued to write after I returned to Indiana, but I felt it wasn't fair to either of us because of the distance, and I had no plans to return to Arizona. In the beginning, the reason I felt comfortable with you was because you were engaged. I felt safe from getting involved since I didn't ever plan to get married."

"Do you still feel safe?"

"You can't ask me that."

"I just did."

"Okay, you can ask, I just can't answer," Guy said with a hint of a smile.

Although there was a real bond between Guy and me, neither of us ever mentioned the word "love." I was certain what I felt for him truly *was* love. He made me feel appreciated and I loved his honesty and wit. I felt secure with him and trusted him completely. We continued to enjoy each other's company and had fun with no pressures. That was important to me, because there was an abundance of pressure in my relationship with Dale. Either it was the pressure of his jealous nature, the number of letters I sent, the length of them, or the time in between them—always some criticism of how I didn't measure up. I often felt Dale was too demanding, but in the back of my mind, I was afraid of what he might do to himself if I tried to end the relationship because now he was in a deeper depression.

March 5th 1931

My Dearest Beloved,

How's your work? Are you as rushed as you were? I'm always wishing I could come there to see you. You can never know how wonderful I think you are not to seek other company to take my place. Why are you so far away from me? It seems I've been holding onto life by the mere thread of your affection.

I thought once that I couldn't write this, but it might be quite some time before I can come to you to unburden these loads of torment. Beloved, I've been faithful to you, devoted unto worshiping with all my being but before I go on, I want to say that life holds nothing for me were you not there to share it.

As I worked here one day, a shadow fell across my path and then was gone. It came back again at last to take shape as a woman. I saw her just as a woman, older than I, life-worn, toil-worn, care-worn, and sad. This shadow crept closer upon me, horror of horrors! It seemed to want to embrace me, but I fought, and it passed away. Truly I was grateful for her little message of love and hope. But on the morrow it came again and pleaded. My soul thought that it must not touch me. It pleaded unhappiness by the unfairness of life. It wasn't for want of love.

Anna dear, I've not been a deeply religious man, but I did thank God that I'd given my heart to one of His children. That I was able to tell the shadow that happiness is not found that way. That people love us, if we in turn love them. That's why I've not written. It exhausted me with all the forces within me.

Sometimes it's unbearably hard not to be able to meet your expectations. I've pleaded for work, demanded, studied and sought after it. Surely the Divine doesn't make men to be as miserable as me. This awful lonesomeness, my need for the means to bring myself to you with our happiness has combined into such a monstrous obstruction that I couldn't bring myself to pour out such a miserable tale to you. I think I'm sick, really sick, and not physically. I'm beginning to question if my dreams and enthusiasm have carried me past the point of normal thinking.

Thank you for my birthday cake. The family was over last night for my twenty-fourth, and we had a good supper and your lovely cake. Please tell me you love me.

Forever Yours,

Dale

I received Dale's letter in which he described the vision he experienced, but I didn't understand it, and it troubled me. Deeply troubled me. It was definitely strange. It appeared he was sinking even deeper into depression, evidenced by the chaos and disorganization in his letter. I was beginning to wonder how he spent most of his days.

I didn't feel I could totally ignore his birthday. After all, we were still engaged. I sent him a cake because he'd always appreciated them in the past. I also sent him two letters which arrived the same day, and he seemed happier because I'd responded to him. I told him I'd help him with college expenses, if he needed it. On the lighter side, I told him of my plans to get together to play cards on the weekend with Alvin and Jiggs.

We wrote less often since Dale had little news to share. At that point, he'd been out of work over eleven months and had no financial reserve left. He continued to apply for positions daily, and even though his efforts didn't lead to a job, he was still hopeful something would come his way soon.

In his letters, he began asking repeatedly who my friend Jiggs was, because he couldn't remember me mentioning him before or meeting him when he visited. My mistake. Huge mistake. I should've realized that mentioning the name of a male acquaintance he didn't know would set him off. Once again, I'd have some explaining to do.

At times, my relationship with Dale dragged me down, and instead of writing him a letter trying to pull up his spirits, I found myself avoiding the task. I didn't know what more I could've done to let him know how our romance had eroded to the point there soon would be nothing to salvage. I doubted I could ever feel about him as I once did.

I grew increasingly more comfortable in my relationship with Guy, and we spent time together each week since we lived on the same street. I enjoyed making Guy his favorite dishes, knowing that good food is a sure way to attract a man. Sometimes, I dreamed of him thanking me for dinner with a smothering of kisses all over me, slow and intentional, wherever he wished to place them. I felt restless, and it sometimes drove me insane that

Guy lived just down the street, but too often our schedules prevented us from being together as much as I'd like. I dreaded to think school would be out for the summer in a few short months, and Guy would go home to Bloomfield. I took every opportunity to be with him, since I'd rather be with him than anyone else in the world.

I avoided Dale's inquiry about Jiggs, feeling he'd soon figure it out and it would only cause him more concern since he was already *rightfully* insecure about someone stealing my heart.

April 20, 1931

Dearest Anna,

I had a miserable night last night. I had a coffee too close to bedtime and had a hard time falling asleep. After I finally got to sleep, I dreamed of you. It was pretty vivid and at first, not so pleasant. The gist of it was that you sent for me, and when I came, you were talking to someone. At the moment I saw you, I felt there was a tension or an antagonistic feeling toward the person you were having a conversation with. In some way, I felt that whoever it was you were with should not have been there. You seemed troubled, but were not embarrassed. I looked into your face, and I asked you silently if you had been true to me and as silently, you answered. The queerest part is that you were rich and the person with you was too. I didn't sleep well the rest of the night and almost fell asleep at lunch time today.

When your pictures are ready, will you please send me one? You didn't tell me who Jiggs is. How do you know him? I need to get

*this in the mail. I miss you more than you'll
ever know.*

I love you, my Beloved,
Dale

Dale wrote he finally found work. It wasn't a steady job, but it paid fifty cents an hour. He'd have the money for the tree-trimming he'd done a few weeks earlier and also be paid by fall for the work he did on his uncle's house. Altogether, he could afford his entrance fees and books for the first semester. He planned to place applications for work in Bloomington since some of the students would be leaving, and there would be job-openings for summer work.

At long last, Dale had the money and the plans to join me in Bloomington. A year before, I would've been elated at this news, but now I dreaded it. We hadn't seen each other in six long months. I felt he was more of an acquaintance than a fiancé. I worried about life in Bloomington once he arrived. I had asked him to set a date when he'd be coming, but he hadn't responded and I was getting concerned.

Chapter Thirty-Six

*I*n spite of the plans, Dale had trouble setting a definite arrival date, and it irked me. More than anything, I was determined to get this over with and move on.

> Bloomington, Ind
> June 1, 1931
>
> Dear Dale,
>
> I'm trying to finish my work here and pack my belongings. I want to let you know not to come, as I'll not be home. I don't know why you can't give me a date when you plan to be here. I'm extremely busy now and can't just hang around waiting. Do you actually want to see me? What's the problem that you can't commit to a date? I ask you, and you don't seem to get it right.
>
> As Ever,
> Anna

Hamilton, Ohio
June 4th 1931

Dearest Anna,

Will you please excuse me? My wits are wool-gathering. I received three letters from you yesterday. Though they're all short, I haven't been able to see through any of them. No, I'm not a dunce, I'm perfectly lucid, but in a way, I don't choose to read them. The first one gave me a shock, but I'm glad I had your telegram telling me you wouldn't be home. I've given that part little thought, but the whole letter was an expression of doubt. I wrote last night and I was tired, yet it may have been better than this. You see, I thought you expressed a doubt as to whether I wanted to see you or not. My heart says you couldn't care for me while doubting my word.

You asked me to set a date when I could come, and I'm truly sorry I disappointed you. I just couldn't tell when the work would be finished since it's outside work which depends on the weather as to when it would be completed. What are six months? Six years? Or even six ages? Eternity? Do you add heartache to my already unbearable misery? I don't care about those miserable letters except that I wish you had put me under a train and ended it. You can't take away my memories. You couldn't even stem the tide of love I bear for you. Can Death?

Anna, it'll be one of my few rare joys to see you this next weekend. I'm as miserable *as I can be over hurting you. I beg you to forgive me, if you can, for truly I didn't mean to.*

Love to your heart,
Dale

I probably should've thought more about his reason for not setting a date. I hadn't considered the weather being a factor. I was concentrating more on getting my own work completed quickly, so I could free up a few more hours to spend with Guy before he'd leave for Bloomfield.

Hamilton, Ohio
June 6, 1931

Sweetheart,

I guess I didn't make myself clear. I've been working for Aunt, so if I get a chance, I work other places which are the only places I get cash for my work right now. I won't get paid for this last paint job until it's finished, hopefully this weekend. I wish I could give an exact date and time, but it all depends on when we finish this job. It's coming to a close, but weather can change things, as you know. I just have to take the work when it comes my way, as I've been so long without any.

I'm honestly happier than I have any right to be I guess because I'll be seeing you soon. Anna, don't you think it's humiliating enough to be in my circumstances without doubting my sincerity? It's not only torment but torture to have you suffer the inquisitiveness of your friends in regards to me, when I can't even send

a token of my appreciation for your regards,
except for these miserable letters. Though it
hurts me to think so, if you can't be proud of me
as a man when a beggar, you won't be when
I'm a prince. I love you because you've helped
me build me, at your own cost sometimes.
         All My Love to You,
           Your Dale

After I read his last few letters, I tried to understand how Dale was feeling and the only word I came up with was "desperate." It made me weary to get through them, and he was much more complicated than I'd ever imagined. When I reflected on his words, "If you can't be proud of me as a man when a beggar, you won't be when I'm a prince," I knew he was right. He'd wrapped himself completely around me and become far too dependent. When I thought back to the early times and remember how excited I was to receive his letters, now it made me cringe to read them. I became even more aware of the tension, the unhappiness, his deep depression; all of it was suffocating our relationship.

Chapter Thirty-Seven

$\mathcal{A}$t the end of June, Dale came to Vallonia for the weekend. I'd been feeling so downhearted, but knew I had to somehow get through it. I'd always looked forward to his visits, but this time, I found I had to force a smile when he arrived.

"Dale, come on in. Breakfast is about ready."

"Sweetheart, what's the matter?' His manner was intent and of deep concern for me. His demeanor was kind and gentle. "May I kiss you first before we go in?"

"Sure, of course. I'm sorry."

"I feel so bad about our communication problems over this last week. I hate it more than anything when there's tension between us. I feel helpless because you're so far away. All I want is to be by your side, to talk it over with you, and feel everything's all right again," he said.

"I assure you, I'm just preoccupied. I've had so much on my mind. I needed to know what day and actually how many days you planned to stay in Bloomington. I want to relocate to a girls' rooming house, because Laura is coming home for the summer. I can't afford the apartment by myself. What about you? Where will you be?"

"Well, Ken offered to take me back with him to work in Champaign, Illinois. I'm hoping it'll last until school starts. I'm saving every penny I can lay my hands on because I want to be with you at IU."

"Good morning, Mr. and Mrs. Fosbrink."

"Good morning, Dale. Come on in the kitchen. We're ready to eat," Dad said.

"Looks wonderful, as usual. Is this more of your great sausage recipe you made last time?"

"Surely is. Want some coffee cake?" Mother asked.

"Yes, please. Never can turn that down," Dale said raising his brows and flashing an approving smile at Mother. Then, turning to Dad, he said, "What's the work for today, Mr. Fosbrink?"

"Dude and I are going to haul a load of melons to Brownstown this morning."

"I'd be happy to help."

"That's all right, son. You came to catch up on some time with Anna here. She could use someone to settle her down. We've noticed she hasn't been herself lately."

"Okay, Hezekiah, nuf said."

"Aren't you going to ride today?"

"Dad, come on now. Have you ever known us to pass up a chance to ride when the weather is so perfect?"

⚜

As we mounted the horses and slowly began to ride, Dale said, "I'm so happy to finally get to ride along beside you."

"We certainly have put a lot of miles on Spiffy and Nellie these past few years," I said making awkward small talk. "You know they both love it, but Nellie's getting pretty old now. I hate to think the time will come when she won't be around."

"I know. They're like your best friends."

"Sometimes, I think they are."

"Anna, you've never told me who Jiggs is, and I've asked several times."

Here it comes. I was annoyed Dale asked again about Jiggs. I'd intentionally been trying to avoid answering, but I was stuck now.

"'Jiggs' is the nickname for Guy."

"Is that the man you introduced me to when you took me to your office that time?"

"Yes, everyone calls him 'Jiggs.'"

"Is he dating anyone?"

"No, he said he'd never commit to anyone because of his health."

"What's wrong with him?"

"Oh, I don't know. He gets sick a lot, I guess."

"What does he do there?"

"He's in research and does some writing for the dean." *I could feel my face starting to flush.*

"He's older, isn't he?"

"Around thirty, I think."

"I suppose you must be pretty good friends. Didn't he go over to your place to play cards one time with you and Alvin?"

"Yes, that was some time ago." *Will this never end?*

"Anything I should be concerned about here?"

"Do you doubt me?" I was hoping he wouldn't ask any further questions, because I was uncomfortable and knew I wasn't being honest.

⁊⊱

We spent much of the day riding Nellie and Spiffy. The haunting memories as we rode along were powerful and painful. I wasn't sure where I'd go with these feelings of wanting to break off the relationship, but I only knew it terrified me to have to face the reality of it. I could see and feel his passion for us to be together in Bloomington and his desperation to be everything I wanted him to be. I felt the weight of responsibility that he only moved forward in life for my sake. Dale was finally coming out of his depression, but I was headed into it.

⁂

I returned to IU and enrolled in summer classes while Dale again took a job pruning trees. He moved into a boarding home next to Ken, Opal, and the baby in Champaign, Illinois. He was excited about the work and hoped he would have it at least until the beginning of September.

It didn't take long for him to lose his enthusiasm for his new environment. He described the boardinghouse conditions as cramped and wasn't sure just how much longer he'd be there. It was still hot and muggy, and he had to share a bed with another man, Merle somebody, one of the gang he worked with. Ken was still the boss of the team and looked out for Dale in many respects, but knowing my brother, he wouldn't grant any special privileges just because Dale and I were engaged.

As time went on, I felt my deep love for Dale withering because of the time we'd been separated, and honestly, because of my growing relationship with Guy. I realized I'd always felt sorry for Dale. He had faced so much sadness in his life and I understood why he responded to me so sincerely and desperately. I wanted to let him down easy and didn't want either of us to experience the anguish of a breakup. I wanted him to be the one to give up on us, so I wouldn't have to do the inevitable. But in reality, I knew he'd never be the one responsible for our separation.

Chapter Thirty-Eight

ale sent a note asking me to type job applications for him to send to businesses around the campus. I was already feeling overwhelmed trying to meet my own deadlines, let alone assuming his work as well. I had my own demanding schedule and the chaos in the rooming house was almost too much to cope with. I wrote back that I was struggling with my own responsibilities and disappointed in his request of me.

Champaign, IL
July 15, 1931

Beloved,

How have I disappointed you? How otherwise when I'm that to me also? Does one ever learn? Truly, I'm grateful. There is in writing, always a danger of misunderstanding but how else can we converse? If I turn to you in a different plane, I'm startled out of my wits by abuse.

Are we never together? Why did I write? Well?
Must I explain? You ought to know by this time
what's lacking in me to fill your heart.

The very soul of me will suffer; will long-
ingly wait your reply. Meet me as I've gone out
to you. 'In the Dark, In the Dew' where have
you been? Anna, we've been too long apart. My
thoughts have been centered on college because of
what may open up for me in education . . . life!
This must not occur again. I'm asking you to
come to me in the natural way, like the blossoms
that unfold overnight, permeating everything
with sweetness and gladness. You can hurt me
only so far, to rob me of a few beautiful miser-
able years living. You're helpless to change that
love I bear you. You can't even alter it in any
way. If your heart is aching like mine, it'll leap
with joy and unbounded happiness to hear me
simply say: I love you.

Forever,

Dale

After reading his letter, I wondered if he thought I owed it to him to fulfill his request. Or, maybe he just wanted me to feel guilty. And, then he quoted the beginning of one of his favorite poems, but I failed to see the connection to "In the Dark, In the Dew." I didn't get it. It made little sense. Had he lost it completely?

I wrote back telling him I was sorry for any inconvenience to him, but thought the long dissertation wasn't necessary. I wasn't trying to hurt him, it was just that I was tremendously busy, always loading way too much onto my schedule thinking I could accomplish more than was realistic. I assured him that I was aware the demands were self-imposed, but I couldn't seem to do it any other way and be able to succeed. I also told him I felt there had been times when he didn't persevere with commitments he started.

Champaign, Ill
July 21ˢᵗ 1931

Dearest Anna,

Thank you for your letter which I received today. I think it mighty good to make the grades you do and work so hard too. I'm sure you're tired at the end of the day also.

Perhaps the dissertation was uncalled for, as you say. After thinking a day on what you've written, I think I can give a more coherent answer. I had a savage impulse to hurt you last night, and now I hope I haven't, for you can only see things through your own eyes and heart. But please, don't be too egotistical to think you can judge me by your standards. Well, let me tell you this, you've made a mistake. You owe me an apology and I want it!

I'm certainly sorry that you've been put out about my asking for help with the applications. I was simple enough to think that it would look better in type than in pencil, which is all I have. How can you be important to me if I can't ask anything, confide anything? Don't apologize for me to anyone. If you consider your choice is that bad, change. That's what a courtship is for.

No doubt you're surprised at what you've found here. If I can't ask of you, if I can't turn to you, I don't want you. It isn't a weakness to live in one another. You know that my heart

has been sealed with your confidences. I'll not burden you any more often than absolutely necessary. Ken says he'll be going to Bloomington weekend after this and I'll stop over to see you. I want to hold you and kiss away your doubts because I love you . . . forever.
> *Dale*

> *Bloomington, Ind*
> *July 21st 1931*

Dearest Dale,

Somehow, we seem to be in discord about our communication. I'm sorry but I feel under so much pressure lately and am trying to keep my head above water. I'm sorry if I hurt you or you thought I was angry. I'm not. I just feel I've loaded so much onto my schedule there's no time for much of any kind of pleasure in life. I just think we've had too much distance from one another to feel the happiness and softness we both need right now. Please accept my apology. If there's something that seemed mean-spirited, I'm sorry.
> *Lovingly,*
> *Anna*

After I mailed the letter and thought over offering my apology, I felt it probably was not what I wanted to say. I truly felt less sorry than annoyed. The entire situation was emotionally draining and tedious.

Chapter Thirty-Nine

Sitting at my desk, I was absorbed in thoughts about how I'd treated Dale. Once again, my familiar friend, Guilt, surfaced, and I began to feel I'd been somewhat of a monster. I decided I could manage the applications with greater ease than he possibly could and began to fill them out. While doing so, memories of the romantic private times we shared flashed in my mind and I found myself longing for the romance we once had. I reflected on how much Dale had endured through the loss of his mother, relentless poverty as a child raised in a run-down, abandoned shell of a cabin, and the life he was about to welcome. How could I be so heartless and just abandon him at this point in his life. I knew all too well the extremely tough year without work or money had taken a toll on him, and he deserved a good shot at something better. After struggling with myself about what I should do, I wrote him a shorter, kinder, note, wanting to ease my guilt as well as the hurt for us both.

Champaign, Ill
July 23, 1931

Dearest Anna,

I feel that both of my letters and the first one you wrote were wrong. Mine were wrong, for I was hurt and angry. It shouldn't be that way. I'm going to apologize to you for mine.

I think you are as dear as can be to write such a sweet letter. I was, and still am, in a terrible mood. I do regret the second letter and though I think I meant most of it, I hope you'll forgive me. I wanted to hurt you. I know you have the second letter by now and I want to hear from you again. It's my aim to be as nice to you as you will permit. I want to say more but all I want is to see you and hold you.

Loving you,
Dale

Dale's letter of apology was kind and sounded so much more like the man I'd fallen in love with. I admitted to myself that I missed him. The pressure I felt and the tension between us somehow dissipated, and once again I was actually looking forward to seeing him. Ken dropped Dale off at my Bloomington boardinghouse mid-afternoon. I was waiting at the door when he walked up the steps. As soon as I laid eyes on him, the anxiety caved within me, replaced by more familiar loving feelings.

"Hello, my beautiful darling," he said softly. "I've been counting the minutes until I could hold you in my arms again. I thought we'd never get here."

He gently held my face with both hands, looked into my eyes, and pressed five or six kisses on my cheeks, forehead, lips, and neck. We embraced in silence for what seemed a long time, just quietly holding each other.

"I've missed you terribly, Dale. We've had too many problems in our relationship lately, and I'm thinking I'm at fault."

"No, it's not just you. It's likely both of us. I get overly tired myself. I sit down to write, and sometimes what I write is not at all what I intended to say. It seems lately I'm not the man I want to be. My life has been in turmoil for so long, and this past year it's been especially awful."

"I know you've had an extremely rough time. I can't even imagine what it's been like. I hope the future will now seem brighter for you."

"Certainly, I'm looking forward to that brighter future."

"I have several applications typed up for you to take home. I included your good traits such as being responsible, hard-working, conscientious, and respectful. I think it's important to include those in the applications. It sometimes makes a difference."

"I can't thank you enough for doing this, and it makes me proud you said those things about me on the application."

"It's all true. You *are* all of those things."

"I hated to ask you for this favor, because I know how busy you are. It seems I depend on you more than I should."

"It's all right. It's done now. Please forgive all my complaining. By the way, I also included the addresses where to send them. It's all there," I said pointing to the address list.

"I'll get right on it as soon as I get back to Champaign tomorrow. But for now, all I want to do is hold you and look at you. Then I'd love to go for a walk. I want to see the campus, if that's agreeable with you?

Holding hands, we slowly strolled along the walking trails lined with small limestone boulders accentuating the grassy edges. The majestic tall trees around the campus impressed him and he began telling me their scientific names. I would, of course, never be able to remember the names to repeat them, only the common ones, if that. He remarked about the magnificent limestone buildings and the various shades of green trees and grass against the gray-white stone. I showed him Memorial Hall with its Romanesque structure and peaked tower; it was my favorite of all the buildings. South Hall and Maxwell Hall were also impressive favorites as well. I pointed out many of the buildings, telling him what activities took place there.

We went over to the cute little pitch-roof bookstore with its green-and-white striped canvas awnings. It had a front porch entrance with double French doors and drop-down wooden sashes, which were used to secure the building when not in use. At the end of the brick walkway was a bridge made of wooden planks and constructed just barely off the ground leading to the bookstore entrance. We held hands as we teetered on the planks headed toward the front porch to peer in the windows. Of course, Dale said that would be the place he wanted to visit right away. He was sure he could lose himself in there for hours.

With all of those romantic feelings now surfaced, we strolled back to Memorial Hall and sat on the stone bench along the pathway under a huge oak tree.

"I've enjoyed seeing the campus with you and am getting even more excited about being a student here."

"I know you're going to love it and I feel certain you're going to be so busy, it won't take long for you to feel comfortable here."

"It's now my dream to eventually get a degree in psychology and maybe even teach. The more I think about it, the more I'm feeling that's the right direction for me. What do you think about that?"

"I have no doubt you can do it. It'll take a lot of work and perseverance on your part. But, now that you seem to have that determination, just keep reminding yourself of what it is you want most in life. Wake up every morning with a positive attitude, and remind yourself of your goal."

"Getting back to us setting a date for the wedding, when do you think we can get married? What are your plans for the event?"

"Dale, with both of us now focusing on our education, I can't see that happening anytime in the near future. Maybe way down the road. I know you're anxious, but I'm just not ready."

Later we headed over to Cauble Coffee Shop on Kirkwood Avenue for a sandwich. It was an enjoyable time together the rest of Saturday afternoon, but I felt dishonest even talking about a wedding that I believed would never occur.

Dale stayed at Alvin's apartment for the night. Sunday morning after breakfast he came to the boardinghouse to meet me. Much to my surprise he suggested we go to church together and it pleased me. But, honestly, as for the brief discussion of our wedding, I knew in my heart, it was too little—and too late.

Mid-afternoon Ken and Opal arrived to pick Dale up and head back to Champaign. I truly enjoyed the time with Dale, but realized we'd lost the spark we once had. Once, we had been best friends, shared our deepest secrets, and greatest desires, but now he seemed more like a friend or a brother than a lover. The love I felt for Dale would never sustain a lifetime in marriage. I knew I could never marry him, but he was so happy, I just couldn't bring myself to crush the hopes and dreams of his new adventure, at least not on this trip.

Chapter Forty

Dearest Mine,

Just a short note to let you know we got back to Champaign at 11:30 last night without any problem. I've been filling out several applications for work in Bloomington tonight and had to go to the post office to get stamps, so this isn't going to be a long letter. I want to thank you for everything. I loved every bit of it and am feeling excited about my life. I'm ever so much in love again. So happy to have seen you, my beautiful, you can't even imagine what it did for me. I hope you make out well on your exams.

I will forever love you,
Dale

His letter was so full of excitement and anticipation for his future at IU with me, yet our relationship was headed for a disastrous event when he would arrive. That scene played in my mind over and over, even though I tried not to think about it.

My twenty-first birthday would occur in one week, and I was looking forward to spending it with Guy, since we were both still in Bloomington. When August 6, 1931, arrived, Guy asked if he could take me to the "Swing Out," a dance at IU the following night.

"What a great idea! I'd love to go to the dance. What a special way to celebrate a girl's twenty-first birthday."

"I thought we should kick up our heels on the dance floor, since it's the last dance of the season."

"I'm so excited. That'll be a huge treat. You always make me laugh."

"I make you laugh?" Guy said, looking puzzled.

"Yes, I get a kick out of watching you. You get all loosened up and silly. You flail your arms and strut around. You're so funny."

"I hope I don't look ridiculous or embarrass you."

"Never! It tickles me to watch you dance. You seem to have such a good time, and you're so much fun—I just love to be with you."

Even though Guy did look ridiculous, I found any embarrassment to be worth dancing with him because his fun-loving personality came out. Often when a dance ended, we'd laugh and hug, then he'd put a protective arm around me as we returned to our seats. I loved both the public display of affection and the feeling of safety I felt in his arms.

The "Swing Out" would be a special night out, since I was aware it might be a long time until I'd be able to be with Guy again. Summer school would be out the next week and final exams were on their way. This meant Guy would be going home within a few days, and Dale would be arriving in Bloomington. The morning of my birthday I received an unexpected telegram.

AUGUST 6, 1931
ALL ARE GOING HOME THIS WEEKEND
WILL STOP AFTER YOU SATURDAY
AFTERNOON RECEIVED YOUR LETTER
TODAY WISHING YOU A HAPPY
BIRTHDAY WILL SPEND PART OF IT
WITH YOU DID YOU RECEIVE THE
SPECIAL LET ME KNOW RIGHT AWAY
IF YOU CANNOT GO HOME LOVINGLY
DALE

I wired back immediately, telling Dale I couldn't possibly go home for my birthday. I had too much studying to do for finals, including a complete book to read. Early in the afternoon of my birthday, the florist delivered three dozen extra-large, beautiful gladiolas with no card. Since I was studying in the dorm library, one of the girls I lived with called me over to the entry foyer while the delivery girl waited, holding a magnificent bouquet of red gladiolas and a message "Happy Twenty-First" on the card with no signature.

I asked, "Who sent these to me?"

The delivery girl said, "You ought to know. A handsome young man ordered them for you."

Naturally, I thought Guy had sent them. The girls I lived with began teasing me, threatening to tell my boyfriend on me. In a few minutes, the good humor evaporated when Dale knocked on the door. He'd borrowed Ken's car and clearly expected me to drop everything and join him, even though I'd wired him not to come.

"Anna, are you ready to go home?"

"Didn't you receive my wire?" I was angry, but trying not to show it. I could see he was angry, too, but I didn't yet know why. It scared me.

"Yes. I did. But I'm taking you home. Hurry up. Go get ready."

"I can't go home." I couldn't believe he was ordering me about, but remembered he was in fact, still my fiancé.

"I got the wire, but I'm not taking *no* for an answer."

"Hold on, let me go put some things together. I'll need about an hour."

"An hour? We're only going for the weekend." I could see he was simmering already.

"Alright, I'll hurry. Just wait in the lobby. I'll get my things together as fast as I can."

My heart sank. My birthday was ruined and the fun that Guy and I had planned for the following night would not happen. What's more, it might not ever happen.

I needed to get in touch with Guy to cancel the dance date. I tried to call, but in my frantic attempt to reach him, I must have mixed up his phone number. I decided to write a note for the girls at the house to read to him when he called. I couldn't do anything about it, so I left with Dale, who was impatient with the whole situation.

I guess because of my silence, Dale felt the tension and realized that I wasn't at all happy about making the trip home. He kept driving faster and faster. I was upset with him, since it was Ken's car he was driving.

"Dale, what's wrong with you? Slow down. You're driving like this is some kind of race car in the Grand Prix."

"Alright, is this slow enough? Twenty-five miles an hour? Is this slow enough for you?"

"That's better. I don't understand what's wrong. Why are you acting like this?"

"You didn't bring your flowers along."

That startled me. I thought some of the girls at the rooming house actually did what they were threatening to do . . . show him my flowers which I thought Guy had sent me.

I stammered, "What-t-t do ya' mean? What do you know about the flowers?"

And away we took off racing again, with the color of his face nearly the color of his red hair. "I must be awfully stupid to think I'd be the only man sending you flowers."

"I don't know what you're talking about."

"I think you know exactly what I'm talking about. Who is it? That Jiggs fellow? Is that who you thought sent them to you? Is that why you didn't want to come with me?"

"Stop it, Dale. Stop hollering at me. You make me wish I'd stayed in the dorm."

We sat in silence most of the way to Vallonia. All I could think of was, I'd be missing the dance with Guy and wondered what he was thinking when he called the dorm and I wasn't there. More than anything, I wanted to be with Guy, and I missed him already.

Then, feeling not only uncomfortable, but also guilty, I said, "Dale, I'm sorry. The flowers arrived just before you did and there was no card with them. I didn't know if they were from my family or who they were from. They were beautiful and thank you for think-ing of me."

"You're welcome, but I guess they'll be dead when you get back there. Hopefully, someone will be enjoying them since you won't be."

It was a difficult weekend with Dale. I knew he was upset because he made a poor attempt to hide it. I'm sure Mother also knew something was wrong. Neither Dale nor I were talkative the entire weekend. The tension was obvious and the conversa-tion was strained.

"Dale, you seem so quiet. Are you not feeling well?" Mother asked.

"I'm fine. It's your daughter. She seems to be losing interest in everything."

"What on earth are you talking about? I'm not losing interest in anything." I snapped back.

"Just drop it and stop yelling at me. It was merely an observa-tion on my part."

Dale abruptly got up from the table and took off out the front door. I didn't chase after him because I knew why he was so angry. I was angry, too. I'd lost my chance to deepen my relationship with Guy at the "Swing Out" dance. I'd wanted those flowers to be from Guy, so I never once considered they could've been from Dale. No wonder he was seething and admittedly I *had* lost interest. Clearly, I had another man on my mind. Neither Dad nor Mother asked any questions about the scene at dinner, but I'm sure they had many, and I expected to hear about it later.

The ride back to Bloomington was worse than the ride to Vallonia. When we got in the car to leave, Dale didn't hesitate to start in with accusations of my having an interest in someone else. I knew he couldn't handle it if I admitted there was, and I dreaded the long ride ahead of us. I wasn't sure I'd convinced him of my loyalty, but I *was* convinced about one thing . . . my twenty-first birthday turned out to be the worst birthday celebration of my life and the fifty-mile trip back to school was nearly intolerable.

Chapter Forty-One

When I returned to the dorm, the girls excitedly told me what had happened when Guy came to take me to the dance. This of all times, Guy didn't call, he just showed up. When he arrived for our date, he saw the big vase of red gladiolas on the table in the hall. The girls told him how pleased I'd been to receive his flowers. They read him my note, but I hadn't said why or with whom I'd left to go home, just that I was sorry I had to leave so abruptly.

He said, "I didn't send her the flowers. It must have been her boss."

That statement confused everyone. Guy left a big box of Maude Muller chocolates for my birthday present and asked one of the girls to give it to me when I returned. Even Guy hadn't considered that the flowers were from Dale.

When I returned to Bloomington, I couldn't wait to call Guy.

"Could you come over to meet me, so I can talk to you about my leaving so abruptly when we already had made plans?"

"Certainly, when and where?

"Well, I know it's getting late, but I need to talk about missing our date. Can you come to my place?"

"Is twenty minutes all right with you?"

"That's fine. I'll be waiting in the foyer."

We met, and I immediately started to explain why I'd left. I assured him nothing was wrong at home, for that had been his concern.

"I want you to know I didn't expect Dale to show up. Not at all! I'd sent a telegram for him not to come, because I had too much studying to do."

"That's understandable. I was just concerned there was an emergency at your home, that's all."

"I have to tell you, I felt too guilty to eat any of the chocolates until I got an acceptance of my apology from you."

"No apology is necessary. Now that I know the whole story, I think it's a funny situation, knowing how you must have been squirming the whole time."

"Will you please stop laughing at me?"

I was embarrassed because of the whole mix-up and misunderstanding, but also because of my feelings for Guy. I didn't want him to think less of me. More than anything, I didn't want to lose him.

"Anna, you have to admit it's funny."

"Maybe funny to you, but I was upset the entire weekend."

"Can't you see that it's a funny predicament for anyone to be in?"

"Well, maybe now that I look back on it, I guess I can. At least if you can't see that I owe an apology, then I can start in on the chocolates. And, by the way, thank you for them."

Eventually, I began to see the humor in what happened— almost as if it had been scripted and I even began to laugh at myself. A few days later, Guy and I said farewell. We decided our dating days were over since Dale had told me he intended to come to

IU next month to "look after his interests." That statement from him greatly concerned me. It left me feeling that he'd definitely threaten my freedom. I didn't want him checking my every move once he arrived at IU. I was conflicted, yet at this point, I knew Dale's "interest" was losing interest!

☙

At the end of the summer semester, I went home for a short break to relax a bit after finishing my courses. I hoped to return to my job in the Education Department with the professors when school resumed, but knew it would be difficult being near Guy in the office with my romantic feelings for him. Dale's arrival on campus concerned me more than ever as the date grew closer.

I couldn't get Guy out of my head. I teased my brain with ideas of how to keep me in his thoughts. I wrote him a letter while he was still in Bloomington, telling him I was enjoying the break. I told him I hoped we could continue our friendship and looked forward to seeing him when school resumed. My heart leapt when a letter from Guy arrived not even a week later.

Spider's Web
August 23, 1931

My Dear Glorianna,

You didn't give me an excuse to write, but I've done lots of things without any apparent excuse, so in writing now I'm probably being as consistent as ever. Besides, as Calamity Jane famously said, "Who said things have to make sense?" I don't like people who fabricate reasons for the things they do.

But for one thing in your letter, I'd probably not be writing this one. Your

desire to be friends and of service if possible, happens to be just what I want, for
in spite of my own contention that it is
impossible for a man and a woman to be
friends, I find myself hoping it isn't true. I
believe in it as much as ever, however.

Since you left, I've been living a life of
indolence and insipidity. It seems to agree
with me for I've gained three pounds since
you left. If I don't see you again for two or
three weeks, I'll have to reach way out to
scratch my chin at this rate. No, I think
I'll have to change my motto from "love me
and leave me" to" kiss me again, I like it."
No, by jolly, I'll keep up the game anyway.
Let me live in a house beside yours and be
a friend of . . . and make bean flippers
for your little boys. And when they wonder why they have red hair, I'll tell them
it is rust, that they must wear their hats
in the sun and the rain. No, I'll probably
live thousands of miles away and come
once a year to bring presents to Dale Jr.
and little Guy L. and talk business and
politics with their daddy.

Well, now how are things down on the
farm? I'll bet you've started padding your
roll, and your mother is losing money on
you every day. I wouldn't care if you ate
two or three big watermelons for me . . .
today, though, I have one in the ice-box,
and if I eat that and you eat one for me
too, I'll be in a rather bad way.

Don't leave this lying around where someone might see it who ought not to. My insurance is paid up, but it won't do me any good unless I collect it myself.
Guy

I was thrilled Guy had written to me in Vallonia, and I missed him more than ever. Guy had such a funny sense of humor. It was amusing, but sometimes a bit odd. I found interest in his reference to the little red-haired boys, but now that I knew him a little better, I hoped that meant there was a tinge of interest in living near me. Come once a year to talk business with their daddy? Would it be the daddy or me? I also wondered about the "Spider's Web," and just what that meant. Guy was so clever, I wondered if it meant we were trapped in a sticky situation. Maybe? But the nicest part of the letter was how he addressed it. My *Dear Glorianna*. I loved reading it over and over. It was different and had a nice ring to it. I welcomed the seemingly affectionate name he'd given me. It was much nicer than "Peaches." Guy was constantly in my thoughts and, some nights, even in my dreams. As it turned out, while I was dreaming about Guy, Dale was planning a very real arrival at IU and into my life.

August 29, 1931

Dearest,

I can't wait to join the ranks of other college students, but more than that, I will be able to be with my beloved to study and explore everything in my new world. I plan to come with a friend to the IU campus for the weekend. I don't want to give up any plans because I hope to stir up a job in Bloomington. I might be around longer than I originally

expected, maybe a couple of weeks. Please send
a letter right away because I need to know if I
will be able to stay with Alvin again.
I love you always,
Dale

When I received Dale's letter, I panicked. My anxiety hit an all-time high, and I felt short of breath. My script was shaky as I nervously tried to compose a message on the back of his envelope. I immediately sent a telegram after changing the wording several times hoping to make it sound convincing. I told him I'd be sending him a letter and *not* to come until he received it. I wasn't sure just what to do, but knew for certain I'd have to give some explanation because—he was just about to find out he was part of a love triangle.

Chapter Forty-Two

Dale's long-awaited, but now dreaded arrival, had caused me many sleepless nights. I was afraid I could lose them both, but I was most afraid of losing Guy. Dale, who would love me to the end and through all eternity, needed me more, but, Guy had set me on fire, and owned my heart—whether he knew it or not. At this point, I had to write Dale and tell him the truth.

Bloomington, Indiana
September 2, 1931

Dearest Dale,

It's with great difficulty that I'm writing to tell you how much I've cherished our time together, but I cannot continue. I'm deeply sorry. I've been seriously troubled with feelings of doubt about our relationship. I've felt ill and been unable to sleep for weeks. I'm overwhelmed with the situation of

having come to the realization my feelings
have changed, and to pretend differently
would be dishonest. To tell you the truth,
this makes me more unhappy than I ever
dreamed I could be. You're right. We've
been apart too long. I've made desperate
attempts to recapture even a fraction of the
intense feelings I once had for you, but the
fire in my heart soon disappears. I need time
to think about my true feelings and ask you
to be patient with me because I'm not sure
of them anymore. I will be leaving campus
to return to Vallonia tomorrow.

I'm deeply sorry,

Anna

A few days later, Dale sent a telegram stating he'd be stopping over at my house in Vallonia to talk on Saturday. For the first time ever, I was shaking inside over the thought of seeing him and glad I was home alone. When he arrived, he was obviously upset and his deep sadness clouded his features. He reached out and wrapped his arms around me, gently kissing my forehead, then my cheek.

"Anna, Anna, Anna. What's happening to us?"

"I don't know. The feelings I have are just not right. I can't even think straight anymore."

"I felt something was wrong from your letters over the past weeks, and now I know why."

"It isn't fair to either of us, Dale, to continue while I'm feeling the way I do."

"Please don't do this. Please, I beg of you. Don't give up on us."

"I'm so sorry. I truly am sorry."

"I can't bear to hear you say these things. It's our life. It's our happiness. What's happened? Why?"

"I know it's difficult. It's hard for me also."

"I've been so happy and looking forward to being with you. It's finally all coming together. I've been so excited to finally be going to college."

"I know, and I'm sorry. I don't know what else to say."

"All I want out of life is to be with you. I love you more than life itself. Please just give us a little more time. We've been apart too long; we just need more time together."

Dale held me in silence while gently touching my face, then as tears filled his eyes, he asked me to walk with him. He held my hand while we walked and talked as he struggled with our life story of the five years and the loving experiences we'd shared. Sadly, all the memories riding horseback side-by-side in the woods and the time we hid out in the cabin in Starve Hollow, sheltering each other in our love was now too painful to hold in our hearts.

"Anna, doesn't any of that mean anything? Did our times together mean nothing to you?"

"Of course, they did. But so much has happened in our lives since then."

"Do you no longer feel the trust that bound us together in the beginning? Where's the promise? What happened to that?"

"I don't know, Dale. All I know is that, for me, the long separation has taken the thrill and excitement out of our relationship. Over time, I've grown up and changed. I'm no longer that little girl I once was. I see and feel things differently now."

"I'm pleading with you to give us more time. You're my life! My world! I don't know how I can go on. I'm so in love with you, I can't even imagine my life without you."

"I've been trying for a long time now to restore those loving feelings, but in my heart, I've not been able to get them back."

It was a tearful experience for both of us and although he pleaded for me to change my mind, I felt it unfair to stay with him. I knew what I'd said was devastating, and while I watched from my living room window, I could tell he was wiping the tears from his face as he walked down the lane toward his cabin. His posture and stride, so different than I'd ever witnessed before. Now left with an overwhelming feeling of loss, he appeared a broken man whose world had suddenly collapsed. I worried about him going to the cabin for the night. It was such a lonely place. As he disappeared into the darkness, I sank into the chair by the window and began to sob. I had just said farewell to my lifetime friend who would be out of my life forever.

⁌

In spite of our breakup, Dale went on to Bloomington and arranged to stay with Alvin until he could work out a plan. He'd hoped to find work, but initially had little success. According to Alvin, Dale learned where Dr. W. Lowe Bryan, President of IU lived, and brazenly set out to personally visit him. When he reached the president's house, he felt fortunate to find him at home. Dale introduced himself and told him he was an orphan and desperately wanted to attend college, but had no money. The president was a kind and generous man and took a liking to Dale almost immediately. He realized how desperate he was, but after talking to him at length, he also found him to be quite intelligent. He not only helped get Dale enrolled, but arranged financial help to get him started. He also offered to help him get a job waiting tables in order to continue at IU. His wife, also taken with Dale, hired him to do lawn work at their home.

I found this information interesting, because he was finally taking the initiative to act on his own. However, his ulterior motive disturbed me when I learned he'd told the president he was an orphan in an effort to manipulate him in a desperate attempt to enter college to be with me. Why was he calling himself an orphan when his dad was still alive? Certainly, it must have been to see if he could get sympathy for his situation and help with his tuition.

That deception was a concern, and once again, I recalled what his father had done to their neighbor in Starve Hollow. Did he feel that deception was okay? What happened to his claim that he must always be truthful?

⁓

I returned to IU with Laura and rented an apartment on Atwater Avenue. After Dale went home to get his belongings, he returned to Bloomington on September 8th, along with hundreds of other students. He wandered around campus in the pouring rain with his suitcase, looking for the all-male rooming house on East 10th Street. After he checked into his residence, he sent a note to thank me for "every little bit of my goodness," which I took as sarcasm. He confided he was so bewildered, and overwhelmed with doubt, that he didn't know if he could make it or not. A great part of him didn't even want to be at IU.

The once independent young man, who'd traveled to distant strange places with certainly greater risk than this, was finding his confidence weakened. He'd been depending on me to help him, show him the ropes, study with him, and share the wonderful experiences of college. Now he faced college completely alone and had to figure it out for himself. Although Dale was extremely depressed, he somehow, without prodding from anyone, decided to try to complete a semester.

I sent Dale a note, wanting to restore some peace of mind to ease my heart as well as his, for I realized he was devastated and felt betrayed by my rejection. It saddened me to think of the heartache I'd caused him, and it consumed my thoughts. I wasn't only grieving the loss of a friendship for someone I had known since I was eight years old, but also the deep love I once had for him. In my heart, I knew he always loved me more, but I didn't have the maturity to understand that there is a delicate balance in love. The last time I counted the letters from him there were nearly six hundred, many of them professing his deepest love to eternity, but that didn't change anything. We both had built a fantasy about how "someday" our lives would become more deeply entwined. The someday had finally arrived, but it was too late for me.

With his motivation for attending college shattered, I worried whether Dale would overcome the grief and loss enough to keep up with his courses. I felt for him to overcome the poverty, the lifestyle he was accustomed to, he'd need to put this behind him and find his own reasons for pursuing a college degree. I hoped he'd be able to focus on his work to make something for himself because he was intelligent and capable enough to do so—if only he could muster the confidence. This was his test as to whether he could stand on his own two feet or not, and he wasn't well prepared to do so.

Chapter Forty-Three

Occasionally Guy called to ask me out, but I kept refusing him, because I didn't want Dale to see me on campus with another man. I only saw Guy as we met in the office or when I saw him briefly at church looking down on him from the balcony to his usual seat in the sanctuary. My fantasy transported me to imagine I was sitting arm-in-arm next to him.

I was back in full swing in the Education Department, trying to concentrate on my work as well as my courses. My girlfriends and Laura were concerned, offering me support and help to overcome my sadness and loss. They assured me they felt I'd made the right decision.

It was difficult, because when I saw Dale on campus, some days crossing paths several times a day, it always stirred memories we'd shared during the past five years. At times when we encountered each other, he would nod or give a tilt of his head. Other times he'd just look away pretending he hadn't seen me. I felt certain he was likely experiencing an even worse depression than I was, so I wrote him a note to show I cared and offered suggestions for help. I wanted to say or do something to help him, but also to make myself feel better.

September 13th 1931

Dear Dale,

Again, I'm deeply sorry about our relationship and the split up. I want to encourage you to talk to someone to see if they can give you some guidance and support. Maybe a pastor or a priest could help you. You need to pour this out to someone who can be objective. I know you're going through tremendous heartache, but I'm not the one to help you right now. It needs to be someone who can give you a better perspective on what's happened.

Please know, I want more than anything for you to get through this. You're a very special person and have a great mind. You just need to get this behind you somehow.

Anna

Bloomington
October 4, 1931

Dearest Anna,

For quite some time now, I have wanted to write a little note to you. This isn't an answer to your note, for I dare not reopen it. However, I do want to speak on it.

I went to see Rev. Cartwright. From our discussion, I managed to grasp a few sane thoughts that helped me a great deal. Also, now that I have work, seemingly as long as I desire it, my mental attitude has changed. The next few months do not promise despair. Some of the hopelessness has fallen away. To be sure, I realize the magnitude of the task ahead of me, but it seems less worrisome. The lateness of the year will hinder much progress in my work, but in the spring, I feel circumstances will be ever so much better. It so seems that I've lost much and gained much.

At the first of our trouble, you turned to me for patience and help. I felt I had little power to help, of patience, none, because of the irresistible surge forward of events. It's my earnest desire to remedy these things. I have at last discovered a way to help, so simple that it's difficult. To cultivate a nobler kinder attitude and a more generous spirit, perhaps is the best way I can say it.

I think this is all, though, poorly said. Thank you for your kindness. You may consider our engagement in the way you think best. I have an engagement in my heart with you that's still unbroken.

To that aim, I've set my purpose for . . . I love you.

Dale

In spite of Dale's pleas, I'd reached the point that I wanted to be released from the engagement and return his ring. I asked him to come to my apartment. When he arrived, I met him at the door, but didn't invite him in. Dale still appeared a broken man. With deep sadness in his eyes, a halfhearted smile, his expression was obvious, and he seemed to anticipate what I was about to say.

"You said you wanted me to stop by to see you. You look lovely, as always."

"Thank you, Dale. I felt it was better for you to come over so we could talk."

"From the tone of your voice, I feel this is probably not what I want to hear. I was hoping you'd say you were willing to give us more time."

"No, I feel we need to dissolve our engagement, so I'm returning your ring. I know in my heart this is the best thing to do. You need to be released, and so do I."

"I hope you know you've been my world, and I still love you with all my heart and soul. There's such emptiness within me now. I know I could never love another as I love you—never."

Then standing at the door with Dale, I extended my hand with the engagement ring to return his lifetime gift, but I could see he truly didn't want to accept it. While trying to hold back the tears, he leaned toward me as he reluctantly took the ring, then gently kissed the back of my hand. I'd broken his heart, and I hated the feeling. After he left, I closed the door and began to cry. Admittedly, even though I loved Dale, I wasn't *in* love with him. I found I couldn't shut out the beautiful memories we had made together and realized then, I would always care about him. The sadness associated with returning the ring continued to haunt me, but I was relieved it was over. I hoped both of us would eventually find our true happiness.

Dale wasn't ready to give up, however.

On Sunday November 1, 1931, Dale took a copy of the *Church Student Paper*, published weekly by the Wesley Foundation, and used it to convey a message to me. He'd folded it in half and in half again, wrote my name on one side, a message to me on the other, and placed it under the door knocker of my apartment.

Call me back, Beloved,
I am begging you,
Do not send me away to my end.
I cannot go on without you.
Let me finish the semester here.
My heart hurts so, Oh God, I can't go on.
You shall not miss these next two months given
to me
And I shall thank you all my life.
I love you. Call me,
Dale

This message was unexpected, and it only confirmed he was still struggling with our broken engagement. Wanting to forget his pleading note, I quickly locked it in my letter box and tried to concentrate on my studies. With his message looming in my thoughts, the hurt I'd caused him once again guaranteed more sleepless nights.

⟡

Monday morning when I returned to work, I saw Guy who was all smiles as he approached me.

"I see you're no longer wearing your ring. Does that mean you're no longer engaged?"

"Yes, we've broken off the engagement."

Guy leaned over and whispered in my ear, "Well then, let's celebrate and go to a dance."

His invitation took me by surprise, but I composed my expression and looked up at him. I flashed a smile and said, "Sure, why not? Let's dance!"

When I accepted his invitation, I was happier than I'd been in months. I'd missed Guy something awful and couldn't wait to be with him again. I was thrilled he'd asked me for a date, but also that it was finally out in the open. My friends told me I looked radiant.

My feelings of depression began to diminish. I occasionally ran into Dale on campus and he often childishly ignored me as we passed in the halls. I made the mistake of telling him this as we passed each other one day, and he responded in a mean-spirited letter.

November 24th 1931

Dear Anna,

You're wrong. I've not meant to ignore you when we meet. I can't hurt you. I love you deeply, earnestly, sincerely. I've made the greatest sacrifice I know how for your happiness. I didn't half realize its magnitude. I must believe you're sincere in your search for happiness. Sometimes I think you're trifling, playing with your power for applause. If so, take whatever you wish and bathe your vanity.

I've laughed at my accursed soul. It's such a comic farce. You've given me all you had to give any man. I beg of you to recognize how steeped in misery and wretched I am. Must you extract the debt in full? Oh, God! How I've suffered nearly beyond my endurance. I don't know how to do more. You asked me to help you, and I can only follow my heart.

I wish you a happy Thanksgiving Day and lots of rest.

I love you,
Dale

P.S. I've tried to be brief and have rewritten this many times, and yet, it can't express my affection for you. I don't know, Anna, why you're gone. I can't be friends with you. That's

just too hypocritical, insincere, and unjust.
You're the judge, my Beloved.
I love you,
Dale

I was doing my best to move on with my life and my work, but the few letters Dale sent, drenched in so much anger and hurt, plagued my thoughts. It seems he tried every angle and manipulation he could create to get my attention and sympathy, hoping to heal his wounded heart by winning me back. Often his letters began with a sweetness, but as he poured out his feelings, the sweetness was tarnished by his frustration that he couldn't get what he wanted, and his words were soon filled with self-pity and anger.

Chapter Forty-Four

Soon after Dale sent the letter accusing me of "bathing in my vanity," he called me. I answered the phone call, but politely declined the invitation to go to a show with him. Not wanting to perpetuate his agony, I told him I had too much work to do and needed to study for exams. I asked him to stop calling me. Then, there it was again, his abrupt and hostile yelling response.

"What the hell is wrong with you? Does it give you pleasure to torture me by holding out this way?"

I interrupted his screaming rant and politely said, "Good-bye, Dale."

December 5, 1931

Dear Anna,

I'm sorry for my rudeness over the telephone last night. I owe an apology, though I doubt if it's worth your acceptance. Would you resent it if I took the liberty just to chat with you a brief moment? I've been writing up quite a difficult

psychology experiment, but couldn't finish it.
Besides, one of the boys is coming tomorrow
night to work with me. I've much work to do. It
seems to be piling up.

I've felt the need of a quiet little talk with
you, yet I'm not sure enough of myself. There's
been much gone out of my life, leaving an over-
whelming bitterness. I'm determined to proceed
regardless of all costs to myself. I love you. It is
as simple as that. A long time must pass before
I can eradicate you from that place in my heart.
I fear a lot of fond memories will go with it. I
must build new ideals if I can.

Oh, My Beloved Anna, the gentle curves of
your white bosom. God's own flowers. You've
been my wife in His eyes. You may hate me for
this, yet I shall love you in return. My hope lies
in your happiness. Forget me. I'm not worthy
of your recognition. I wish I'd known how to
live, but I didn't. I'd like to spend a pleasant
hour with you Sunday afternoon. I'll call you.
Lovingly,
Dale

I read his letter over several times and felt this one, unlike some
of the others in recent weeks, gave in to his sensitivity for our love
and loss. And, unlike others, there was no attack, but just a large
dose of self-pity and a self-serving reminder that I was his wife in his
eyes and God's.

⁂

I'd been studying when I received a phone call from Guy asking
if I had any plans for the afternoon. He thought it would be nice

to spend a little time with me if I were free. Pleased that he called, I invited him for supper. As Guy and I spent more time together, I wanted to learn more about his life. After supper, Guy moved to the sofa where I joined him. As he pulled me closer to him, he put his arm around me and gave a little squeeze.

"Guy, I wish you'd tell me about your boyhood."

"What is it you'd you like to know?"

"I don't know. Start from the beginning."

"Let's see, I was the second son born of ten children. My older brother Reede weighed eleven pounds at birth, but when I came along, I was premature and so tiny I could fit in a shoebox and a tea cup fit over my head."

"Are you serious? I never heard of such a thing."

"What's more, the doctor who delivered me at home said my chances for living were so slim, he told my father to come to the office the next day to pick up a burial certificate because I'd never survive."

"I'm certainly glad that doctor was wrong. How *did* you survive after that?"

"I have to give credit to Mother's constant nurturing and loving care. I grew up pretty well and was able to graduate from high school, but admittedly was never strong. And, what's more, somehow I turned out to be the tallest kid in the family."

"That's incredible. You'd think you'd be just a little bitty thing. Did you miss a lot of school because you were sick?"

"I had a lot of colds and problems with my lungs. I mean *a lot*. I had a hard time with lingering coughs after I got over a cold. I always tried to be careful to avoid people with colds."

"That's pretty hard to do, since everyone in the winter seems to be coughing and sneezing. So much sickness on buses and trains, in school, and everywhere."

"You're right, but I try to keep a strict schedule to make sure I get plenty of rest. Sometimes that was pretty hard to do."

"Once you told me you attended school in Arizona, didn't you? How did you end up there?"

"First, I went to Indiana University after high school for a twelve-week teacher's course in 1919. I passed the exam, so I could teach. Isn't it something to be a teacher when you're just nineteen?"

"I'd say so. For sure, it is. You certainly got an early start with your career."

"Then my doctor advised me to go Arizona because of the dry climate. He thought it would help my bronchitis."

"Did it?"

"I guess it did. Everything was dried up there, which eventually and fortunately included my lungs."

"I can't imagine going that far away from family. Way out there, living in nothing but dirt and sand. Was it scary to move there when you were so young?"

"No, that never occurred to me because my brother Reede went with me. Mother wasn't in favor of me going by myself, so he joined me. The summer of 1920 was so hot in Phoenix, there was nothing we could find to cool us off. We opened all the windows and hung wet sheets and towels on lines trying to stay cool. Since there was always a breeze in the valley, it did help a little. Then, I moved to the outskirts of town and lived in a small tent on the grounds of a one-room schoolhouse."

"Well, it sounds like you had free housing anyway."

"It was, until I left there to attend the University of Arizona in Tucson. Reede had already returned to Indiana by that time. He didn't like the hot weather, and I was healthy, so he went home."

"So, why did you come back to Indiana?"

"When I was on my own, I never wanted to get serious with anyone, because I felt it wouldn't be fair since my health was so unpredictable. But as I told you, I met Olive there, and we were engaged for nearly two years until I learned I needed to have gall bladder surgery. I was advised I should have it soon, or I'd die.

Since it was presented to me in that way, I decided to have the surgery right away, then return to Bloomfield to recover. I didn't care enough about Olive at this point to bring her back to Bloomfield with me, so I broke off the engagement."

"I know how having an illness that takes your strength, and changes your life, is difficult to get over. Emotionally and physically."

"Did you also have some kind of a long illness too?" Guy asked.

"Yes, but I was young. I had malaria at age five and was confined to bed for a few months. I received so much attention, my family teased me, saying it left me spoiled. But my situation is no comparison to yours."

Hearing about Guy's past, I felt a kinship with some of his life experiences, his growing up in a family with many children, and also his strong desire to get an education. But, there was no comparison in our health problems. Unlike Guy, my illness occurred when I was young, and it didn't have a lasting effect on me. Guy's health would always be in jeopardy. However, I wondered if his mother's protective concerns about his premature birth and subsequent frequent illnesses fostered his insecurity about never putting his health at risk. He'd broken off one relationship because of his health, and I wondered if his health would keep him from developing a committed relationship with me.

Chapter Forty-Five

With Christmas approaching, Guy and I shopped in Indianapolis together. I purchased a few Christmas cards on one of our outings and sent one to Dale, thinking it was a nice gesture. His hostile response shocked me, and I felt his anger in the note he wrote on the card.

December 24ᵗʰ 1931

Miss Anna,

    Thank you kindly, but you know I can't appreciate this thinly veiled pretense. I've asked you to respect certain wishes. But you choose not to for reasons of your own. I ask again simply; I don't wish you to remember me through this trivial junk. I need no stimulating to remember our engagement at this time of year. All the rest can go to hell. Is that plain? Don't pretend!! For my sake, save something of you that I

*idealized! I'm nearly broken. Isn't that enough
to feed your vanity? A little more? I wish you
all success and someday perhaps content.*
~~Lovingly,~~
Dale

My card came back in an envelope addressed to me. Lovingly was crossed out. The anger lingers.

Dale and I continued to see each other occasionally on campus. A month later, we happened to meet on the steps of the library, and he told me he still wanted to make things right.

"Anna, could you meet me at Alvin's apartment after class? I have to help him with a photography project, but I'd like to talk to you."

"Why, what's the matter? Is there something wrong?"

"I need to talk to you, that's all. It won't take long. I promise."

"I have a book review to finish, but can meet you for a few minutes. Is two o'clock okay?" I said.

I reluctantly agreed to meet Dale and when I arrived at the apartment, I briefly talked to Alvin about his new assignment at IU in the photo lab. He hastily took his jacket from the closet and was preparing to leave, so I felt he wanted to give Dale some privacy.

"I'll see you two later, I have to pick up some supplies for my project," Alvin said.

"Well, Dale, here I am. What is it you wanted to see me about?"

"I'll be straightforward with it. I miss you more than you can ever imagine. My life is upside down and I want you back. My life has completely gone to hell."

"Dale, you know as well as I do, it's over."

"Maybe it's over for you, but it's not for me. I'm still deeply in love with you. Don't you understand?" He said raising his voice.

Then suddenly his demeanor changed. He appeared angered

and the abrupt change scared me. He grabbed my shoulders and began shaking me. "What's wrong with you? Why are you holding out on me? You're just doing it to torture me, aren't you?"

"No. That's an absolute NO! and you have no right to touch me. Now, stop shouting like a crazy man. Everyone on the block can hear you."

"Why are you being so stubborn about this?"

"I'm not being stubborn and this isn't getting us anywhere. I need to leave. I knew I shouldn't have come."

"Hold it, I'm sorry, honey, come on, I didn't mean to say those things. I didn't intend to lose my temper and I didn't mean to hurt you. Can't you see, I'm a broken man?"

He grabbed my arm trying to prevent me from leaving the apartment. I jerked loose and raced down the stairs while hearing his plead for my return. "Why can't you give just a little? I'm begging you to come back to me."

Once again, our encounter ended badly, and we parted before anything was resolved. Dale claimed he still had a deep love for me, but obviously his anger stood in the way of reason. He expressed his frustration with hostility, and his anger showed lack of emotional control. More than anything, he said he wanted to come across in a loving way. However, when he began to express his love and understanding, his anger surfaced, and he said things he didn't intend for me to hear. In my eyes, his behavior demonstrated that if he couldn't control me and my feelings, he certainly couldn't control his own.

As I reflected on my relationship with Dale, and the one I was developing with Guy, I came to better understand the difference between them. Guy was neither jealous of my time spent with others, nor did he question my other relationships, while Dale's obsession was suffocating. Then, Dale's next letter took his obsession and anger to an even greater level than I had believed possible.

CHAPTER FORTY-FIVE

January 8, 1932

Sweetheart,

This endearing name still haunts me, but its use may soften the mood. I do regret that you've taken my invitation as a chance to wound me. I thought you cared, and I still think you love me. Perhaps you know that I love you, and knowing that to see me, would give you another chance to show your diabolical cunning and womanly cruelty.

Two perfectly normal, rational beings without a damned bit of sense. We both know that we've had ideals in each other; that we've experienced more absolute happiness with each other than we'll ever gain out of life again. We've simply thrown away our greatest gift, you perhaps for social reasons, I in retaliation.

We're mere secondhand men and women now. Never again will we feel the absolute trust and purity of a beautiful, newly awakened life. We may be fathers and mothers someday, but I'll not respect the woman though I love the children, and you? Can you love another man without a heart? Having given everything you possess to me, can you give him anything but the satisfaction of masculine desires? You can't even be his first wife and neither can I be her first husband. Nor he your first husband because I've been that in every sense. That I've cared for you, tenderly, loved you more than you'll ever be again; that you've stood by me, loved me, honored me with all of you, all of which has now robbed us both.

I truly thank you for this half year of college. I'm sure I wouldn't have made the effort but that I thought it would place you and me on a higher plane, give us a model foundation to start life.

I've found contentment here because I love to study, have overcome much opposition, more than you credit me for. But I don't care for it now. I know that I'm simply throwing away a career. Dad's heartbroken, though I've merely explained that I'm only pausing to replenish my resources. Right now, I simply must get away.

Much of my silence and bitterness is to be laid here. Your redeeming quality is that you're very sensible and determined. I know every inch of you, everything but the right key. You're ashamed of me. And you're the most miserable coward alive because you love me and will not come to me.

You care only for the social life here, its glamour and praise. You've refused my recent advance because I wounded you. For God's sake, Anna dear, don't you see that your leaving me has disrupted my whole life? I've suffered so terribly and fallen into misery, I've laughed and cursed myself, God, Dad, everything and everybody but my Mother.

I'll love you to the end. Anna, please accept my ideals, faults and attributes and my heart. Will you be my wife?

I love you,
Dale

It was a shock to receive this letter from the one who proclaimed his love for me for all eternity! I felt his bitterness and anger and sat stunned for what seemed a long time, just staring into space. Then, eventually, a complete resolve to free myself from Dale's obsession and manipulations slowly overcame me. Even though I would care about him forever, I knew then, our romantic break was permanent. I'd never go back.

Chapter Forty-Six

During the winter months, I saw Guy at work, and he often walked me home and stayed for dinner. He now lived across campus from me, so it wasn't as often that we could be together. Frequently, however, when the weather was nice, we'd hop the interurban and spend the day in Indianapolis. We loved going to the toy store, taking in a show, and having dinner at the Claypool Hotel, but the best part was being with Guy, no matter what we were doing. He was handsome and wonderful company, and I enjoyed being seen arm-in-arm with him. This relationship was so different for me, so natural and easy, I loved every minute we shared.

It had been months since I'd heard from Dale. We had been together for five long years, had shared many good times and I often wondered how he was doing. I wondered if the scars from our broken engagement were beginning to heal. I never had any unkind feelings toward him. Near the end of the summer while I was still in Bloomington, Dale wrote once again.

Hamilton, Ohio
July 28th 1932

Dear Anna,

    Out of the chaos and wild disorder of time and events comes a day marking off another year. My erstwhile companions of Solitude and Poverty, wish that my greeting be simple and unadorned. Wishing you happiness, success in your affairs, and may I add my compliments to your goodness and benevolence which are your beauty and charm.

August 6th 1932, Birthday #22
Sincerely,
Dale

I was surprised to receive a birthday card from Dale, but he'd been on my mind for weeks. I'd wondered how he and his family were doing since our breakup, for they were the ones left to help him put his life back together. I also wanted to share some family news with him.

Bloomington
August 22, 1932

Dear Dale,

    I want to thank you for your birthday card. It was nice that you remembered me. It set me to revisiting better times when we shared so much laughter and family experiences in Vallonia. I've kept all of your letters locked in a wooden box under my bed at home, but never can bring myself to open them to refresh the memory of their messages. I don't write many letters any more, but when I do, it's a bitter-sweet memory as I take the pen you gave me and once again, begin writing.

I'm sending this brief letter to you to tell you about a year ago, Laura married a nice fellow who is becoming a minister. We were so excited for her when she decided to start a family. However, I'm saddened to report she has since lost her baby, and the family, of course, is terribly upset. Laura is home in Vallonia, but I stayed on in Bloomington to complete a summer course. I'm planning to continue college, but don't know if I'll have a job for the fall or not. I wish you well, and send my regards to your family.

Do you have plans to return to the university to continue toward your degree?

As Always,
Anna

Vallonia, Ind
September 5, 1932

Dear Anna,

It's late. A mouse is keeping me company and is amusing himself by gnawing holes in a box by the chimney. Wasps have built a nest on the window sash, and now one is seeking the source of the light. There's the familiar hum of insects outside. Now and then a cricket chirps from his hiding place beside the door. The clock . . . I set it by guess, ticks serenely as though the time past had not gone forever carrying with it much happiness. A night bird calls eerily.

I came here yesterday. During my last visit, I was struck by the feeling of a lingering presence inhabiting this old cabin, a faint echo of laughter, a haunting sweetness, a touch of feminine tidiness. I noticed that it still lingers, as though you and I had not been gone from here only yesterday.

You asked about my plans and if I would be returning to IU. Dr. Bryan and his wife sent for me about four weeks ago. They have been most kind to me. I did two weeks' work for them and will finish there this week. I work Saturdays, wait tables as last year, and do a few other jobs when the time comes.

I wonder if you're in need of encouragement. In your brief letter, it would appear so. Go on, if you possibly can. Even if you lose your job with the professor, don't be bound by obligations too much. I wish so much to see you accomplish what you desire. Don't even lose one semester, for the task will appear too hard to accomplish if you stay away. Don't give up. Keep your ideals in mind and forget the rest.

You said that Laura lost her baby. I thought I ought not stop by, even though I was in Vallonia, since your family would be so upset. That's why I'm writing. It's too much to have the baby die after so much pain and being so near death. If I were her husband, Merlin, I'd be stark-raving mad.

I may have been selfish in wanting you, but I tried to redeem myself when I set you free.

I could have done better if I hadn't loved you so much. At any rate, you can see why I desire you to cheer up and go ahead.

I hope I haven't made a mistake. You're too good, too beautiful. Please don't resent this, for you see, I live by this. If you glean a little courage from these lines, I'll be so happy to have helped you. Let me thank you for your letter. You were kind where I was not, and I am ashamed of my bitterness. Please let us regress into the past a moment and let me say,

I love you,

Dale

So, it appeared Dale continued to visit the memories of our time spent in the cabin along with the loneliness which lingered within that small, dark, place he fondly referred to as home. It did please me, though, that Dr. Bryan seemed determined to help Dale move toward his goal at IU. I thought they must have seen the same potential in him that I did, and could help him earn his way at the university without injuring Dale's pride. It had been eight months since I received that biting letter in January in which he'd poured out his bitterness in great detail. I recalled, in October after our breakup, he said he'd figured out what he needed to do was to cultivate a nobler, kinder attitude and a more generous spirit. Now this, a letter much softer and kinder than the last, suggested Dale was beginning to emotionally recover and move forward.

Chapter Forty-Seven

I returned to campus in September of 1932 as planned, but found I wouldn't have a job in the Education Department, due to the budget crunch as the Depression progressed. I did, however, secure a secretarial position at twenty-five cents an hour with Lillian G. Gary, a Latin professor, who had the reputation of being the most difficult person on Earth to get along with. In spite of her reputation, I agreed to live with her, doing the cleaning and cooking in exchange for my room and board. I was able to win the professor over, and in no time, we became friends.

Guy and I worked in buildings a distance apart that didn't permit the close encounters we'd grown to appreciate the previous year. However, we continued to meet for casual dates until sometime in October, when Guy abruptly stopped contacting me without any explanation. I didn't understand, and was deeply hurt by it. We hadn't had any disagreements, and I felt we were at least good friends. Had I misread the depth of our relationship? I'd completely and quietly given my heart and was so invested in Guy; I wanted our feelings to be mutual. One balmy evening in late October, while appreciating the sunset as I walked along North Washington Street, I saw Guy walking toward me, and I felt my heart flutter a little.

"So nice to see you, Guy. I've been wondering about you and hoped you weren't ill again. I couldn't imagine why you suddenly disappeared." I was so excited to see Guy, instantly I felt a sudden shiver and my pulse was racing. I knew he still had that same effect on me.

"No, I haven't been sick, just busy working and teaching, I guess. I was wondering if you wanted to get reacquainted."

"Sure, I'd love to. I've missed you and couldn't understand what I may have done that caused you to stop coming by."

"I'll give you a call when we can meet, if you like," he said, dodging my question.

Two weeks later, Guy took me to the Book Nook to sip on a soda and talk. I was overcome with happiness he'd showed up in my life again, but I found it extremely difficult to keep my mind on anything else while waiting those two weeks for him to call.

"I know I probably owe you some explanation of why I've been out of touch, other than the weak excuse of being too busy because of work. The real reason is, I found you were meaning too much to me, and I needed to step back."

"I'm glad I'm beginning to reach a special place in your life," I said.

"It concerned me since I don't feel my health would ever permit me to marry. I know this is nothing new to you, because I've told you this before, but I don't want you to feel I'm leading you on."

"I don't feel you're leading me on. I think I understand how you feel, but I hope you know I wouldn't turn my back on you if you were sick. I hope at some point that you'll believe I'm sincere when I tell you this."

"I want to continue seeing you, if you're agreeable to it."

"Certainly, I'm agreeable to it—even looking forward to it."

"I'll call for you next weekend, if that's all right with you."

He took my hand from across the table and helped me with my chair. We walked back to Miss Gary's house, and he said he was relieved and happy I was back in his life. He didn't know I never stopped being in love with him. Once again, I was totally happy with the world.

As we spent time together and I learned more about Guy, I realized his resolve wasn't easy to bend, and he was determined to keep his space. Always, I hoped not to overstep my boundaries, but to keep in mind to respect his. More than anything, however, I wanted us to be together and for him to finally make a commitment.

⚬⚬⚬

"Anna, I do hear what you're asking of me."

"But, I just want us to be in a relationship I can count on. Can't you commit to us being together?"

"You've asked me this question several times and the answer hasn't changed."

"I have? I've asked you that same question?"

"Yes, you've asked me to commit to a relationship. You ask the same question but not always with the same approach. But, for me to make a commitment, is something my conscience has told me all along isn't right."

"But why? What's wrong? Why isn't it right?

"I worry about the condition of my health. I don't feel I can make a lifetime promise, because I might not ever be able to make good on it. I've experienced so many serious episodes of bronchitis, I'm leery of the next time I will find myself in that situation."

"You're making your health issues an insurmountable obstacle."

"When I get sick, I get deathly sick. I've been at death's door too many times to feel confident in giving in to a commitment."

"I'm sure you do get deathly sick, but I'll stick by you, no matter what."

"Those episodes leave me in such a weakened condition I need all of my strength to rebuild my endurance. I want to spare you any hardship it may cause, if we were in a serious relationship."

"I understand that fear is constant, but please know I'll always be there for you."

"I want you to be my friend, but the varmint you've treed hasn't been captured."

"Ha! Funny!"

In my determined way, I knew what I wanted, so I ignored his self-imposed wall—the wall which was reinforced over the years, with the onset of each episode of bronchitis.

November and December brought weekend dates with college football games, dances, shows, and shopping. Guy came to my home for Thanksgiving, but he spent Christmas with his family. He said his parents, all ten brothers, sisters, their spouses and children hadn't been together since 1923, and the house bulged with relatives sleeping on the floor with blankets they'd brought from home. He said they weren't used to all of them being in one place at the same time. Even when growing up, their mother had rented an apartment for some of the older children to live together. The apartment was close by, eliminating some of the congestion in their home. He often said they were a tight-knit family; they always looked out for one another, and even after childhood, the ten children were happy to be together whenever they could.

⁂

Occasionally, Dale and I saw each other on campus. He encountered me late one afternoon and said he'd been hoping to bump into me. He said he continued his courses in psychology and was determined to succeed, even taking additional evening classes.

"I'd like it if you'd come with me to chat over a soda at the Book Nook. I've wanted to talk with you for such a long time now."

"Sure, that's fine with me, but please understand, I'm not giving you any romantic encouragement. I'm only offering friendship, which is what I offered before, but you refused," I said.

"Well, now, I'll take whatever you have to offer. I just want to share some of the strategies I've been using to become more aware of my reactions to what people say. I'm so excited how this new knowledge has made a difference."

On our way to the Book Nook, I noticed his face as he beamed from ear-to-ear when I accepted his invitation. I was hopeful this would be the good one—the encounter that would leave us both more at ease.

"You're looking happier than I've seen you in a good long while," I said.

"You know I've always loved sharing my plans and achievements with you because you give honest, straightforward opinions, which I appreciate. And, what's more, your belief in me and my potential gave me what I needed to believe in myself."

"I know sometimes my opinions might come across as harsh, but I mean them to be encouraging."

"I wanted to tell you, I'm making excellent grades in my most difficult subjects."

"I had no doubt you'd be successful. You're a smart guy."

"I've learned so much about myself in psychology. I sometimes wonder if I chose this field, because I was the one who needed to examine my thoughts and behavior the most. Did I ever say that before?"

"Isn't it strange how things work out for us sometimes? It's probably the greatest message God gives us, if we'd only pay attention. Do you remember in Psalms? 'May He give you the desire of your heart and make all your plans succeed.' Don't you see, by your desire to reach your goals, He's helped guide you to achieve them?"

As I sat across the table from Dale, he began speaking softly as he leaned in closer and reached out to touch my fingertips. I could see it was still hard for him not to make physical contact.

"I'm trying to acknowledge my anger and understand where it came from."

Looking down at his clasped hands he slowly moved back and sat erect, then looked me straight in the eye, and began shaking his head. "Again, I sincerely want to apologize to you for my violent temper when we were at Alvin's apartment. How stupid could I have been to think that would change your mind and you'd want me back? I was embarrassed at my behavior."

"I have to say, you did scare me. You'd come close to it only once that I recall, but I'd never seen you so enraged. That aside, just look back, your entire life has been full of tough times. No wonder you get frustrated, but the key is to learn how to change it."

"I keep hoping to recognize what sets me off and catch it before I react, but that's the difficult part."

"It may take you a good while to actually figure it out, and change it."

"Yes, I know. I can more clearly see why our love affair soured for you as time went on. I've been able to step back and look at myself and how I reacted to you. How I made demands on you and pressured you when you tried to resist. I thought I acted that way because I loved you so much. I wasn't thinking about you. I was only thinking about myself. I want you to know I still do love you."

"I'm happy you've gained insight into yourself through your studies. I think most people never recognize or give thought to what they need to acknowledge or try to change. It's hard work, but it's more fulfilling to enjoy happy relationships, no matter who it's with."

"You're right. I'm now so aware of that. I have many regrets. How I wish I could turn the clock back for us."

"But you know, for us Dale, there were so many other challenges. It was hard to keep fires burning when we were so far apart.

There were many differences in our backgrounds, religion, politics, and upbringing—all of those things made it harder for us."

"I know. There was so much that could've split us up. But, even though all of those differences made an impact on our relationship, we never fought about them—quarreled, but never fought." Dale smiled and chuckled a bit.

"For me, the only huge difference was, I was so determined to get an education at all costs, and I knew you didn't care about college. Once I was here, I realized my feelings for us were waning."

"Like I said, I have many regrets. All I knew was that I loved you with all my heart and soul and wanted you to love me back in the same way. It's hard for me to believe how immature I was and how badly I behaved during our courtship."

"I have so much respect for you. You're a good, good person, kind and sensitive. You have a great mind and will become someone who's to be respected for your wonderful accomplishments in life. I've wanted to say these things to you. I respect you and am proud of you for your courage and success."

"Thanks for joining me to talk things over, and also for the compliments you've so generously given."

"You're welcome. I just knew you could do it."

For the first time, Dale didn't need to control me, and I didn't need to make him feel better or inspire him to do anything. Even so, as we parted I noticed his smile when he looked back at me, nodding his head with approval, as though he remained hopeful. It felt better to have had our chat, one that had ended on a positive note. I didn't know if Dale could ever understand that I loved another man, one who loved me, but didn't need to possess me completely.

Chapter Forty-Eight

$\mathcal{M}$y sense that Dale saw a glimmer of hope in our last encounter was verified in the letter I received from him soon after our meeting.

May 12th, 1933

Dear Anna,

I hope you'll be pleased to receive this, for I feel that I can write it in a new spirit. As you might know, I've given a great deal of thought to our last meeting. I lost my newborn hope and found it again in my solitude here after a good battle.

Perhaps this new joy showed itself which made you speak, or made you realize it quicker than I. My approach was crudely rough, which wasn't at all in keeping with you. I may as well go on, for nothing can change except toward the *better. The impetuous fiery love of youth has long since gone out, finding in its place is born a love which can never die. The kind of love which sustains perpetual hope, even as I may be writing my doom. No, we couldn't go on long, for sooner or later I'd have to take that lovely girl who walked beside me into my arms and into my heart again. It's inevitable. Here then, is what I wished to say across those invisible barriers.*

Is it impossible to begin again, Anna? I know a great deal stands in the way, but is it not possible to close that book and try a new one? It'll not cost you. I promise. I thank you again for that night, I enjoyed it.

I love you as always,
Dale

I wrote back to Dale to tell him I preferred to stay friends, if at all possible. I still had concerns for him because we'd known each other for many years, shared many experiences, and written each other hundreds of loving letters. Even though I wanted him to do well, I couldn't allow myself to become involved again. I didn't want to lead him on, and truthfully, I wanted to protect myself and my growing relationship with Guy.

⚬

At the end of May, Guy left Bloomington since his work had finished for the summer. I was still on campus taking summer classes while living with my friends in the rooming house. Guy and I wrote often, but I missed his companionship every day.

During the months of June and July, I concentrated on completing three more summer courses while continuing to work for Miss Gary. I took no time off other than an occasional weekend home to see my parents. Guy was able to get to Bloomington twice, and it was always a joy to be with him, but so difficult to endure the emptiness I felt when he left. I realized I was falling more deeply in love with him with each passing month.

⁂

I hadn't expected to hear from Dale again, but about two months since he had last written, I saw him coming back from the cinema late in the afternoon. He was a good distance away, so I waved and continued on to the library. When I arrived home, I found his note asking me to meet him.

July 12th 1933

Dear Anna,

I've been to see State Fair which I thought was much better than the book. In fact, I read the book only partway through. You saw me coming back; I still have half a sack of popcorn! Have lunch with me Saturday and go to the midnight show. Or the evening show. Or read some of my junk and let me talk to you. Something to break the monotony. Please, Anna, I'll look forward to it.

Always.

Dale

When I didn't respond to this request, he wrote again two days later.

July 14th 1933

Dear Anna,

Would you accept an in invitation to lunch with me this coming Sunday or dinner at 8

*p.m.? I'll be very disappointed at this early
notice if you don't find it convenient. Please let
me know as soon as you can. Until then, I have
a heart full of hope.*

Sincerely,

Dale

Short notes from Dale continued to arrive, and although I read
them, I refrained from sending a response. It seemed he was still
having a difficult time letting go, so I felt I shouldn't offer even a
glimmer of hope. I worried, though, that my silence may have made
me appear cruel.

July 19th 1933

Dear Anna,

*I hope the third time is a charm, though
as you know I put little faith in such as black
cats, yet however glad I am that none has
crossed my path. Curiously enough, I find
myself rather expectantly awaiting tomorrow
night, and I thought I might even remind
old Fate to do his stuff. But perhaps I've
been too prompt. Did you not say you come
every night to the library? I've been there two
nights looking for you.*

*If you do decide to come, I'll probably
get there at 8 p.m. I'll be disappointed if you
aren't there.*

Sincerely,

Dale

I didn't meet Dale or respond to subsequent letters. I needed
to silence the entire affair once and for all. The third time was not

a charm for him, but Dale did send me a card for my twenty-third birthday. He didn't sign the card this time, and there was no message inside. I only knew the sender by the postmark from Hamilton. He'd given it all he could give. Finally, he stopped writing.

Chapter Forty-Nine

*J*n September of 1933, I continued taking courses and working for Miss Gary. Guy received a one-year fellowship through May 1934 in the School of Education. He planned to work on his doctorate, and receiving the seven-hundred-fifty-dollar fellowship made it possible for him to stay on campus and us to continue to date. Over the holidays and the cold winter months, we met less often than we'd hoped. Fortunately, Guy stayed healthy and spent most of his waking hours working on his doctorate, while I kept pace with my courses. We celebrated New Year's Eve in Vallonia with my family, then Guy returned to Bloomfield on New Year's Day to be with his.

I was so happy to be able to have Guy with me to enjoy the celebration of New Year's Eve, and felt blessed and satisfied as I reflected on the maturity of our growing relationship. I realized that I felt more secure and content, which was something I had not been accustomed to in my previous relationship.

January 3, 1934

Dear Glorianna,

How would you like to kiss the cook? I'm still at home, but Mother is away visiting, so I'm the housekeeper and cook for a couple of weeks. It's too cold to do anything, but sit around the stove today and write you a note if I can get these fingers working.

I can't tell you how much pleasure it gave me to see you last week over the holidays. I feel that I know you better now. I hope you didn't learn me well enough to be thumbing your nose at me now. Ha! I thought certainly you'd write Sunday evening or Monday at least, to tell me how many A's you made; you let me down. I couldn't have written yesterday . . . no not from depression, from pondering the wonderful time I had just had. I'm afraid you have me in the hollow of your hand.

Cautiously,

Guy

I loved that Guy was finally starting to come around, telling me I "had him in the hollow of my hand." That's just where I wanted him. On Monday night, February 12, 1934, three and a half years after we'd been dating, he stopped over to see me.

When he held me in his arms and kissed me, he said, "I'm going to tell you something you must've known for a long time. I love you, and I will love you, forever and forever and forever!"

"Guy, you don't know how long I've wished I could hear you say that you love me." This was a red-letter day for me. Finally, at last, he said it! I absolutely adored this man!

"Couldn't you tell how I felt about you?"

"I hoped you loved me, but you kept saying how you didn't want to make any commitments. I thought it might be because it would be easier if you wanted to stop seeing me."

"Well, I simply couldn't come out with it, even though I've felt it in my heart for a long, long time."

Recalling the thrill it had first given me, I said, "I just knew you were the one I wanted to be with from the moment I laid eyes on you that time when you first came into the office. Remember? I felt my heart skip beats and had butterflies in my stomach."

"So, I had that effect on you right from the first day?"

"Yes, I'd never felt that way about anyone before, and I remember it as if it happened yesterday. You *had* me, right from the first day I saw you. I think about that day often."

Guy wasn't only pleased to hear that, but was pleased with himself that he finally had the nerve to tell me he loved me. I was happier than I'd ever been in my entire life. He gave me a box of Maude Muller chocolates and a Valentine's card since he wouldn't be seeing me Wednesday, then kissed me again and told me he loved me. I went to sleep with a smile on my face and wrapped in sheer happiness.

The next letter from Guy confirmed I was starting to get to him, but I needed to remind myself to be patient. It had taken a long time to get him to this point, and I didn't want to take anything for granted.

March 3ʳᵈ, 1934

My Dear Glorianna,

I decided to stop home in Bloomfield for the weekend and wanted to respond to your note. Your letter brought you tantalizingly near, almost as near as you were last week. I was very much in the mood for making a reply at the moment, but was afraid to trust myself. Perhaps I'd have said some things that wouldn't have seemed at all appropriate in steadier, more sober moments. You do me that way when you're near, I must confess. I'm not a bit sorry for anything last week, though at times I've felt that possibly I should be. I had a wonderful time with you, even for two or three days after you left.

With your planning to take nineteen subject hours besides your work, I'll not feel right in taking much of your time, so I've been thinking that when I come up I oughtn't to keep you up later than 9:30 or 10:00. I know you won't like that, but you'd better think it over and decide to agree. Your grades are very good, and I want to help you keep them that way.

Yours Too,

Guy

His letter tickled me, especially when he said he had a wonderful time with me, even for two or three days after I left. When I thought about the two relationships I've had in my life, they were so completely different. Dale couldn't possibly know how I admired Guy for his honesty, ambition, and sense of humor. Guy and I were developing a mature and deepening relationship as two adults. I was so lucky, and so in love.

Chapter Fifty

$\mathcal{G}$uy accepted a job working on a two-month project in Indianapolis, while I moved ahead with the unimaginable task of the nineteen subject hours to secure a teaching license. I included the "Methods" correspondence course he'd previously taken and used his notes and test results. We referred to it as "our" course.

It had been weeks since we'd been together, so Guy planned to spend Labor Day weekend with my family. I was so excited he was coming to Vallonia, I could hardly stand myself. Dad drove me to the train station, and when he finally arrived, I jumped out of the car and ran to his open arms.

"Hello, my handsome darling. Let me look at you. I can't believe you're finally here."

"I can't believe I'm finally here myself. It's been such a long time, and I've missed you terribly. Now *I* have those butterflies," Guy said with a chuckle as he grabbed and kissed me.

"Let's hurry. Dad's waiting for us in the parking lot."

"Hello, Mr. Fosbrink. Thank you for coming for me. I certainly appreciate it."

As we sat in the backseat of the car on the way to my house, Guy put his arm tightly around me and whispered in my ear that he loved me. It gave me goose bumps all the way to my toes. It was such a thrill to finally be with my handsome boyfriend and experience the familiar fluttery feeling of excitement in my stomach whenever he was around me. I was certain it was going to be a great weekend.

"Hello, Mrs. Fosbrink. Golly, what an amazing variety of food you have on the table. I could make a meal on just the tomatoes, corn, and potatoes and make off with at least half a loaf of your hot bread."

"Well, you're gonna want to save room for Anna's butterscotch pie and watermelon after dinner, aren't you?" Dad said.

"Certainly, I can't pass up either of those. I hear that pie of Anna's is out of this world."

"Who told you that? Is word getting around up your way about her pies?" Dad teased.

"No, Anna told me that herself, so I asked her to make one to prove it."

Guy took my hand as we strolled down the lane after dinner and watched the sun gradually dropping behind the wooded hills. It began to turn a little cool as the sun was setting, so we returned home, snuggled next to each other and sat on the swing, talking about our plans for the future, and how much our love had grown. It was so wonderful having Guy with me. I found him even more charming and irresistible. I was thrilled to be wrapped in his arms and share an abundance of sweet kisses.

"Golly, Anna. Aren't you excited to have a job teaching? In a few weeks, you'll be a North Vernon high school teacher. That must be one terrific thrill for you."

"I *am* excited. It's probably only for one year to fill in for another teacher, but I'm pretty nervous about it. Sometimes taking over for another teacher can be rough. If it weren't for you persuading me to take all of those courses, I wouldn't have the job at all."

"No, it's because you pressured yourself to take those nineteen credits along with your job that got you there. I didn't suggest you do it all at once."

"Now that I look back on it, it does seem pretty crazy. But, if it weren't for you giving me your answers on the 'Methods' course final exam, I'm not sure I would have made it."

"Thanks for giving me some of the credit, but you managed to stay committed the entire time you were at IU. I had nothing to do with that."

"Yes, you did, my darling."

"How so?"

"Always wanting to know how I was doing. How many A's I made. You probably don't even realize it, but when I was tired and grumpy, your praise and encouragement made all the difference in the world."

"I want to find more permanent work after I finish this current project. My problem is that my teaching experience isn't recent enough, because I spent all that time working on my Master's, instead of getting a job teaching. Big mistake, I guess. Now look what a mess the Depression has made for everyone. I can't get a teaching job anywhere," Guy said.

"I think if you just keep trying and continue making contacts, something will turn up."

"Anna, you amaze me. I've wondered how you seem to get everything you go after. What is it about you? Other than being beautiful, intelligent, outgoing, determined and adorable?"

"It's Arcada, I guess."

"So, what's that? What's an arcada?"

"I'll take you there tomorrow."

Saturday morning after breakfast, Guy saddled Nellie and Spiffy for a race to the hills. We arrived at the place I called "Arcada."

Almost immediately, Guy noticed the big heart carved on the front of the sycamore in full view opposite the fallen log.

"Looks like those aren't my initials in that heart," he said.

Suddenly, the memory of Dale carving the heart flashed in my head. Instantly, visions flooded my mind like fairy dust, sprinkling memories of the times we'd spent here together, just talking for hours. Then, I realize how powerful our love had been—and I wasn't completely over him. I shook myself from the vision of happier times as my eyes began to fill with tears . . . and I said, "No, Dale carved it a long time ago."

"Well, do you mind if I whittle a little of my own creative work to change it?"

"Please do. It needs to be changed."

Guy took out his pocket knife and began to disguise the initials with a new design, replacing them with his initials. "So, what's it about this fallen log you're sitting on?"

"Well, it's not only the log to rest on, it's the location. It's how the sun casts shadows through the trees, it's the essence of the forest, the serene feeling I have when I'm here. Arcada is my sanctuary where I come to meditate and pray to God for health, prosperity, and love. It's where I recharge my inner strength from the universe. It has a spiritual, almost mystical quality. I feel this spiritual connection has blessed me and granted me the opportunities I've desired. That's why it's Arcada."

"Golly, Anna, what a wonderful sanctuary. Do many others come here?"

"Not that I know of. As you can see, it's pretty far away from everything and everyone. I've never seen anyone here. Not ever, and I'm glad no one else comes here. I feel it's my personal piece of the world."

"It certainly is that, so quiet and peaceful. Thank you for bringing me along. It gives me more of an understanding of your spiritual side."

"Hezekiah knows I come here. I brought him here a few times when we were out riding. I don't know that he senses the same peace here that I do, but he seemed to like resting here with me."

"Is he a spiritual man?"

"Yes, both Mother and Dad are religious. Grandma was, but Grandpa wasn't."

"Why do you call your Dad 'Hezekiah,' anyway?"

"It's just something I made up to tease him, and it stuck."

"I think it's more endearing for him than a tease, don't you?"

"Probably so. He refers to himself sometimes as Hezekiah. Maybe he prefers that over 'Ulysses,' who knows? My birth name is actually 'Anise Marie' but everyone started calling me Anna or Ann. Now you're calling me 'Glorianna,' and I like it."

"You like when I call you 'Glorianna?' My 'Glorious Anna?'"

"I do, and you can call me that anytime."

"Looks like most of us have nicknames. You seem to have more than most. So, how did your brother get the name Dude?"

"I'm not sure, but I think he liked bugs and Mother called him 'Doodle Bug,' so we called him that. Then as he grew up, the Dude part just stuck. His real name is Raleigh."

"It's funny how we start giving people nicknames rather than their birth name.'

"Now, how did you get the name Jiggs?"

"My sisters, Fontella and Reba, started that when I was younger. They thought it was funny to call me Jiggs. Don't ask me why."

"It kind of suits you."

"You think I look like a Jiggs?"

"I've never seen a Jiggs, so wouldn't know if you looked like one or not. I always think of you as distinguished-looking, but Jiggs suits your personality and your funny way of expressing yourself."

We had a wonderful Labor Day weekend together riding horses, enjoying a picnic by the river and just being with my brothers, sisters, and parents for delicious meals Mother prepared for us. As our love grew deeper, and the intense feelings we had for one another so apparent, we found it harder and harder to be apart. I didn't know how much longer we could continue the agonizing separation we felt each time we had to leave.

Mother and Dad both told me how much they liked Guy. Dad in particular liked his sense of humor and how down to earth he was. Mother made a point of telling me she thought he was a handsome and mature man. It was a relief to both of them that I had broken my engagement to Dale.

After our splendid weekend, I took the bus to North Vernon to again live with the Sanders family, who had recently moved from Indianapolis. I was happy to be reconnected with them and be able to rent a room while I'd be living there. It amazed me to see how everything was falling into place. I was excited to begin my journey as a junior high school teacher. I thought back over the wonderful time I'd had with Guy and taking him to Arcada, but I was puzzled as to why I'd been so affected by seeing the heart on the tree that Dale had carved. I hadn't been there in a long time, and I wasn't still in love with him, but why was I so emotional about the flood of memories that triggered the tears?

Chapter Fifty-One

*I*t took no time at all to settle into my new life with the Sanders family and my first year teaching high school. After the wonderful visit with Guy over Labor Day, it was difficult to keep my mind on track. Each day we were apart, my desire to be with him became more intense. Our time together seemed to have been ages ago. All I wanted was to be back in Guy's arms and hear him tell me how much he loved me. My students couldn't have given me a greater welcome, and my job was even more pleasant than anticipated. But still, more than anything, I missed Guy.

October 25, 1934

Darling Mine,

It surprised me to hear your voice on the phone last night and for certain I will be there to meet you for the weekend. I'm planning to leave here Friday at 4:30 and arrive in Indianapolis about 6:45. I can meet you

*at the Claypool Hotel mezzanine or leave
word for you at the P.O. there in the lobby.
I can hardly wait. Don't let us lose a single
moment. I'm going to be real selfish and take
every spare minute you have. I love you with
all my heart. I can't wait to see you, I'm
beyond excited.*

Forever,

Anna

We met Friday at 7:15 pm at the Claypool Hotel. Right there on the mezzanine, he wrapped me in his arms in a long passionate embrace, giving me the same thrilling feeling as if it were our first date.

"Guy, thank goodness you were able to be here. I was so afraid we'd miss connections."

"I wouldn't have missed this chance for the world."

"I'm so happy now. Finally, I can see your face and hold you. Do you know of a place where we can go that's not so open, somewhere we could have some soup and just sit and look at each other?"

We settled on supper at The Lincoln and located a cozy booth which offered us privacy.

"Anna, my darling, I have a little surprise for you."

"How nice. I love surprises. What is it? I can't wait to see it."

"Here, open your hand and close your eyes." He put the surprise in my hand. "Alright, now open your eyes."

"It's a key. What's it for?"

"I've rented a room for the weekend over at the Linden Hotel. I stopped there earlier this afternoon, and it's quite nice. I have a surprise waiting there for you."

"Are you serious? We're staying there for the weekend? Together?"

"I suppose we could. That is, unless you prefer that I stay with Aunt Myrtle at her place, and you stay by yourself."

"No, let's stay together. After all, we're not little children. It'll be fun," I said while softly clapping my hands with excitement. With a huge grin and a little bounce up and down on the padded cushion at the table, I quickly covered my mouth so I wouldn't attract anyone's attention and whispered, "I love you Guy, I'm so excited!"

It surprised me that Guy had actually rented a room. It was obvious he was beginning to cave. Labor Day weekend he shared his feelings more openly and said he felt much more comfortable with us being *alone* together. As we walked arm-in-arm to the hotel, we hoped we wouldn't run into anyone familiar. Even though I didn't say it, I felt this was the commitment I had patiently awaited and wanted for three long years.

The Linden was quieter and out of the way, yet within walking distance from the Claypool. The weather suddenly turned cold. As we walked to the hotel, I began to feel the chill. Guy opened the door to usher me into the room, and I found it was surprisingly cheerful and warm. There was one double bed with a large heather-green wool blanket and a lamp table next to an overstuffed beige chair.

As he took me in his arms, he chuckled a little, hesitating to kiss me when he saw my teeth were uncontrollably chattering. I wasn't sure if it was from nervousness or from being freezing cold, but Guy held me close until the chattering stopped. Then, secluded in our own private space, we shared our affection, offering our sweetest, most passionate kisses in an expression of our love for one another. We held each other in silence for what seemed endless time, knowing we shared the contentment of finally being together and alone.

Then, Guy whispered in my ear, "I don't want either of us to have any regrets about this weekend. I want you to be certain about us and our love. Do you understand?"

Then Guy began kissing me passionately again for what seemed like a blissful eternity.

"I do and I feel the same way. Neither of us wants to have any regrets. We can take our time. We're here to enjoy two fabulous days and we have all weekend to play together."

Giving in to temptation, we slipped off our outer clothing and quickly crawled into bed snuggling together in our warm welcoming room. We lay silently in each other's arms for a long time while enjoying each other's soothing touch.

Suddenly, Guy in his always playful and teasing manner, abruptly raised up on his elbow and said, "Golly, Anna, you said we could 'play' all weekend. On my way here, I stopped at the toy store and bought something to play with. You know how I love toys. I was going to give it to you for Christmas, but on second thought, I wasn't sure what your mother might think."

Guy reached over to the lamp table, grabbed a sack then dropped it on the bed between us. I opened the sack, took the newspaper off the gift, and dropping my jaw in shock, I gasped and looked at his handsome smiling face.

"Guy? What's this? It's cute, but is there some meaning behind it?"

"Don't you like it?"

"You've caught me off guard. Is there some story to this baby carriage?"

I fell back on my pillow putting my hand over my mouth and began laughing hysterically. He was laughing, too. I could tell he obviously was tickled with himself.

"I thought it was a great toy and might be something you'd like."

"I love it, but I'm curious as to why a little baby in a baby carriage?"

"You know how I love toys, and I just thought it would be fun to give it to you."

"I do love it and also think it's funny, but can you imagine the look on mother's face if I *had* opened this present on Christmas?"

"No, I'd probably not notice hers, because I'd be looking at your face and the huge question mark over your head. I have to confess that in a weak moment, while at the toy store, I just envisioned you pushing our little baby in a blue carriage like that someday. So, I bought it. That's all."

"Am I to understand that statement to mean someday we'll be married?"

"I'm not proposing, but it seems that's the direction we're headed. Don't you think?"

"Guy, you are one heck of a funny fellow. Now, get back under the covers and let's cuddle."

Lying in the arms of my wonderful man brought me unimaginable peace and complete satisfaction. All day Saturday, we took advantage of the golden opportunity to lavish our deepest feelings and expressions for one another. To be wrapped in the love and affection of the man of my dreams overwhelmed me, and truthfully, this time, I wasn't worried and had no regrets.

Sunday, we spent nearly two hours window-shopping and roaming the streets of Indianapolis since everything was closed. It was a crisp, sunny fall day, a little warmer, and we loved every minute of being together, reminiscing about our private time at The Linden. We lunched at the Claypool before I had to take the train back to North Vernon. During my ride back, I blissfully daydreamed about the wonderful relationship I shared with Guy. I congratulated myself on the triumph of having patiently awaited those years until he joined me, and now we shared such a beautiful, fulfilling love. I didn't know how I could have possibly loved him more.

Guy wrote that everything during the next day irritated him, and even though he had no fuss with anyone, his inner turmoil colored everything. He felt alone and missed me more than ever before, and the opportunities for us to be alone weren't often enough. His sensible judgment told him he shouldn't see me at all for a while, but then confessed he didn't have the slightest intention of being sensible. At the end of the letter, Guy became more serious. I caught my breath and my eyes welled with tears when I read, "If I read you correctly, you are seriously in love with me, or am I jumping to conclusions?" Believe me, Guy wasn't jumping to conclusions.

October 31, 1934

My Dear Glorianna,

Listen, I want to thank you for the very splendid good time I had with you. It was perfect. I know you are busy getting settled back in with your students, but I hope you will soon write to me. When you don't write, I realize how much you are to me and how I depend upon you. I have to talk to your picture in the evening when I get home from the office. I tell it what I did, whom I met and other things I know you would be interested in. Of mornings when I greet it, it smiles back as if to say, "Did you think I'd left you? I've been right here all night." I can't wait until the next time we are together.

I plan to go to the World's Fair in a few weeks also. They say the "Century of Progress" is spectacular. I'd very much like to see "the dream cars" and tour the "Homes of Tomorrow," but will have to take a look at the famous fan dancer Sally Rand. That should be pretty special. I wish you could be with me to share the experience.

Again, a Thousand, Thousand, Thanks,

Jiggs

I found it amusing when Guy wrote that he depended on me. There was no comparison between the way Guy depended on me and Dale's demonstration of neediness and suffocation. It was difficult to be separated from Guy so much of the time, especially with such long absences between our visits. We missed each other every day and constantly tried to arrange times we could get away to meet again for a weekend, but Guy was working at the Plainfield Boy's School, and his projects kept him on location many weekends.

Monday, Nov.19, 1934

My Dear Anna,

I've had a terrible cold for about ten days, but today, I'm feeling a little better and hoping by tomorrow it'll be pretty much gone. Our administrator was here today for the meeting of the adjustment board, a conference on the new boys. I just wish you could sit in on one of these meetings.

We have a real problem boy, about fifteen years old, IQ of about 85, probably a paretic caused by syphilis, with definite signs of hallucination and emotionally unstable. My heart came up in my throat more than once during his examination. Such boys have no business in a penal institution.

I am counting the days until I'll be with you for Thanksgiving. I'll take the train to Seymour and the bus to Vallonia, arriving around 5:30 p.m.

Forever,

Jiggs

It had been a week and a half since I'd heard from Guy and I was getting worried. I always worried when I didn't hear from him because I often feared the worst. His unpredictable health was a constant threat to our future, and had caught me in its grip as well. Much like my mother, I was born a worrier.

November 23rd 1934

My Dearest Guy,

I hadn't heard from you in eleven days and had been so worried that you were too sick to write. Darling, you don't know how you worry me for days and days by not writing. You see, you hadn't written me where you'd be or anything, so my mind was going crazy with worry.

Your letter sounds as though you not only have your hands full at the reform school, but your heart as well. I'd love to hear more about it when you get here. I'm so happy you're coming for Thanksgiving. Will you please bring your hunting togs with you? I love you with all my heart and can't wait to be with you. I'll be looking for you in Seymour.

Anna

We enjoyed a traditional Thanksgiving Day dinner with my family in Vallonia. Several of my brothers and sisters were able to join us, and Mother created her usual fabulous spread. Hezekiah, our beloved and most appreciated patriarch, was unusually loquacious and lighthearted, which kept us all laughing much of the weekend. The weather was uncooperative for any outdoor activities, but the house was warm and there was never a lack of chatter *or* laughter. It was wonderful to be with Guy for three days, but always feeling the emptiness once we had to say good-bye, I stayed on with the family until Sunday to soften my loneliness.

December 5ᵗʰ 1934

My Darling Love,

Thanksgiving was wonderful with you close to me all the time. I miss you so much I hardly know what words to use to describe how deeply in love I am. Twenty-five hours and five minutes ago, you kissed me good-bye. A few hours being with you spoils me. Even though there wasn't much to do because of the weather, I enjoyed every single minute we had together. I'm so in love.

By the way, wasn't Dad funny? He was in rare form and I got such a kick out of him. What a character. Please take care of yourself and stay well. Hopefully, we can meet in Indianapolis for the weekend of Dec. 15ᵗʰ. In fact, I'm counting on it.

Until then, I love you,

Anna

I was so excited when Guy called Friday afternoon and asked me to meet him at the Claypool in Indianapolis. I always kept my overnight bag packed, sitting by my bedroom door in anticipation of meeting him on a moment's notice. I grabbed my bag and left immediately for the train. I hurried to reach the hotel for our meet-up at six-thirty p.m. I barely made it there in time, but Guy was nowhere to be found. I had a sinking feeling after searching for thirty minutes, and the anxiety worsened with each stroke of the ticking clock in the lobby. When he didn't show up by eight-thirty, I began to panic. I checked for messages at the desk several times, but there was nothing there for me. I didn't know what had happened, and if I should stay or head back home. By nine-thirty I began to feel sick inside and was afraid there was something dreadfully wrong.

Then, a telegram arrived from Guy. He was sorry to disappoint me, but plans were changed at the last minute by the administrator at the boys' school. That wonderful feeling of excitement to be together had turned to my deepest disappointment. With my eyesight blurred by tears, I somehow made my way back to the train, but the ride back to North Vernon seemed to take forever. It was hard to get over the disappointment of not seeing Guy, and although I had my heart set on being with him, I was relieved to know he was okay. He called on Saturday to tell me he was sorry for the abandonment, but reassured me of his love and we'd make up for it the next time we were together.

Chapter Fifty-Two

Guy hated to disappoint me again, especially since he stood me up in Indianapolis two weeks ago, but he was unable to make it to Vallonia for Christmas. Instead we had our celebration Saturday, December 29th while several of my brothers and sisters were still at home, and many of us were able to ring in the New Year together. We had no problem making up for lost time and as always, loved every minute we were together.

January 6th 1935

Dearest Guy,

I'm spending the weekend catching up on some rest while the Sanders have gone visiting. I have papers to grade, but put that task off to catch up on some reading of Dorothea Dix while listening to music. I'm still reliving the wonderful time spent together last week and am taking advantage of the quiet moments here to do some intense daydreaming. It's so cold today it's hard to get motivated. But I know I'll have to drop down from those air castles and get back to reality if I'm to get anything accomplished.

I hope you have a safe trip to Richmond to check out the new job. Please take care of yourself and try to get some rest.

I love you from the bottom of my heart,
Anna

January 7th 1935

My Dear Anna,

I received your letter. Such languor and lassitude! It permeated the whole letter and left me so lazy I haven't yet dispelled the feeling. I can imagine you dreaming, radio-ing, and reading Dorothea Dix, wondering if I will ever come home, throw you over my shoulder and onto the bed. As for me . . .

I stayed last night in your room,
And felt that your self was there;
I lay in your bed where you lay
And toyed with locks of your hair.
I day-dreamed of dozens of things:
Things we might do and say,
Then fell asleep and dreamed
The rest of the night away.

I'm glad you can find time to rest and relax. You've had too little time for that in last three or four years. Then too, I want

you to have time to write me letters tell-
ing me how lonesome you are and how
much you need me. That's the kind of
jealous person I am. I think of you not
a dozen times a day, but all the time.
Wherever I go, I find myself looking for
people who might resemble you, but the
results disappoint.

Another thought. My dear, I adore
you, my life I live for you, and I'll love
you forever,

Guy

In February, Guy wrote that his job doing research for the state at Plainfield Boys' School was on hold. The "Works" bill didn't fare well in the Senate and was returned to the Appropriations Committee. He was sending out applications in every direction imaginable and searching out every professional contact he had in the past, seeking any available opening. By the end of March, Guy still hadn't had any success finding work.

To take a break, he decided to go to Gary, Indiana, with his sister Ava and her husband Dave to spend a few days. He was look-ing forward to a comfortable ride in their new car. On the trip, it rained all day, and the car leaked in two places during the five-hour journey, so they all ended up soaked. I was concerned Guy would become ill again having just recovered from a cold a few days prior.

❧

Following in my footsteps, it was my sister Kay's turn to be a contestant in the state Latin contest in Indianapolis on Saturday. I wrote Guy a note to let him know I'd be in Indianapolis with her and hoped to see him there. I told him I would stop at the Claypool Hotel to check for messages as I always did. When I arrived, I found

I didn't have a message from him, my concerns escalated. My constant fear of his health hovered over our future.

April 1st 1935

Darling Anna,
It is about a week since I wrote you and now, I dislike telling you, but I'm writing on my back. I've been having a rather hectic time. Thursday, I almost had pneumonia. Don't let that scare you, for it's over now, and I'm getting along all right. I'm sorry I didn't get word to you at the Claypool, but I was just too miserable to write.

I'm tired.
Bye darling,
Guy

By Sunday, April 14, I was just about beside myself with worry since I hadn't heard anything from Guy and wasn't even sure where he was. I received a note from his brother Bill, dated Friday, April 12, telling me Guy's condition progressively worsened, and he was in critical condition, hospitalized with pneumonia. I immediately took a bus and rushed to the hospital in Indianapolis. I found Guy debilitated and shaky with a high fever and a terrible cough. He wanted to talk, but couldn't get enough air into his lungs to speak. His color was ashen, his lips were blue and he struggled for every breath, yet he tried to smile. Although I was sure he wanted to make me feel he wasn't so bad off, I was terrified to see him so sick and frail. I prayed and asked dear God to make him well, help him, and answer our prayers to save him. I sat quietly holding his hand until his doctor came to put a needle into his lung to draw off the fluid since the pneumonia wasn't clearing.

I had to tear myself away to return home for work. I hated leaving him there so sick, and I hated being so far from the hospital. I'd never have thought how someone could suddenly become so deathly ill. My heart ached. I felt alone and frightened. All the way back to North Vernon, I tried not to break down and cry. Once I arrived at the Sanderses', though, I went to my room, buried my head in a pillow, and cried myself to sleep. I was so scared, so worried about the love of my life. All I could do was pray he'd survive this. Over and over, I begged God to protect the one I loved, to save him for the wonderful life we could have together.

The next day, I received a letter from Guy's sister, Ava.

April 15, 1935

Dear Anna,

I'm sorry to have to write you of this, but I've been so busy taking care of Guy. His condition turned worse after you left Sunday, and he has fallen into extremely grave condition. My brother Bill stayed with me at the hospital while Dave drove to Bloomfield to get the folks. It's fourteen hours round-trip by car, and we didn't think Guy would last until the folks got here. They arrived at 10 p.m., but he didn't want them to come into the room. However, Mother insisted she had to see him. He couldn't talk, but just lay there and grunted with each struggling breath. Everyone is deeply concerned and as we watch over him, we cannot see any improvement. Our prayers are constant. We'll stay with him and care for him as long as he needs us near.

All our love to you. Ava

After reading Ava's letter, I became even more distraught about Guy's condition. I could think of nothing else, and I constantly prayed for his recovery. When I returned to the hospital Friday night after work, Guy appeared to have made a slight improvement.

"I'm so happy to see your beautiful face. I was hoping you'd come back. I've missed you terribly." His voice was barely a whisper. He held out his hand and drew mine to his lips. The kiss was as warm and tender as his sweet smile. I leaned over and kissed his feverish dry, cleanly shaven, pale face.

"Guy, you've had me worried sick. I can't keep my mind on anything but you."

"I'm so sorry, my sweet. I would've rather been anywhere but here. This has been the worst time I've ever had. I just couldn't seem to shake it off. It's totally taken me down."

"Do you feel like your lungs are getting any better now?"

"Jerry, Dr. Rand's assistant, said I'm improving, but he's still worried, because I'm so weak. He warned about a relapse. I still can't get out of bed. It takes all my energy just to brush my teeth, and I'm done for the rest of the day."

"You look like you've lost a lot of weight. Are you eating?"

"Yes, but I get tired before I get full and have to quit. Everything is such an effort."

"I'm here now and will feed you, if that's agreeable with you."

"Of course. I'd love for you to help me. I'm feeling better already just seeing you. I love you and have spent many hours longing to be with you."

"It looks like the nurses are taking good care of you. They've shaved you and freshened your linens."

"Yes, there's one named Rita, and she has red hair. You know how I love red hair." I finally laughed, releasing the tension. Leave it to Guy and his sense of humor to put people at ease.

"I know. Now it's time for you to rest up a bit before supper."

"I hope you can stay for a while. I've missed you so much. It's so lonely here all day just lying in bed. Not even any toys to play with. Sometimes I lie here and think I can do something, but the least little thing wears me out."

"I plan to stay until Sunday afternoon. I'll be here in your room or the lobby. I want to make sure you eat, and be confident you're getting better before I leave."

Now I could clearly see what Guy meant about how vulnerable his lungs could be to weather changes, and how rain or cold could take him to death's door so unexpectedly. It frightened me to see Guy so ill, but also how quickly his respiratory weakness could become a grave condition and a threat to our future.

More than six weeks after Guy was admitted to the hospital, he was released by ambulance to Ava's home in Gary. Guy asked her to send me short notes about his progress so I wouldn't worry about him so much. She said one week after release from the hospital, he rose from bed and stood for a few moments. Though still weak and pale, a few days later, he was well enough to sit up for a few minutes, and the persistent dizziness was decreasing. He would stay with Ava until he could return to Bloomfield and the care of his parents. After three weeks at her home, Guy was finally able to return home to Bloomfield, but the doctors confined him to bed. Weeks of good nutrition, rest, and gradual exercise helped him to recover. With each passing day, Guy emerged from his bed stronger and with improved endurance. It took another month to fully recover, but when he did, he was determined that finding work was his top priority.

That spring, I completed my teaching job in North Vernon and, while I felt it was a great experience, I was pleased it came to an end. It had been difficult to keep on top of my teaching and grading at school with Guy so ill and far away. At times, I wanted to give it all up, to be with him, and help him get well. However, in his family's care, he made good progress. I began to feel more confident that Guy would soon be back in good health and in my arms planning our future. With his illness behind us, I returned to Vallonia for the summer to help out with the family and catch up on some rest and reading, while Guy continued to work toward complete recovery.

Chapter Fifty-Three

$\mathcal{A}$lthough the last letter I received from Dale was on July 19, 1933, we'd occasionally seen each other on campus until I graduated, but we rarely spoke to one another. I never thought badly of Dale and the hurt was because I wanted out of the relationship. I hadn't heard from him in almost two years. I felt certain he'd be graduating from IU in May, so I wrote him a letter conveying good wishes for his many accomplishments and to congratulate him on his success. In the letter, I also briefly shared some of my teaching adventures and told him about Guy recently coming so close to death and of my concerns for our future. I was surprised when he answered my letter so kindly.

> *Bloomington, Ind.*
> *June 11th 1935*

Dear Anna,

I was gladly surprised to get your unexpected letter, in fact, so much so that I even felt

the good wishes you were sending and heard their genuine silvery ring. Thank you.

I have the desire to go one more year to be well enough prepared to meet the world as it should be met. Haven't you glorified my accomplishments just a little? You see, I've had all sorts of good luck, good friends, and good jobs. It's sweet of you to make me feel as though I'd done it all myself. I'm so glad that your first year out has been a real success and that you have a promise of another. Now that you've had the experience, next year should be less nerve-wracking. But, when are you going to take that real vacation you deserve?

I wouldn't want to argue with you, seeing as how it's been some time since we chatted together, but your last page seems quite fatalistic. It seems almost as though you're willing to take life as it is.

It does make me feel good to hear you say that you hold only pleasant memories of me, but, Anna Dear, all your impulsive generosity can't possibly dismiss the fact that I was gloomy, selfish, and terribly ignorant. I do thank you, though, for throwing your blanket around the past in such an utterly forgiving manner. And now, somehow I don't feel you'll charge me with a lack of ambition. Work, Anna, and whatever stray bits of happy moments come along, are treasures; it's these little things that are big! I'm thoroughly happy as I plan another year here. I want to be well prepared for the world. I have my writing to amuse myself, hosts of friends, *and more money than any mere student has a right to have.*

Now, I see that I've come dangerously near to philosophizing, and, what's more, have written an overly long letter to one who has not even expressed the desire for an answer. Please, when I come from camp, which will be the first week in July, if you do ever come prowling around this spot, let me know. I should like nothing more than to hear more of your success about which you've been rather stingy in your letter. Until the future, then, I'm always,

Sincerely,
Dale

The letter from Dale was friendlier than many received in the past, and it pleased me to know he was more content. He'd moved on and developed many relationships, which wasn't surprising. People seemed to genuinely like him, maybe because he was honest and sincere. I was happy I'd sent him the letter to let him know I had such respect for his academic accomplishments, especially in a challenging subject such as psychology. I knew he always respected my opinion and was pleased to hear it from me. During our relationship, we both found what it was like to have the sincere desire to support and inspire one another to achieve our goals. For Dale, he learned he could survive mental and financial depression. As I looked back at all of the resistance and excuses, doubts, and struggles, I had no regrets. I helped push him toward what he referred to as "too much of a stretch" for him to accomplish. But, once Dale decided to reach his goal for his own benefit, his persistence paid off.

I was home for the summer, helping mother with the garden and canning. Guy was continuing to make gains, feeling stronger every day, and we continued to write. I'd been hoping Guy would visit, but he wrote he didn't feel up to traveling to Vallonia for the July 4th holiday because of the heat. I was disappointed, but a letter from my Chi Omega sister, Dorothy, lifted my spirits.

July 1ˢᵗ 1935

Dear Anna,

    I've been thinking it would be so nice if you'd come to visit me and stay a few days. Bea has gone to Kansas to be with her family for a couple of weeks and if you can get away, we could have a great girl visit and catch up on life. There are some good shows here in Bloomington that I haven't seen, and we could look up some of our old Chi Omega sisters and friends to get back in touch with them. Let me know what you think.

Dorothy

July 3ʳᵈ 1935

Dear Dorothy,

    That sounds wonderful, and I'd love to come. It's especially good timing for me because I just finished the canning with Mother, so I can be there Friday by train at 4 pm. I'm so looking forward to it. It would be nice to see Alvin if he's still hanging around campus. If this is fine with you, I'll see you Friday.

Anna

On the train to Bloomington, I daydreamed of my wonderful experiences going to college, working with the professor in the Bureau of Education, the Latin professor Miss Gary, and meeting Guy—the love of my life. So many exciting times. How I missed those days! Dorothy met me at the train station, and as we headed to her house, we picked up our friendship as if a day hadn't passed.

"Thank you so much for inviting me to stay with you. This is a real treat, and I'm so glad you thought of it. I brought you a loaf of bread Mother and I made this morning and a lemon loaf cake with white icing."

"Yum. They smell wonderful. Come on and have some supper with me. Let's go to the kitchen, I have something to tell you,"

"What is it? What's going on?"

"Well, yesterday as I was crossing campus coming back from Alvin's apartment—by the way, Alvin's excited to see you tomorrow—I ran into Dale."

"How is he? What's he been doing?"

"He said he had a letter from you, and he seemed pleased that you wrote to him."

"Yes, I wrote to congratulate him on his accomplishments. It's amazing how well he did, once he started college."

"You know he's in Scabbard and Blade, don't you?"

"No, Dorothy, what's that?"

"It's a national honor society that encourages cadets to keep their grades high while still in the military. I'm not sure, but I think it's ROTC, or something. He was in his uniform and looked 'so military.' He just arrived from camp yesterday and was on his way to a Scabbard and Blade meeting when I ran into him."

"He did mention in his letter he was going to a camp, but that's all he said about it. I wasn't sure just what kind of camp," I said.

"I told him you were planning to be with me for a couple of days over the weekend. He turned out to be quite a nice guy, after all—well-respected and popular. He's quite different than I remember him, but it had been a number of years since I'd seen him. Alvin and Dale became good friends when Dale moved here."

"Did he say what he's going to do? Is he going back to Hamilton?"

"No, but he did say he'd love to see you. I think he just might come over here tomorrow."

"Dorothy, that's a bit unnerving. Writing him is one thing, but seeing him is quite another." I had mixed feelings about seeing Dale and felt a little anxious inside.

"I think he's still carrying a torch for you. He seemed so pleased that you were coming here and hoped I'd ask you if it would be all right for him to come over. What could I say? No?"

"No, I guess that wouldn't be polite. But, you know Guy and I are serious, and we do plan to marry at some point in our lives, so I hope Dale has no expectations."

"How is Guy, anyway?"

"He's doing better. He was deathly ill in April, and it's taken over three months for him to recover. I was so scared that he wouldn't make it. But, now he's back looking for work. It's awful out there. Jobs are so scarce. He's trying to get on as an academic advisor at one of the CCC camps. He thinks he can manage that physically."

"What's a CCC camp?"

"You know. It's those Civilian Conservation Camps where they send unmarried men to learn forestry, build roadways, to conserve and protect our resources. That sort of thing. They pay them some money, but most of their pay is sent home to their families. Guy is hopeful to get hired as one of their advisors because he feels he can handle that kind of work."

Dorothy and I talked nonstop the rest of the evening and into the wee hours of the morning. After breakfast, we strolled over to the Chi Omega sorority house and stopped to see Alvin on our way back.

"Hey, Anna, it's so nice to finally see you. It's been a long time." Alvin leaned over and kissed me on the cheek.

Chapter Fifty-Three

"Yes, it *has* been. You look great. What are you doing these days?"

"I work as a journalist and photographer here in town. I'm fortunate to have the work. Pay isn't great, but it covers my expenses as long as I'm careful. What about you?"

"I just finished a year teaching junior high school in North Vernon. It was a great experience. I had a lot of fun, and I found I love teaching. Since it was a temporary position for a year, I've lined up another teaching position in Rushville starting in September."

"Are you still with Guy?"

"I am. He was deathly ill in the spring, but is doing better now, thank heavens."

"Yes, I did hear that. Dale said he was close to death in April. Did Dorothy tell you Dale is back and knows you're in town? He wants to meet with you."

"So, I heard."

"Do you mind if he shows up? He's planning to come to my place in about a half an hour."

"No, that's fine. I guess it would look like I was on the run if I left now."

"You don't have to stay if you feel uncomfortable, but I know he's looking forward to seeing you." Looking out the front window, Alvin said, "Hey, as a matter of fact, it looks like he's coming up the walk right now." Alvin opened the door and motioned for Dale to enter.

"Hey, Dale, come on in. Of course, you know Dorothy. And our sweet Anna here."

I hoped I didn't look too surprised when he walked in. He appeared more muscular, maybe even a little taller, but glancing at his feet I thought it was probably the boots. He was tan, looked quite handsome, and I recognized he was even wearing that new Zizanie men's cologne. Such confidence. What an attractive difference!

"Hello, my dear, Anna. You look beautiful, as always. It appears teaching school is agreeing with you."

"You look wonderful also, Dale. It appears that life is treating you well."

"It is, and I have a good many exciting plans ahead of me. Would you care to take a walk with me? I'd love to tell you about them. Maybe you can give me some advice."

"Of course. Dorothy, would you and Alvin mind if Dale and I take a walk for a few minutes?" Even though I didn't want to seem rude, I wanted to be alone with Dale for a little while.

"Not at all," Dorothy said. "Anna, why don't you head back to my apartment afterwards?"

As Dale and I walked over to campus, I thought back over our lives together. Mostly, I remembered the good times we'd had, but as we walked, I struggled to block out the more painful memories during our breakup and let them go.

"Anna, you're still on my mind and in my heart so much of the time. I hope I'm not making you feel uncomfortable, but I wanted you to know, I felt I was more in love with you than any human being could be. For many months, I kept praying you'd come back to me and give me some encouragement to begin it all over again. It was my fantasy, and I'd dreamt it every day and write of it at night. Then, I'd remember why it ended as it did, and I'd beat myself up that I could've been so ignorant and self-ish. At times, I thought I could've written a book about our lives together, our Starve Hollow love affair, and the laughter and the tears. At times, I still think I might."

"Oh, Dale, we did have a special relationship, but I feel our lives turned out as they were supposed to. I'm so proud of you. And, just think what we've both done with our lives. You're suc-cessful, and so am I. We've reached an equality now that was never there in the past. Look where we started and how far we've come. Little old Vallonia High. Who would have thought? What great memories!"

"I wanted to tell you, Dad suddenly passed away in February. I regret

I wasn't with him when it happened. He was so good to me, and I miss him every day. He would've been so proud to see me graduate."

"I'm so sorry. I didn't know."

"At times, I get choked up when I feel his spirit around me. Sometimes, when I'm sitting and reading a book, I sense he's sitting with me as he used to do when I was a young boy and we'd read together in the cabin."

"He's with your mother now, but I feel certain he's always near. He grieved her loss for so many years, and life was such a struggle for him, being so poor and having to raise you and your sisters alone. I'm so sorry."

"Thank you, but tell me, how is your boyfriend, Jiggs?"

"He's better. He came so close to death, I was terrified. He's getting stronger every day and looking for work now."

I paused, then asked, "Is there any special lady in your life?"

"No, not so far. I do have dates from time to time, but just haven't found anyone I'm crazy about. At least, not since that one that got away. Ha! I have many good friends and good times, so I can't complain. I already have my PhD, but wanted to stay one more year here at IU to teach. Then, I hope to move on to Columbia University in New York in their psych department, if I can get hired. How's that for a goal?"

"It's incredible, just incredible. Remember when you told me going to college was too much of a stretch for you?"

"I do. But, see now what your persistence for me to get into college has done? I thank you, Anna, for all of that. It changed my life. I also thank you for spending this time with me now. You know how I always love talking to you and hearing your opinion. I've always regretted that I handled our relationship the way I did. I owe so much."

"Please, don't beat yourself up. You know, you did a lot for me also. You helped me through some awfully hard times, and your letters were so loving and supportive. There's a lot of good memories there for me."

"I often think of the wonderful family life you have and what enjoyable times I had in their company. What an enviable life you've lived."

"Like I said, Dale, our lives turned out as they were supposed to. It's been good to see you and, especially to see how satisfying life has become for you. Please give my greetings to your family next time you write them."

"You do the same. I want you to know, Anna, I think you are as beautiful and sweet as ever. I doubt I'll ever stop loving you. If you ever should change your mind about Guy, call me, or at least drop me a line. You will be in my heart. Forever."

When we parted, I turned back around to have one last look at my lifetime friend, and found he had done the same. With a smile and a wave good-bye, he threw a final kiss.

≈

Being in Dale's company stirred up all kinds of emotions, both good and bad. I learned a lot about myself during our courtship. I also found our years together had taught me many life lessons: tolerance, understanding, guidance, acceptance, to love and feel loved, to forgive, the power of will, and the importance of education. I had no regrets about my relationship with Dale and the love I'd always have for him, but I've matured and moved on. I felt no guilt about seeing him again because I was certain how I felt about Guy, the direction my life was headed, and how much in love I am. My love for Guy and our relationship could not be more beautiful or joyous.

Dorothy was anxious to know what Dale and I had talked about during our walk. On our way to the show, I filled her in on the details of our conversation, and she made a point that her suspicions were accurate about his feelings for me, even after all these years.

"Anna, that man is still in love with you. Don't you see it?"

"Maybe so; you may be right. We shared our lives, but we are beyond that now and have gone our separate ways. You know

Dorothy, Dale once told me something, a long time ago. He wanted me to read Socrates and insisted that I understand it. He said, 'If what Socrates said was true, this Earth wouldn't be our happiest place after all. Just think, if this is so, and we have reasons to believe it to be that way, you and I will always love each other and know it even after death!' Those words have stuck in my mind, and I've thought about them ever so many times. I wonder if God brought Dale and me together for a reason—a reason we may not fully understand until we arrive in our happiest place above this Earth."

Chapter Fifty-Four

"*A*nna, honey, wake up. The night nurses said you were asleep the entire night and now much of the day. That shot I gave you last night must have knocked you out," Miss Allen said.

"Oh, my goodness. You wouldn't believe the dreams I've had. My entire life passed before me as if I were sitting in a movie theater watching it all."

"We need for you to eat and get dressed. Your children are coming to pick you up. Dr. West said it's time to leave the hospital."

꧁꧂

I'd come mighty close to the ending my children had dreaded for so long. After they completed the enormous task of clearing out my house, they gathered my few most precious belongings before picking me up at the hospital.

I'm eighty-six-years-old now, and have had a good life, but I'm looking forward to moving on to my last adventure. My son arranged for me to live in a safe assisted-living home near him in

Utah. He rented a van to transport my few treasured possessions while my daughters, Peggy and Patty, followed behind with me in the front seat to enjoy a comfortable ride in a rented red Cadillac. It was hard for me, because I knew then, the ride to Utah would be our last road trip together—but I also knew in my heart, for me it would be *my* final journey . . . before I ascended to that happiest place above this Earth and be reunited with my beloved.

About the Author

P.A. Schoenfeld was born in Alexandria, Indiana. At age three, her family moved to Phoenix, Arizona for her father's health. Once she completed her education and received her RN degree, she worked in a number of hospitals from West Coast to East Coast. She returned to the Phoenix area with her husband Donald in 1999. After completing forty-seven years in nursing, she retired as an RN Case Manager in 2009.

It was sixteen years after her mother's death, that her curiosity peaked about a box she had found in her mother's closet. The box turned out to contain a treasure-trove of love letters written to her mother between 1927 and1935. Six hundred and fifty of the one thousand letters were from a secret boyfriend she was engaged to. That discovery set the wheels in motion to write the love story... *The Starve Hollow Affair.*

A sequel, *The Final Air Castle,* is currently under construction.

94337434R00197

Made in the USA
Lexington, KY
27 July 2018